*To Mars,
with best
Rosemary Sturge*

Death

of a Daughter

of Venice

by

Rosemary Sturge

Copyright © 2013 Rosemary Sturge
All Rights Reserved
First published 2013

ISBN-13: 978-1483939995

ISBN-10: 1483939995

This book is available in print from createspace.com and as an e-book and in print from Amazon.

About the Author

Rosemary Sturge has always enjoyed creating stories, particularly those with a historical background. She is currently working on a further novel set in the period of the English Civil War.

If you would like to comment on Rosemary's story please contact her on rosemarysturgestories@gmail.com

To my husband, Theodore, without whom this book would never have got this far, and in memory of my parents, Arthur and Nora Ford, who always thought I might be a novelist.

Chapter 1

In which Harry Brierfield, a young painter in pursuit of a livelihood, receives some useful advice, and witnesses an encounter, little realising where his curiosity will lead him

Later, propped against an unforgiving stone pillar, tied up, helpless, with blood from a cut lip dripping down my shirt front, I naturally found myself wondering how it had come about that I, an unassuming English traveller, found myself suspected of murder by a parcel of nuns in an institution for orphaned maidens? How could I have known, two days ago, that my curiosity about what went on in this building would alter my life, perhaps for ever?

I had my first, best, and possibly my last, drawing lesson that day, on a windy Venetian quayside. Alas, I didn't realize it until he was gone. Well, I hadn't expected it from one of the great ones. There was I, crouching on a stone stair leading down to the water, with my drawing board wedged under the corner of a step, my paper skewered against the breeze with the blade of my clasp knife, when this nosy individual in a floppy black hat came by, and peered over my shoulder. As is their wont. Except that in these parts I usually find they wear those reddish stocking caps pulled down over their unwashed foreheads, and stink of fish. This one smelled of garlic and oranges, and the hat with the drooping brim and wayward feather was a new departure. Which made it difficult for me, Harry Brierfield, penniless Englishman abroad, and would-be artist, to place him. Pennilessness, my father achieved for me, whilst I was still in leading strings, but becoming an artist has proved a trickier proposition. The one thing I supposed I had learned about Venetian men, since establishing myself here in *La Serenissima* two months ago, is that the moneyed sort wear the fashionable tricorne with its stiff curled brim. This is decorated to suit taste and pocket with varying widths and colours of braid — whilst the rougher elements wear those woollen, felted articles, usually red, that their old grannies ran up for them several winters ago, and which have never been laundered and never will be. So his hat disconcerted me. I didn't know what to make of him. 'Signore, you will allow?' He gestured that he would like to take my pencil from me, and I was so busy noticing the contrast between his workaday clothes and eccentric hat, and his smooth manner of speech, that I handed it over without a murmur.

'You have a strong frame for your composition, which is good,' he remarked, crouching down beside me to study the subject of my drawing, 'here between *Santa Maria della Salute* on the left bank, and the palace of our Doge on the right, but you must rearrange your fishing boats a *lee-ttle*, so that they fill the central space more harmoniously. See! I push this old lady with the bronze sail over here, and this one, we turn her through ninety degrees so that she pokes her prow at us, and leads us forward to this gondola,' he sketched it, faultlessly, although there was no gondola plying the water in front of us at that particular moment, 'which draws the viewer into the scene, and which your clients will expect.' He grinned at me, boyishly, although I would have put his age at forty or more. 'It is difficult to sell a picture to a foreign visitor to Venice which does not contain a gondola. I tell you this as a man who has tried!'

He stood up, glancing from my sketch, now much altered, to the actual scene before us. 'You should also, I think, bring the Doge's palace forward somewhat,' he added, tapping the pencil on his teeth. 'Disregard these tumble-down buildings on the right, they are too difficult for you, and also they are ugly. Show more of the side of the palace — the pink and grey tiles, they will add a delicate touch of colour. Together with the *Salute* it will hold your little scene tightly. Simple fisher folk and their craft, squeezed between Church and State, as indeed they are!' He chuckled, 'You argue with me, no? I see it in your expression! — that I am suggesting that you change what is truly there, that you tell lies about Venice. So I will tell you a secret. Your patrons, when you have them, will not want truthful renderings of *exactly* what we have here in Venice. They will want what they *think* they have seen. And if we artists are to prosper in our trade, this is what we must give them!'

So saying, he sprang up the steps, tipped the brim of his ridiculous hat, and bowed slightly, murmuring, 'Zuane da Canale, at your service, Signore,' and was on his way. My initial reaction was annoyance. He'd gone off with my pencil.

I nearly went after him, but what the Devil! Can I go whining after a man that he's stolen my only decent drawing pencil, and I can't afford another? An Englishman, even an Englishman with his pockets to let, has too much pride. Besides, he was already threading his way along the *Riva deghli Schiavonni* amongst the seafood vendors and the stalls selling lace and gewgaws, and, at this season, carnival masks, as if he owned the place. Which, now that it was slowly dawning on me who he was, I supposed he might feel he did. One of my artist acquaintances had told me that over the past five years *Il Canaletto* had sold two dozen paintings to the Marquis of Tavistock alone. So, I thought bitterly, he can afford to be whimsical, and take a few minutes to show a struggling novice some of the tricks of his trade. But even as I watched him dodge smoothly around a hawker with a tray of crabmeat pasties, his passage was suddenly arrested by a vignette which might have figured in one of his own cityscapes. A stout young woman wearing a heavy cloak, and carrying a wicker marketing basket under her arm, blocked the way. She paid no more mind to the great artist than she would have to a stray dog, or a pile of discarded crab claws. She was much too intent on launching a shrill tirade at the young man who had just touched her arm in greeting. He was, as the country folk say back home in Lancashire, 'a reet big lad', with a protruding under lip and a slightly morose expression. Whatever it was she felt for this fellow, surely it wasn't love? Signor Canaletto hovered for a split second, and then slipped behind a stall selling wash tubs, and made good his escape.

I fished the stub of my one remaining pencil out of my waistcoat pocket, took a scrap of paper from my satchel, and began to sketch the couple. Why? Maybe it was the curve of her arm about the round underbelly of her basket, or the way her body inclined towards his as she gave him the benefit of her opinion, and he drew away, as though she was literally spitting fire, and he feared she might singe his peculiar sheepskin coat. A vignette of Venetian life. Perhaps I could work it up into something. I scribbled notes around the margins about colour. The drab inner hide of his sheepskin, contrasting with the deep terra-cotta brickwork of the orphanage of *Santa Maria della Pietà* behind him; her cloak, a stark, solid block against the grey-brown canvas *ombrella* which shaded the fish stall in front of which she'd planted herself.

I felt a sudden spurt of enthusiasm for my chosen occupation, which I confess had faltered these last few weeks. This was why I had come here. For five long months I had travelled about Italy, learning the language, viewing the masterpieces of Naples, Rome, Florence; copying the work of the great masters, and trying my utmost to acquire their secrets with, I had supposed, some success. Now I was in Venice, which I find to be the most beauteous of all cities, putting my newly burnished skills into practice, attempting to capture scenes of its busy canals and bustling quaysides on canvas. And then, I had hoped, I might sell them to some sojourning foreigner, who would turn out to be the Earl of Wigan, or the Margrave of Linz. Or, knowing my luck, a business man from Bolton, with interests in the cotton trade, who once met with my father, and foolishly lent him money. Such funds as I had brought with me from England having run dry, I was, at this point, beginning to think I would sell my spare pair of boots for a good meal, and if things didn't improve soon, I would be parting with them for no more than a paper cone of grilled sardines from one of the hawkers, just to keep the hunger pangs at bay.

When I glanced across, perhaps for the tenth time, at my subjects, I saw it was too late to add further details to my sketch. The young woman was on the move, flouncing away across the *riva*, her cloak filling out like a sail in the breeze, making for the entrance of what I fancied must be the nun's quarters of the huge orphanage building of the Pietà. Delivering something? She might have had all her worldly possessions in that basket, but she didn't strike me as having the right temperament for one about to embrace the cloister. The young fellow who had just been exposed to the rough side of her tongue stood watching, as she yanked the bell and waited for the heavy oak door to open. Presently it did, and a vinegar-faced Sister with a sacking apron over her habit let the girl in. So she lived there, or was, at least, expected to stay some time. The door closed. Well, a story there, no doubt, but, I told myself, I had no means of ever discovering it. How wrong, as it turned out, I was about that.

I turned my drawing over, and began an outline sketch of the fish stall, roughing in the bowls of shellfish on the plank counter, and the barrel of live eels under it.

It was just as well I did, because presently I became aware of heavy breathing, and looked up. It was the fellow in the sheepskin coat. As well as being the size of a house, he had a head shaped like a turnip lantern, an impression heightened by his ample mouth and widely spaced front teeth.

He spoke. 'I — I see you make a drawing?' I translate him freely. This is not exactly what he said, but the gist of it. He had an unusual manner of speech, Venetian with a guttural overlay of something else. Germanic? Slav?

'Just trying out a few ideas for a painting,' I replied, adding, as smoothly as I dared, 'Were you requiring a picture?' He didn't look like a connoisseur, and I did not for a moment expect to sell him one. But perhaps it was his old mother's birthday, and even if it wasn't, my sales patter might distract him from tipping me into the canal, which I feared could be his intention.

'I, er, think you saw me, speaking with a young woman?' He was a slow thinker, this mangel-wurzel. Up from the *compagnia* perhaps? That would explain the ill-cured sheepskin. His coat stank. I nodded, trying to convey the impression that whilst nothing escapes the keen eye of Harry Brierfield, limner to the moneyed classes, I had only noted their encounter because I was sketching the fish stall at the time.

'You are here some time?' he queried, 'An old man may come. Little old man, legs much bent, and a hat. Tassel on his hat. And he asks — you say, never seen me? Never seen me speaking to the young woman? I — we have some business to settle. I don't want him ... putting her off.'

I wondered — who would not? — what business he hoped to settle that the intervention of an old fellow with a tassel to his hat might prevent. If it was an amorous liaison, the girl hadn't seemed enthusiastic, but it was not my place to point this out.

'My dear fellow, nothing easier!' I promised, keeping my hand flat on the paper so that the breeze didn't lift it, and expose the sketch of the couple on the other side. And sounding, to my own ears (such was my relief that he wasn't going to thump me) like my elder brother, Frank, being expansive after two or three brandies.

'I am most grateful,' he said, and digging deep into the pocket of his disgusting coat he produced two coins, and dropped them onto the open flap of my satchel. Then he clumped off along the quay in the direction of the Arsenal.

Bribery, by Our Lady! (I could use this expression here, though I would never do so amongst our Protestant neighbours in Lancashire) I knew, of course, having travelled around Italy these last months, that this is how things are done here, or, as in this case, left undone, but this was the first time anyone had tried to bribe *me*. My guide book is eloquent on what to do if one's travelling coach is set upon by brigands, but neglects to say how an English gentleman should behave if offered monetary inducements for his silence. I suppose I should have drawn myself up to my full five feet and nine inches, which would have been awkward, as I was sitting on the steps below him, stating in a loud clear voice, 'Sir, you insult me. I am the younger son of a *milord*, and my word is my bond!' I looked at the coins. I looked after Sheepskin Coat, rapidly disappearing into the distance. I asked myself what that same *milord*, Sir Francis Brierfield of Brierfield Hall, Lancashire, would do in these circumstances? I decided that, provided my mother didn't get to hear of it, he would take the money to the nearest hostelry and demand of the landlord a tankard of his best, and a portion of the rabbit pie. A man should have respect for his father's judgement. As a businessman, my father is not a pattern to walk by, but as a snapper up of unconsidered trifles he is an exemplar for us all.

    I went back to my sketch. The shade cast by the *ombrella* in the weak February sunlight presented some interesting technical problems, but I needed to hurry. Thundery clouds were massing over the bulk of *San Marco* and the *Campanile* to the North. The two coins found their way into my pocket. Pride does not buy sustenance. If the old fellow with legs much bent, and a tassel to his hat, did come by, I never saw him.

Chapter 2

Within the Orphanage of Santa Maria della Pietà, Paola, a young musician, out of loyalty to her friend, exhibits some unwise behaviour

The rehearsal had been going on for hours, and I was longing to stretch my cramped limbs. Loose sheets of music fluttered across the music salon's highly polished floor, and came to rest under our feet. Some ninny in the wind section had dropped them. I looked up, and caught Marta's expression, half horrified, half brimming with mischief. I might have known! She was signalling with her eyebrows. 'Paola, can you help me gather them up, while the old dragon has her back turned?' Sister Angelica was deep in consultation with two senior choristers, heads bent, pencils poised, over a tricky passage in the third movement. I should have learned by now to let Marta get out of her own *imbrogli*. But I laid my fiddle down carefully, and stood up. Disaster! My foot had gone to sleep, I stumbled onto the hem of my neighbour's gown, backed off and knocked into a music stand, then dropped those sheets of music I'd managed to scoop up, and collided with Marta. Then we both got the giggles.

Enough! All afternoon Sister Angelica had been a thundercloud at the back of the room, whilst overhead, real thunder rumbled. At this time of year cold winds from the Alps meet with warm air travelling up the Adriatic from the hot lands of the south, and conspire to pour a bucket of cold water over Venice.

'Paola, Marta! Get out!' Sister Angelica's name belies her nature, and such meagre stocks of patience as she possesses had been thoroughly exhausted that afternoon. 'I will not have you silly creatures disrupting rehearsals!' Grimly, her mouth a thin line, she paused, devising our punishment. The thirty musicians of *l'Orchestra de Santa Maria della Pietà* held their collective breath. Twenty four hours on bread and water? Scrubbing out the privies?

'You will go,' she decided, 'to Sister Porteress, and ask for brooms. The rain has passed over, but the *cortile* must be awash. You will sweep it free of puddles before the school children come out.' There was an audible sigh, as our comrades exhaled. Disappointed? I'll wager they were, and the rehearsal having dragged on interminably, as jealous as cats.

'Yes, Sister.' Eyes lowered, but heads high, the two of us walked out of the room. Seventeen years old, and behaving like silly chits from the schoolroom? Yes, in truth I was a little ashamed, but I did not intend anyone to know it.

As it happened, brooms stood ready, propped against the archway leading into the cloistered courtyard. Of the Porteress there was no sign, but she must have been confident of conscripting a couple of miscreants like us to use them. Giddy with relief and fresh air, I stretched my arms above my head and yawned hugely.

'Saint Paola of Rome, dear patroness, I promise to use some of my concert money to light a candle to you! Marta, why couldn't you drop your music sooner? I have my courses, which means I have a headache, backache and bellyache, quite apart from my bowing arm being about to fall off. I was ready to swoon back there.' 'I would have,' said Marta, her black eyes snapping with devilment, 'if I'd known this was the worst punishment the old crow could come up with!' She took a broom and hopped down into the *cortile*, where pools of water lay in the worn hollows of the ancient grey-brown paving stones. I stepped down after her, and for a moment we stood side by side, taking the rare opportunity to examine our reflections in a puddle. No looking-glasses for us, the nuns do not permit them. There is perhaps a chance that you would like to know how we looked? Anyway, I shall tell you. Marta is small and olive skinned, with spirals of wiry black hair escaping from beneath her lace-trimmed cap. Everything about her is lively and quick, and it's fortunate for her that her fingers dart like swallows in flight when she plays the flute or the oboe. Otherwise her equally nimble tongue would have got her thrown out of the orchestra long ago. Our orchestra of girl musicians, famous throughout all Europe, of which you have surely heard? I'm taller, with rust coloured hair scraped back from my long, pale Venetian face. They call me Paola Rossa, because of my red hair, to distinguish me from all the other Paolas and Paolinas lodged beneath the Pietà's roof. I don't have any other interesting features, not that I see them often, except as now, reflected in rainwater. My friends tell me I have a long, slender neck, an advantage for a fiddle player, they think, and fine eyes. These, they describe as grey, with a hint of green, something like our Venetian canals on a wintry morning, I suppose.

'That rehearsal was shockingly bad!' pronounced Marta, losing interest in her reflection. 'Don Antonio is getting worse, I swear it. He kept half explaining things, and then losing the thread of what he wanted to say. And *then* to go off, to see his banker, of all things! — leaving poor Barbara to beat time, not really knowing *how* he wants the piece played. When old Dall'Olgio sent to say he's sick, and Don Antonio would be acting as Musical Director, I should think Sister Angelica was fit to do a murder. She can't bully him like she does Dall'Olgio.'

'Our dear Sister Angelica fit to do a murder, surely not?' I laughed, skimming the surface of the puddle with the stiff bristles of my broom, and sending bits of our reflections flying off in all directions. 'I'm surprised she let us off so lightly. Although I'm sure she meant us to feel lower than beetles, sweeping the yard for the school children.'

'Instead of which we thank the Blessed Saints for favours received!' Marta began to dance around the *cortile* making fleeting passes at the puddles with her broom. The skirts of her red woollen chorister's gown swirled out around her, and the water flew into the air, catching rainbows from the weak rays of the sun, now struggling to emerge from behind the thundery clouds. Beyond the walls of the orphanage, out on the *riva*, or down one of the little side streets leading to *San Giorgio deghli Greci*, someone was playing an accordion, hawkers were crying their wares, but here, within the Pietà, we could have been deep in the cloister of some closed Order, cut off from the world.

'Have a care!' I grumbled, as droplets splashed my skirt. 'We'll be in more trouble if we go back with our gowns soaked through. You're supposed to sweep the water into the drain, Marta. Like this!'

'I know. So dull. It's nearly Spring, Paola, Spring! Can't you feel it, can't you smell it? Even here in horrid Venice, stones piled upon dreary old stones, and few signs beyond this poor lonely lilac bush to witness the season?' She paused to examine the fat buds on the little tree, which struggled for its existence in the centre of the paved courtyard.

'I don't know about Spring,' I replied, sweeping briskly now, to make up for Marta's lack of industry. 'I can certainly smell the drains!' They were always like this after a thunder storm, whatever the season. The rain had stirred up the muck in the pipes where they ran off from the privies into the canal.

'Ugh! Venice is disgusting. I can't understand why people flock from all over the world to see it, when it smells so bad.' Marta wasn't born in Venice, as you'll easily guess from this remark. She claims to know exactly where she comes from, a town called Rovigo, in the south of the Veneto. She can even tell you her dead parents' names, which is a good deal more than the rest of us orphans can.

'Saint Anthony save us!' I muttered, seeing movement on the other side of the *cortile*. 'Here comes one of the lay sisters with the school children, and we're nowhere near finished!' As usual, we had been talking when we should have been working.

'No, it's Sonia,' said Marta, who sees better at a distance than I do. '*Ciao*, Sonia! Hold those *ragazzaglia* back will you, while we finish sweeping?'

A plump young woman — Sonia always had a good appetite — her figure straining at the seams of her dark work gown, held up a warning finger to the gaggle of little girls at her back.

'Don't move off this step, until I call!' she admonished, and came bouncing down to join us.

'What's this?' she jeered, her round face split into a malicious grin, displaying her splayed front teeth. '*Choristers* doing chores? I thought you lot had servants to blow your noses for you!'

'Oh, we do!' simpered Marta, striking a pose. I should mention that Marta claims her parents belonged to a troupe of travelling players. 'But when we saw these puddles, and thought of your dear little charges getting their feet wet, we went straight to Sister Angelica and *begged*, on our knees, naturally, to be allowed to sweep this courtyard.'

'Liar!' Sonia wasn't deceived. 'You've done something you shouldn't have, and upset the old *vacca*. This is your punishment, right?'

'It was a very successful ruse,' declared Marta, with her usual airy disregard for the strict truth. 'I deliberately dropped the pages of my wind part, because Paola has her courses, and needed air. We're nearly finished here, so your little pets can run about and scream and shout to their hearts' content. Come on, children,' she gestured to them. 'Make a line behind me, and I'll teach you a new dance. It's called the yard sweeper's dance!'

The children, round eyed little girls, bundled up in cotton overalls, looked anxiously at Sonia, to see how she was reacting to this unusual invitation, but seeing her standing with her hands on her bulging hips, grinning, the bolder spirits ran forward and formed a line behind Marta, each one holding the one in front around the waist. Then Marta began to dance and sing, 'One, two, three, *and* swish!' as she danced around the courtyard, swooshing at the puddles with her broom. Some of the water went into the drains, and the rest was redistributed over the flagstones, now warming and drying in the late afternoon sun. The little girls soon picked up the rhythm, and the line wound around the courtyard, singing and dancing.

Then the more timid children, who had hung back, came pattering down the steps with eager, pleading faces, and made a shorter line behind me, so that I too was forced to dance and sing, despite my bellyache, and our two lines went snaking around one another. Sonia settled her rump on the low wall around the lilac bush, and folded her arms, creasing up with laughter at the pair of us, making fools of ourselves. Soon, however, I was able to plead a stitch in my side.

'Enough, children,' I puffed, breathless, 'go and play!' I flopped down on the wall beside Sonia.

'Sonia, how are you? I haven't seen you for weeks. Sometimes it's hard to credit that we live in the same building.'

I was feeling guilty about this. Sonia had been my friend for much longer than Marta. Once we two had been little shrimps like these, in ill-fitting overalls, bullied by the Sisters and the older commoners who worked in the school, dragooned into crocodiles, or made to hem handkerchiefs until our fingers bled; cuffed around the ears for every misdemeanour. Ah, happy carefree days!

'Well enough.' A note of grievance crept into Sonia's voice. Alas, for Sonia. She had so longed to be a chorister when we were nine or ten, but although she could catch a tune, unfortunately she straight away dropped it again, and as for playing the recorder, she never did sort out her fingers from her thumbs.

'You and Marta swan about with the Chosen Ones. I'm just a hard working commoner. Still, I'm promoted, did I tell you? Since Sister Teodora came, I'm a schoolroom helper. No more wiping babies' bums for me!'

'You like working with the school children?'

'It's not so bad,' she acknowledged, grudgingly, 'not that I want spend the rest of my life teaching little girls to form their letters, and hearing them stumble through the catechism. The best part is, they let me go out into the town now, on my own, not even a lay sister to chaperone me! Errands for the school, and for the nuns, if they want something. This morning Sister Domenica had me go way down beyond the Piazzetta to get some threads for the older girl's embroidery classes. I'm not going to let them coax me into a lay sister's habit, but it'll do until something better turns up. Which is a possibility,' she added, mysteriously.

I waited, to see if she would say more, but she didn't, so I said, 'Sister Teodora, she's the new one?'

Sonia nodded, a gleam in her eye. She always loved gossip, and knowing things about people, especially those things that were none of her business. 'The Order's sent her to try to raise standards in the school. She's certainly raising dust, changing things, questioning how things are done. You can imagine how certain people like that! You heard about the row with your beloved Sister Angelica?'

I waited for her to tell me. To be honest, we choristers live in a world of our own, and what goes on amongst the commoners, or in the school, largely passes us by. We're too busy singing Masses, or practising for the next concert, and trying to avoid Sister Angelica's displeasure ourselves, to notice what dealings she might have with anyone outside the music department.

'It was all to do with these,' said Sonia, indicating the children now clustering round Marta, who was letting them have turns with the broom. 'Every year the Head of School sends a list of candidates for the *Coro* to Sister Angelica, and every year she crosses half of them off without even giving them a trial. Sister Teodora asked why, and was told that *nowadays* it's a matter of *appearances*. You lot give so many public concerts now, it isn't enough to be musical anymore. To join the Pietà's angelic choir, girls have to look the part. So, no blackamoors, like Bella over there,' she nodded towards the group of children, 'no hare lips, no squints, no skin complaints! Sister Teodora says — '

I wasn't destined to hear what Sister Teodora said. One of the senior choristers, Giulietta, was flapping a tentative handkerchief at me from the cloister step.

Giulietta is so short sighted that she probably only picked me out amongst that crowd by the colour of my dress.

'Marta!' I yelped, 'we're sent for!' As Marta came scurrying, I turned back to Sonia, 'We must meet, have a proper *rattle tattle*,' I said, using our old familiar Pietà dialect, 'where and when?'

'Tonight? On the *terrazzo*, after supper?' she suggested, 'There's something I want to show you. You always made better sense of written stuff than I did. There are words in this thing that I can't make out at all.' She plunged her hand into the pocket of her gown, and produced a handful of assorted buttons, half a string of glass beads, and a coin, which glinted gold in the weak sunshine. *Gold?* What could Sonia be doing with a gold coin? She'd just mentioned running errands all over town, so unlike the rest of us, she did handle money, but surely, however many embroidery threads were needed, Sister Domenica wouldn't entrust her with — ? But before my thoughts could catch up with what my eyes had seen, Sonia's plump fingers closed around her prize and disappeared back into her pocket. 'Oh, I haven't got it with me,' she said, 'I'll show you tonight. Straight after supper?'

'I'll try!' I called, over my shoulder, as I fled after Marta. Sonia remained, sitting on the wall in a shaft of late afternoon sunlight, smiling her splay-toothed smile, looking as self-satisfied as Sister Benedetta's cat. I never saw her to speak to again.

Chapter 3

The Figlie di Coro receive an interesting invitation. Paola seizes the opportunity to meet her friend, with unexpected consequences

We arrived back to find Sister Angelica absent.

'She's arguing with Sister Teodora, the new one, in the corridor,' hissed Albetta, who sits next to me in the violin section.

Barbara, our orchestra's leader, was waiting, anxious to continue.

'Albetta, Paola, *if* you're ready? Starting from the beginning of the second movement,' she said, sounding tired, and not a little exasperated, as she waited while I fumbled for my place in the score. We played twenty four bars, badly in my case. Behind me, as I lost my place, and played two wrong notes, I heard Sister Helga hissing in disapproval to her friend Sister Juanita. Helga is a visiting student from a convent in Germany somewhere, and thinks the lack of discipline at the Pietà is quite shocking. But I was thinking about Sonia and the gold coin. There was absolutely no way that a Pietà girl could be in possession of a gold coin. Had my eyes deceived me? Perhaps it was just a gilded button from some gentleman's cuff, picked up from the chapel floor after a Mass?

Then Sister Angelica reappeared. 'That's enough, girls,' she announced, her mouth a grim line, and a faint flush staining her sharp cheek bones. The clash with Sister Teodora had evidently not ended in outright victory for the music department. 'I don't think there is any point in continuing.'

Barbara, who as well as being a superb violinist is also an able conductor, didn't protest, but just for a moment I thought I saw, from the spark in her eye, and the tightening of her mouth, a tiny flash of temper. This surprised me a little, because Barbara is usually mild and obliging to a fault. The rest of us, mightily relieved, downed instruments and began to pack away. Sister Angelica held up her hand.

'Girls! *Do* stop shuffling your music! I have two important announcements.' She always calls us girls, although some members of the *Coro* are into their thirties and in one or two cases, forties. I don't know how they feel about it, but nobody is brave enough to say anything. Spirits thoroughly crushed, Marta says. She doesn't intend to suffer the same fate. We'll get out of this place somehow, she tells me. I'll be a great opera singer, and you — there's sure to be *something* you can do.

'Firstly, girls, I've just been informed that we are to play at a private celebration. At extremely short notice, the day after tomorrow in fact. Signor Fosca, who, as you know, is Chairman of our Governing body at the present time, wants us to play at his wife's birthday party. The Prioress has agreed.' Sister Angelica's tone made it clear that she hadn't, but even she can be overruled by Mother Prioress, and she in turn by the Governors. The Prioress must have been busy, and instead of coming herself to tell her, asked Sister Teodora to acquaint her with this news. Sister Angelica wouldn't care for that.

'We don't have time to rehearse anything new,' she went on, 'but I'll consult with your section leaders, and we'll make up a short programme from our regular repertoire.'

An excited buzz now erupted. A party, in a private house! A thrilling excursion through Venice after dark! A chance to witness something of *carnevale*, something we rarely *see*, although the sounds of that revelry sometimes penetrate the ordered existence of our orphanage home. It doesn't take much to excite we *Figlie di Coro*. Our daily round consists of singing Mass, practicing, rehearsing, and performing public concerts. Commoners like Sonia may envy our supposed superior status, the extra mugs of well watered wine, and larger dollops of polenta on our plates, but the truth is our lives are strictly confined. *We* never go strolling down to the Piazzetta on a shopping spree. Even if we ever had money in our pockets, permission would not be granted. Shackled to our music stands, that's what we are, says Marta, nothing but slaves to music.

'Girls, *please!*' said Sister Angelica, 'You are not *guests* at this party. You will be there to provide half an hour's musical entertainment, after which we will leave.'

'Must we go?' A quiet voice broke in. The rest of us, frankly thrilled, turned in astonishment. 'Sister, I would beg to be excused!' Barbara was looking distressed, almost on the brink of tears.

Sister Angelica blinked. The last thing she was expecting was rebellion, especially from that quarter. In so far as she allowed herself to have favourites, Barbara was one.

'I… would much rather not,' Barbara went on. 'You know it can be quite horrid. *Out there*. When the carnival is in progress? We're supposed to be a religious house. I don't want… that is, I'm thinking of making some changes in my life. Taking my devotions more seriously…' her voice trailed away to a whisper.

Sister Angelica is seldom disconcerted, but this was clearly news to her. However, she rallied. 'Yes, well, as you know I am not enthusiastic about these secular engagements myself, Barbara, and the city is, as you say, not an entirely pleasant place for people such as ourselves, at this time of year. However, Mother Prioress has agreed this with Signor Fosca, and he has promised a cohort of his menservants to escort us. We cannot let him down. I will speak to you about it later.'

Then she broached her second piece of news. A teacher had been found to instruct those who wanted to learn the mandolin, so please to give our names to Cecilia, who would chalk them on a slate. The first lesson would be immediately after supper tonight. Another excited buzz, but this time Sister A permitted it to continue. Even if this Signor Perotti turned out *not* to be over fifty, with a face like a frog, *she* would be there to chaperone throughout.

'Are we going to sign up?' Marta enquired, as we tossed our parts into the cupboard.

'Not me. I don't care for the mandolin, do you?'

'Not a minim, but you do realize the alternative is mending circle with Sister Domenica?'

'No. Look at that queue! If we don't turn up at mending, Sister Domenica will think we're swooning over this Signor Perotti. She'll never check through all those names. I've promised Sonia we'll try and meet her for a *rattle tattle*.'

'Where?'

'On the *terrazzo*.'

'Paola, we're not allowed up there!' Marta was horrified. It's strange, Marta comes out with a lot of rebellious talk, but when it comes to actually breaking the rules that's all it is, talk. She flatly refused to come.

'You'll get caught; don't say I didn't warn you! It's dangerous; they're doing building work up there. Part of the balustrade's missing, there's nothing there but scaffolding. The wind could blow up under your skirts and toss you right across Venice! *I'm* going to sew a new lace collar on my concert gown, ready for the Fosca's party. They have two grown sons, did you know?'

What if they had? Marta was deceiving herself if she thought a lace collar would get her anywhere with the Fosca sons. We may play and sing like the Heavenly choir, but nobody in the Foscas's financial bracket would be prepared to overlook the fact that Pietà girls are the daughters of whores.

Marta and I weren't speaking over supper. We wouldn't have been anyway, because meals are eaten in silence in the refectory, but we normally signal to one another across the table by pulling faces and wiggling our brows. Marta's brilliant at this, she can carry on a whole conversation just by raising and lowering her eyebrows. Tonight she ignored me, and wiggled them at Carolina and Maria-Regina instead. But I'd promised Sonia, and even though she was annoyed with me, Marta wouldn't tell anyone where I'd gone. She probably wouldn't be asked, because Sister A would assume I was darning the holes in my stockings, and Sister D would think I'd taken up the mandolin. As soon as supper was cleared I went and sat in the privy until I judged everyone had dispersed to the music salon or the sewing room. Then I made my way towards the stairs leading to the *terrazzo*.

I told you I never spoke to Sonia again after our meeting in the *cortile*, and that's the truth, but I did see her, in the gloomy East corridor. She was leading a crocodile of little girls, who were trying her patience by attempting to play hop skip and jump on the black and white floor tiles instead of walking in an orderly file. They must have been to a music lesson, because they were clutching treble recorders. There were several lay sisters about, carrying armfuls of fresh laundry, so we didn't speak. Two little naughty ones were poking the mouthpieces of their instruments into the ribs of the two in front, and Sonia was fully occupied with boxing their ears, and trying to keep the file moving in an organised fashion, up to their dormitory. When I managed to catch her eye I pointed upwards, indicating the *terrazzo*. She grimaced, and threw up her hands, meaning give me time to settle these. I watched her broad behind disappear around the bend in the stairs, followed by the troupe of little girls. They were the same youngsters we had seen earlier; at the back of the group I spotted Bella, the one they call the blackamoor. She stuck her head through the banisters, grinning at me and waving.

'Hello, my friend!' she mouthed at me. I knew her, of course. We choristers are expected to take our turn at teaching the little ones, hearing them sing and practice their scales. Bella had a sweet voice, 'pipes like a little bird in spring time,' Marta had commented. But according to Sonia she had no chance of becoming a chorister with Sister Angelica vetting the applicants. Her skin was the colour of polished cherry wood, and someone had tortured her frizzy hair into pigtails so tight that they strained the skin taut over her cheekbones.

'Hello!' I mouthed back, smiling at her. The poor child wouldn't think me her friend if she knew how little I could do for her. No matter how true her voice, or how nimble her fingers on the stops of her recorder, I feared Bella was destined to spend her life scrubbing sheets in the laundry, or ruining her eyesight in the lace making workshop. Nothing *I* could do or say would alter that.

I was suddenly full up with misery at my own powerlessness. As an orphan, abandoned here as a babe, by a mother who was probably only too relieved to be rid of me, I have little say in my own destiny. I certainly have no power to affect that of anyone else. It didn't help my mood when I barked my shins on a linen cart which the laundresses had left parked in a shadowy corner. I hurried on, blinking back tears of pain and frustration. At the foot of the north stairs I passed Sister Benedetta, our teacher of Religion, but she had a lighted taper in one hand, and an open book in the other, and didn't see me. Or if she did, she didn't stop me, although there was nowhere up that staircase I had any business to be going at that hour.

I hadn't been up there for months. Marta was right about the scaffolding. Our cold wet Venetian winters are very destructive of the building's fabric, and I remembered that the *terrazzo* had been pronounced unsafe some time ago. There had been gangs of workmen the previous autumn, heavily policed by the lay staff, lest they do so much as ask us the time of day, doing demolition work. Nothing seemed to have happened since. All that remained was the wooden floor. The solid balustrade had been replaced by rough poles, lashed together with ropes.

These seemed too flimsy around the edges of this high exposed terrace, and as I stepped into the open my stomach lurched. Occasionally we were allowed up here in the heat of summer, to sit beneath a sailcloth awning and catch the breeze. This evening that breeze was strong and chilly. Marta's jest that I could be blown across Venice did not now seem so ridiculous. I edged my way across to a corner pole, and gazed at the scene below. The light was fading rapidly. Along the *calle*, lamps were being lit. Although it was still early, a few carnival revellers were setting out on evening excursions, torches ablaze, meeting others at the corners, and moving on like processions of fire breathing dragons. Their shouts of greeting and the strains of fiddle and drum drifted up to me. The canals glinted, pewter in the fading light.

I shivered on my eyrie in that wind from the distant mountains, wishing I'd brought a cloak, but even Sister Benedetta keeping a tryst with Virgil, could not have overlooked a chorister dressed for outdoors. The stones of the buildings were still warm from the day's fitful sunshine, and though dusk was falling, householders had not yet ordered their servants to close the shutters. Maids were laying tables; cooks drained pans of vegetables. Parents and children were coming together to eat, and share the events of their day. These glimpses of family life always distress me, a reminder of everything a foundling like me can never have. I turned away, looking out over the lagoon.

And saw something that provoked and intrigued me in equal measure. A gondola lay at the foot of the stone stairs a little way to my right; gondoliers were stationed at each end, leaning on their oars, preventing it from drifting on the current. A servant lent a hand to the embarking passengers. My eyes are not as sharp as Marta's, but I knew the two women were young and handsome from the fashionable cut of their clothes, and their lithe carriage as they stepped into the boat, and ducked their heads to enter the *felze*, the little cabin, velvet lined, that each gondola has, for the privacy of travelling ladies. I could guess that one of them was Anna Girò the opera singer, and the toast of Venice, because I didn't need the sharpest eyesight to recognise her male escort. That old fashioned wig, that baggy old greatcoat, its pockets pulled out of shape by the bottles of potion he took for his asthma, and even at this distance, that great hooked nose. Who could it be but Don Antonio Vivaldi, my violin teacher? He who had walked out halfway through this afternoon's rehearsal.

Perched on high, I found voices carried upwards, so I heard his familiar gruff tones as he dismissed the servant, stepped down to join the ladies, and commanded the gondoliers to convey the party to '*Teatro San Angelo.*'

I don't believe there was anyone who hadn't heard the rumour that Don Antonio, at sixty years of age, and *in holy orders,* had formed an *intimate friendship* with Signorina Anna.

The situation, so the gossips claimed, was that Don Antonio, as well as teaching music for nearly forty years here at the Pietà, wrote operas for the public stage. Anna Girò sang in them. Of late, Don Antonio wouldn't consider other singers, although people said her voice wasn't exceptional. It had even been said that they were living under the same roof. These scandalous rumours had caused some bishop in another town to denounce them, a financial disaster for Don Antonio, who had intended to mount an opera season there. With the result, delightful for me, that I had my dear kinsman and teacher once more. He was terribly hard up, and had to beg the Governors to let him teach violin again.

No, Don Antonio isn't really my kinsman. The jest is his. I'm nobody's kin, but I have red hair, as he did in his youth. People call me Paola Rossa, and that's what they called him too. *Il Prete Rosso,* the red priest. So he jokes sometimes that he and I are related.

'Kinswoman Rossa,' he admonishes, when I pick up my bow and send wrong notes spraying around the practice room, 'for the honour of *la famiglia*, you can do better!'

I am not imagining that I'm his forsaken daughter, or anything goose-ish like that, but Don Antonio has always pretended to see talent in me, more, I fear, than I really possess, and having someone call me kinswoman, even in jest, makes me feel better about my orphaned state.

As I watched the gondola slide out onto the gunmetal waters of the lagoon, I thought, sadly, that even an old fellow like Don Antonio has more freedom to choose his friends (and whatever the gossips say, I stoutly defend him) and go jaunting off whenever and wherever he pleases, than I do, or perhaps ever will.

All this while I was listening for Sonia stumping upstairs, confident that I'd hear her heavy feet and laboured breathing long before she arrived. So when someone at my elbow coughed, I squealed, and clutched wildly at the scaffold.

'My dear child!' exclaimed the Prioress, 'I didn't mean to startle you,' and then seeing I wasn't about to plunge over the barricade, she added, 'it isn't safe up here, my dear.'

'I see that now, Ma'donna,' I managed. Now I really *was* in trouble, just as Marta had predicted. I knew, of course, that the Prioress had her private rooms up here at the top of the building, but had overlooked the fact that I might be visible through the gaps in her shutters.

'I'm sorry, Ma'donna,' I went on, desperately devising a fib — I wasn't going to mention Sonia — 'but I have a headache, and stomach ache, and the practice rooms are stuffy.'

'So you came up here to breathe the air and soothe your spirit by looking down on our lovely city? I understand. Remind me of your name, child.'

I'd hoped she wouldn't ask. 'Paola, Ma'donna. They call me Paola Rossa.' I couldn't see her expression. Her face is always hidden inside a hood; they say half of it was eaten away by disease when she was a child. There was no moon, only a few stars glimmering in the darkening sky above the white dome of the *Salute* across the water, where clouds were building once more. Her voice was low and soothing. Had she really thought I was about to hurl myself off the roof? They say a girl tried, once, years ago. A chorister with a lovely singing voice, but she had some deformity, and the other girls were cruel to her.

'Ah, Paola Rossa. A violinist? Don Antonio thinks you promising, but Sister Angelica worries that you lack application?'

It occurred to me that she, like me, must have seen Don Antonio's departure with Anna Girò, just now, but she didn't seem concerned. Perhaps the gossip truly was just that, gossip.

'Yes, Ma'donna.' Sister Angelica would think even less of me when she heard of this escapade.

'You're not — *distressed?*' She thought I might be considering taking my own life. I'm ashamed to say that while she was speaking, I was thinking how I might use this to get out of my predicament.

'Not really, Ma'donna,' I mumbled, 'just low in spirits.' Which was true. I'd quarrelled with Marta. Sonia hadn't come. I had been feeling sorry for myself, and all the things I resented about my life. I could easily convince myself I was hard done by.

'And sometimes I feel downhearted, being a foundling, and wonder why my mother abandoned me.' I paused, then added, 'Then I realize how fortunate I am, and feel sad for girls who won't have my chances. There's a little girl, Bella — .' I was babbling now, trying to talk my way out of trouble, but the Prioress didn't seem to notice.

Relieved, perhaps, that I showed no sign of jumping.

'Ah, yes. The little blackamoor.'

'It seems *unfair* if she can't be considered for the *Coro*! She sings so sweetly.'

I heard the Prioress take a deep breath. 'Paola, often life isn't fair. You may never know what dreadful straits drove your parents to abandon you. You, *we*, are fortunate to be daughters of Venice, a City which cares for its orphaned children more than most. We must count our blessings, and make the most of the opportunities God and our city grant us.'

We often get lectures like this from the nuns, but she said it kindly, as though she really wanted me to believe it. I'd forgotten that the Prioress was a Pietà girl herself, and had come up through the *Coro* to claim her present exalted position.

Now she sighed. 'We're required now to present so many public concerts. Gone are the days when we were always concealed behind the grille in the singing gallery.'

'However,' she went on, 'We try, *I* try, to do my best for every girl here, rest assured of that, Paola. Bella may have other aptitudes and other opportunities. And now I have work to do, and must go. So must you. The bell will soon be ringing for Compline.' She motioned that I should follow her indoors.

But where was Sonia? I half expected to find her crouching in the shadows by the door, but she wasn't. I had been dreaming on the rooftop far longer than I realized. As I started down the stairs, loud, tinny, and not in the least musical, the chapel bell began to chime, and I had to gather up my skirts and run *strisciando* down three flights, to join the back of the line of choristers, filing in to perform our final duty of the day.

Squeezing into my place in the singing gallery — we still conceal ourselves from the congregation to sing during services — I peered down through the star shaped holes in the metal grille into the body of the chapel. Those present, as is usual at that hour, were all commoners and staff from the Pietà itself. It always troubles me to see the elderly laundresses with their bent backs and reddened, swollen hands; the lace makers, their eyes dimmed by years of close work, some of them barely able to fumble their way to their seats. However, they appear content, accepting the life God has given them, listening to Don Salvatore, our aged chaplain, quavering through the prayers; telling them to go to their rest in peace. I looked down at my hands, holding my choral part, remembering that these women's lot might one day be mine, if I should injure them, or if my sight became too feeble to read music.

I thought of Sonia, disappointed not to be a chorister, but who had found herself a comfortable post in the school. Where was she, with her pocketful of buttons — and a golden coin — and a letter of some kind she wanted me to read? I looked where the school staff sit, by the side altar dedicated to *San Stefano*. One of the ancient lay sisters, Sister Prudenza, had fallen asleep, lolling sideways across the chair which was Sonia's usual place. Sister Benedetta and Sister Teodora were twisting their heads round, smiling at one another, probably wondering whether to wake her before she toppled over.

Perhaps, like me, they were wondering what had happened to Sonia?

Chapter 4

A night scene, wherein several alarming adventures befall Harry

People tell me, including those who couldn't draw a cat sitting backwards, that if you want to sell your work, you must consider your market. I needed to find a way to sell mine, and soon. The alternatives were unthinkable; begging letters to my noble but impoverished relatives, with whom I had quarrelled inexorably, or starvation. But what could I do when others have already cornered the same market, and done it more successfully? Five months travelling around Italy had shown me, that however skilled I may have fancied myself to be with pencil and brush, *Il Canaletto* I am not. What aspect of Venice could I paint that no one else had done better? Or not often?

Over supper and a bottle of *Bardolino*, so generously funded by the youth in the sheepskin coat, I thought I had the answer. Venice at night. Venice as the sun drops behind church steeples, outlining the delicate tracery of ornate domes and bell towers against an apricot sky. The Venice of assignations in shadowy torch-lit alleyways. Disguised revellers cloaked and masked, caught in the light from open doorways as they seek entry to gambling dens, or brothels. *Or*, if my purchaser should happen to be a lady of refinement, these personages could be presenting their *tèssarae* for innocent musical entertainments, or romantic masked balls.

My encounter with Signor Canaletto had inspired me — I kept reassuring myself, he hadn't dismissed my work as rubbish — and my little sketch of Sheepskin-coat and his virago had given me another idea. Mysterious little scenes of Venetian life, might they be the thing with which to woo customers? I had already arranged that evening, to split a bottle or two over a game of cards with a would-be actor acquaintance who shares my dismal lodgings. So I was unable set out immediately to look for likely scenes. But after a supper of fried mullet, and a second bottle of the superior red, in the tavern we favoured, but could only infrequently afford, I vowed to do it. As my brother has often remarked, a good wine puts a rosy glow on things, and I'm not such a fool that I am unaware of this, but I still thought my scheme worth trying. Better yet, Luca, my actor friend, picked up the bill for our supper (he had snared a stint of scene shifting at the opera house). So it was with a full belly and a light heart that I stashed my drawing board in that damp cupboard my landlord calls a bedchamber, in the cockroach infested lodging house off the *Rio San Mosë* where I pay (now and then) to sleep. I took my notebook, and went out to look for suitable subjects.

I'd wandered around Venice after dark before, but always with some fellow dauber or drinking companion along. I soon became glad I had left the drawing board behind, and began to understand why night scenes are less commonly painted. Walking across the great Piazza in front of San Marco, hearing my boot heels click on the flagstones, I was suddenly alone and vulnerable. It was very late. There were shadows everywhere, despite the blazing torches stuck at intervals into wrought-iron holders around the Piazza. Great flags flapped in front of *San Marco*, a strangely forlorn sound, their ropes sawing against their wooden poles. The early evening had been mild and dry, after thundery showers late in the afternoon, but now rain clouds were massing again, and a thin mist was rising above the waters of those canals sheltered from the rising wind. I had lingered too long, listening to Luca's tales of life behind the scenes, and drunk more than was wise. The Piazza, at first sight, had seemed deserted, though a disturbing murmur of voices reached me from the shadowy *logge* on either side. Although it was Carnival season, only occasional groups of masked revellers flitted across the far end of the square. Those I saw sounded drunk and quarrelsome, and I was glad to keep my distance. Most, at this hour, must have already dispersed to taverns or private homes to eat, drink and fornicate. Only a few stragglers remained. Should I sketch those two oriental fellows in turbans, trading who-knew-what, with that sickly-looking individual in a green velvet coat? Not if I had sense. Nor that band of ne'er-do-wells lounging at the base of the statue of *San Teodor* as I turned into the Piazzetta. Men, and some women, picturesque in their rags, they mutter 'Spare some change, Signore?' to every passer-by. In the busy hours of daylight they don't trouble me. Now their mutterings carried an undercurrent of menace, which made me uneasy. If I was the kind of fellow who enjoyed fisticuffs with the lowlife, I would have stayed at home in Lancashire, and waited for our local hostelry to turn out.

I swerved to give them a wide berth, but despite this a woman shuffled forward from amongst the group, extending a claw like hand, and crying out blessings on my head, interspersed with lewd offers of sexual congress. One glance at her skeletal form, the black blemishes on her neck, and burning, feverish eyes, told me her story. Could this diseased hag once have been some innocent young beauty flirting with her lover? Where was that lover now, and by what series of betrayals had she been brought to this? I had fallen in love with a vision of Venice, beautiful as a soap bubble floating on the surface of the water, but I was beginning to know the other side of her. Venice is cruel and ugly too.

Here, in the dark Piazzetta, with the filth of the hag's curses flowing after me, I did seriously consider abandoning my undertaking. But, I told myself, I wouldn't be painting outdoors at night. If I made sketches and detailed notes, I could work up my chosen scenes in my garret.

I turned out of the Piazzetta, along the *riva*. Here, I was relieved to see, there were more ordinary folks about, stall holders packing away, and a voluble group of senators in crimson robes, who had obviously dined even better than I.

I scribbled notes. Some were still legible next day.

Gondoliers, seated, legs dangling over the edge of the quay, counting day's spoils, lantern light silvering the wavelets, covered boats, fretted prows, silhouettes. Sailing barque, a 4 master.

A beam from the ship's riding-light lit my page. Another vignette caught my attention:

Gondola, 3 persons, stepping ashore. Servant holding lamp. Ladies gowns, green, russet, sheen of velvet cloaks. Lucky fellow escorting 2 charmers.

I scribbled the roughest of sketches. They stepped from the boat, and hurried away, huddled in their cloaks, following a servant with a lantern bobbing on a pole, into the maze of tiny streets around *San Zaccaria*.

Pleased, I dismissed my previous fears, telling myself that the notion that Venice is dangerous after dark, even in the carnival season, is grossly exaggerated. Why, I'd seen more alarming sights in Preston, or even Clitheroe, after the ale houses closed. For no particular reason I wandered on along the *riva*, passing close to the spot where I had sat sketching the previous day, coming to rest on the crown of the little bridge over a narrow *rio* that ran down the side of the orphanage of La Pietà. It was very dark now, the slow moving clouds having obscured any stars, but gradually my eyes began to adjust, and rectangles of light from lamp-lit windows enabled me to make out my surroundings. I was gazing inland, suddenly aware of having left the noisy, argumentative, but somehow reassuring, voices of gondoliers and senators behind, and discovered myself to be in an unexpectedly lonely place. I was not paying any particular attention to the bulk of the orphanage building on my right, when from the corner of my eye, I saw a door open onto the small *rio* that ran down the side of the building. A candle held aloft revealed a female figure, who glanced furtively right and left, and then withdrew. I had the impression of a smooth head, and a flash of white. A nun's wimple? I was intrigued, but not alarmed.

Why would a nun be peeping out, from the safety of her cloistered quarters onto this dark and deserted walkway? The head appeared again, and this time the nun — if she was — glanced in my direction before retreating. My curiosity was now thoroughly aroused. I had heard — who in Venice has not? — boastful stories from men who claim to have had amorous encounters with nuns, but I had dismissed these as tarradiddles. Was I about to discover that at least some of these tales were true? I ran lightly down the steps and along the boarded walkway. Prying fool! Flown with wine, I forgot caution, discounted the late hour and the fact that I was alone, in a part of the city barely known to me, and indeed that what went forward here was no business of mine.

The door I had seen open was one of a pair, evidently opening onto the little *rio* to expedite deliveries to the orphanage. Strolling past, as nonchalantly as I might, I smelt the soapy aroma of wood ash and lye, and, puzzlingly, an undercurrent of the rotten sulphurous smell of spoiled eggs. These doors must indicate the laundry of the place. Could they be expecting a boatload of soiled sheets at this time of night?

Just past the double doors, I paused in the middle of the walkway, and turned to look back towards the *riva*, waiting for the woman to appear again, but just as the door began to move outwards, someone coming from behind me, from the direction of *San Giorgio deghli Greci*, barged against me, spinning me round. Then a second fellow charged at me, full tilt. My pocket book flew from my hand as I fell, catching my skull against the weathered mooring post. For a moment all was pain and blackness, then further pain, as my shins were kicked aside. One of my assailants was gasping, battling to catch his breath, as he struggling to untie mooring ropes. The other had already jumped down into a small rowing boat, and was hissing angry words, in a language which might as well have been Greek to me (as indeed it turned out, it was) at the first fellow for his clumsiness. I lay still whilst he succeeded in freeing the painter and leapt down to join his comrade, who was already pulling on the oars, sculling the pair of them out towards the lagoon. Then I crawled round the mooring post and stood up, waiting for the pain to pass. My notebook, with all my splendid ideas in it, was trampled and torn, but the stub of my one remaining pencil, I was relieved to find, was still in my pocket.

My head had begun to clear, and I was bending to retrieve the notebook, when a second band of ruffians, four or five of them this time, running hard from the same direction, charged at me, this time raining cudgel blows on my head and shoulders and knocking me to the ground in their haste to clear the pathway. My head cracked on the boardwalk. My face and ribs were kicked. Trying to avoid my assailants' boots, I half rolled, half fell, over the edge into a flat bottomed barge that lay alongside.

I cannot say how long I remained insensible. At some point I must have drifted from unconsciousness to sleep, and from sleep to sudden jolts into wakefulness. Several times during the night I was roused by voices, by the clatter of passing feet or other, unidentifiable sounds, penetrating my befuddlement. At one point two or more people came ashore from a boat, one of them an elderly man grunting and wheezing his annoyance that the boatman was unwilling to take them any further. The woman (or, I thought, women) accompanying him, offered assistance to help him ashore, one of them discoursing the while about "the second act aria". Evidently opera goers, or even, from the carrying nature of this woman's tones, performers. I considered calling out to them for assistance, but did not. Their footsteps and their voices died away as they walked inland towards the heart of the *Castello* district. It seemed to me only moments later (though it may have been more) that I was jerked awake again. This time the barge rocked beneath me, as though the canal had been agitated by a passing boat, or by some heavy object being dropped into it. A fetid smell of garbage, and other things more vile, which I was not eager to identify, rose from the disturbed waters. I became aware that my head was aching abominably, and my eyes had difficulty in focusing on the few twinkling stars visible in the cloud flecked heavens. At least the threatened rain had passed over, though that was small comfort. Desperate to pass water, and with my stomach urgent to part with its contents, I struggled to my knees to relieve myself over the side. Not long after this, a late band of youthful carnival revellers, returning no doubt from some *ridotto* or drinking club, stumbled past, roaring what I imagined to be indecent songs. A few of these rips paused to empty their bursting bladders into the canal, and whilst they did so, flaming torches wavered briefly in the unsteady hands of their comrades, illuminating the lower courses of the red brick of the orphanage building. I held my breath, and fortunately must have remained invisible to them in deep shadow at the bottom of the barge. Then, thanks be (I think?) to Saint Jude, quiet and darkness returned. I crawled under a ragged piece of canvas I found in the bottom of the boat, and gave myself up to Morpheus once more.

I woke at daybreak to the sound of doors being thrown back, squealing on rusty hinges; pots and pans clashing, and female voices, young and old, calling to one another. The sky above me was grey white, the cloud having thickened during the night, but even so the light was almost too bright for my eyes. My head ached; and my limbs, when I crawled from under the canvas, cried out in protest. Had I drunk too much last evening? *Yes, but that was not the cause of my discomforts.* I remembered now, only too well. I had been attacked, first by one band of ruffians, and then another. Venice at night, in the lawless time of *Carnevale*, a perilous place, just as everyone had warned me. I shall not, I vowed, struggling to my feet, make that mistake again.

I stretched my cramped limbs, another mistake. The boat rocked and I fell, scraping my nose and mouth against the rough hemp of the mooring rope, causing blood to stream afresh. I dabbed it ineffectually with my neck cloth. My clothes were filthy; my shirt front already stiff with blood from my wounds, was now absorbing a second torrent. A buckle had been torn from my knee-breeches, and they were rent over one thigh. Bluntly, I'd seen vagabonds more elegantly turned out. I must, I reasoned hazily, go back to my lodgings and change my clothes, before I was hustled out of Venice as a vagrant.

I hauled myself out of the boat onto the walkway. The door to the orphanage's kitchen was open to the pearly morning air. Within, I glimpsed women in aprons, their heads bound in kerchiefs, chopping, pouring, stirring. The smell of food was both tempting and dismaying. My stomach rumbled, but bile rose in my throat. The last time I'd felt so ill was the night I spent drinking with Frank, my brother; the night I fled Lydia's father's house. But this was no moment to revisit the sins of the past.

I turned back towards the *rio*, and the barge where I had so recently lain. The water was being disturbed by another small, snub-nosed boat, laden with vegetables, which an old man was poling, gondola style, out towards the *bacino*. Cabbage leaves, slats from a broken crate, and other detritus, swirled in his wake, and in the lee of the laundry barge, just below where I stood, a black and white bundle of some sort bobbed beneath the water.

In my dulled mind, I tried to name it. A bundle of washing, clumsily spilled overboard by whoever made deliveries here? A parcel of kitchen waste dropped by the rubbish collectors? Slowly, the bulky object turned in the gently swirling current. A human hand. A head, a face, gleamed in the depths, black hair streaming. The body of a young woman was floating just beneath the surface of the canal.

I don't think I made a sound, I just stood, transfixed, blood dripping, slowly now, from my nose onto my shirt front and my hands. I must have presented a gory spectacle, for when two men in red caps appeared round the corner of the building, and saw me, frozen to the spot, they surged forward to see what I was staring at. Then one of them began yelling.

Instantly, it seemed, people poured forth from the orphanage building, and surrounded me. They formed a small but noisy mob, consisting of the two greasy red caps, the custodians, they claimed, of the barge, a bemused elderly man in priest's vestments, and a gaggle of women of various ages, dressed identically in dark gowns and white aprons: the orphanage's kitchen staff, some of them carrying vicious looking knives. One, older, bent nearly double, with a wart on her nose, came hobbling from the laundry next door, carrying a jackdaw in a cage.

'He's killed someone! This foreign devil's killed someone!' declared one of the red caps. 'He's killed 'er and thrown 'er in the water! Look at 'im, hands covered in 'er blood!' His accent was as thick as the mud at the bottom of the canal.

'Well, fish her out then, Giorgio, you useless *cretino*,' commanded the old woman with the warty nose, 'use yer boathook. Grab a hold of this fellow, Nardo, while we see who he's killed!'

I should have run. Taken to my heels and not looked back, but I am that fool, A Man of Reason. Also, a man who has always supposed, because he is the squire's son, and they always have, that the lower orders will listen to him. Once I got them to calm down and attend to me, I was sure they would realize that the blood on my hands and clothes was my own, and that the body in the water had been there long enough for any blood she might have shed to have washed away. For I now suspected that the rocking motion I had experienced during my night in the barge was caused by this poor wretch's corpse being lowered into it. But the mob, roused by the sight of blood, even though it was mine, not hers, were more inclined to listen to the spiteful old bundle with the jackdaw. The bigger of the two boatmen — I surmised they were brothers — seized my arms in an iron grip, so that I could not change my mind and run, whilst the other climbed down into the barge, and used a pole with a hook on the end to catch hold of the corpse by her apron strings, and pull her against the side of the boat. Then he grasped the skirts of her sodden gown, and dragged her over the side. From there, eager hands reached down to lift her up onto the canal side.

'*It's Sonia!* You've killed Sonia, you foreign devil!' one of the harridans howled, waving a paring knife under my bloody nose.

'Now, Annetta,' quavered the priest, who had taken no part in the proceedings until now, and seemed to be as dazed by it all as I was, 'we don't know that *he* killed her. For if he had, would he not have run away? It could be that he too has been assaulted. Look! His head is bruised and bloody. Perhaps, even so early in the day, they were attacked by assassins. Signore, can you describe them?'

I did my best to tell my story. The priest, whom they called Don Salvatore, seemed willing to listen to my stumbling explanations, but the rest were unconvinced. I was a vile foreigner, too idle and steeped in wickedness to speak their language properly, and had most likely received my injuries when the poor girl tried to defend herself from ravishment. Don Salva should not be fooled, they insisted. Opinions within the group varied only in that some thought I should be thrown into the canal immediately, and others that I should be locked up until such time as I could receive similar treatment from the men of the local Watch Brigade. Don Salvatore lived up to his name, proving to be *my* salvation. Frail as he was, he commanded respect from these wretches, and he forbade them to throw me into the canal. On pain, I hoped, of excommunication.

'No bickering, good people!' he quavered, 'It is unseemly. This poor child, Sonia, is unshriven, and her soul is in need of our prayers rather than curses. I will take charge of this fellow, and take him indoors to the nuns. Giorgio, go speedily and fetch the Captain of the Watch. He shall tell his tale to him.'

Giorgio, the boatman, who with his brother, I soon learned, was employed by the orphanage to fetch and carry laundry, argued that Don Salvatore should not attempt this. I might attack him as soon as I was out of their sight. *They* would take me to the nuns, and see me locked up.

'He's a dangerous swine!' squawked the crone with the jackdaw, although nobody had asked her opinion. 'Bring him through the laundry. I will give you rags to bind him. See that the nuns put him in a room with a stout lock on the door, Don Salva, or he'll be murdering all us poor defenceless women!'

'Now, Signora Amelia, nobody here is going to be murdered,' mumbled the old priest. Though a puff of wind could have blown him off the quayside, he stood no nonsense from this harpy. 'This poor child may not have been *murdered*. It may have been some horrible accident.' He turned to me, 'You were alone? You didn't see this girl?'

'I never saw her before in my life, Father,' I replied stoutly, believing I spoke nothing but the truth, but even as I said it, one of the kitchen workers knelt by the girl's body and turned her over, so that I saw her face clearly for the first time, and realised what I had just said was untrue. I had a portrait of her, still safely stowed in the inner pocket of my coat. She was the young woman who had bandied words with Sheepskin coat, the one he had bribed me to say I had not seen.

Chapter 5

Accused of murder, Harry is unimpressed by the prevailing forces of law and order

They dragged me indoors, along a passage and through a doorway. Then they tossed me aside like a sack of soiled underdrawers, to be dealt with later. My skull came into contact with the edge of a stone step, and I passed out again. When next I became aware of my circumstances, my head was aching worse than before, and my hands and feet were firmly bound. That rabble really believed I had killed the girl! And the venomous old witch from the laundry had kept her promise to give them strips of torn sheeting with which to bind me.

Alas, I fear I have little of the hero in me. I lay still, feeling too weak to struggle, praying that feigning death would somehow help my plight, and trying to remember the name of the British Consul in Venice. No idea, but that Irish fellow would know, the one who acted as an agent for artists wishing to sell paintings to the *milords* doing the Grand Tour. Owen Somebody. McSweeny? I'd met him. At least, I'd had him pointed out to me in some tavern or other. It looked as though I was going to need him, though not, as I had hoped, to find buyers for my paintings. I lay listening to angry, excitable female voices in the distance. My accusers were going over what had happened, yet again, with the priest and a woman with a deep, resonant voice, who seemed to be taking charge of the proceedings. She sounded surprised, shocked, but not vitriolic. Then she gave an order, and I heard wooden patterns and metal tipped boots clattering on the stone-flagged floors. An outer door slammed, cutting off the contentious voices. I risked opening my good eye.

The room they had thrown me into was not some locked and barred cell, as the old woman had recommended, but the vestry of a chapel. A dense aroma of incense and candle grease hung in the musty, dusty air, and behind a faded velvet curtain, partly drawn aside, I could see part of a small altar. Over it hung a portrait of the Madonna with a naked Holy Child displayed somewhat carelessly on her lap.

'Madonna,' my swollen lips tried to form a prayer, 'I need your assistance, immediately if you can manage it!' It was a bad painting, fussily framed in carved and gilded curlicues. The Virgin's smile was smug, rather than serene. Her upturned gaze was fixed on the ceiling, hands folded in prayer, quite unconcerned by the likelihood that the Infant Saviour might roll off her knees. If she heard me, she gave no sign.

Earthly voices were coming closer, but the on-comers didn't glance in my direction. I heard the squeak of wheels turning, and through my eyelashes saw boots and spokes pass by. A wooden bier, droplets of water, and the stench of the canal. They were bringing Sonia's body in here. Poor girl, indeed she deserved to be treated with reverence, not left like a dead tunny fish on the canal side. More feet crossed the flagstones, and halted close by. I saw two pairs of black shoes, one with silver buckles, one with cloth ties, and the dusty hems of two black robes.

'This is the fellow who says he was attacked, Sister Serafina.' I recognised the priest's quavering voice. 'Giorgio and the women from the kitchen — and old Amelia from the laundry of course — are convinced he must be the one who killed her, but he's been badly beaten himself, as you can see. He's some breed of foreigner, which of course convinces them of his guilt. But what reason would he have to kill Sonia, I wonder? Is it not possible that he too was a victim?'

'That remains to be seen, Don Salvatore,' replied the nun, poking me in the small of my back with the toe of her shoe, hard enough to find a bruised spot above my hip. With difficulty, I suppressed a grunt of pain. She bent over me, and I saw keys and a pair of scissors, as well as the obligatory rosary, dangling from a chain around her middle area. An observation I have made during my time in this country is that nuns lack waists. Of course, having embraced religion, I suppose they would not consider it right to employ the tight lacing fashionable ladies favour, and in any case their robes are all concealing. I guessed this one must be the Infirmarian; naturally they would send for her in the circumstances. It didn't sound as though she would be offering me salves for my wounds.

'What kind of foreigner do you think, Father?'

The rise and fall of the hem of the priest's robe suggested that he was shrugging his shoulders in that exaggerated fashion Italians favour. '*Inglese*? *Tedescho*? Giorgio thinks German. His accent is vile.'

My accent was vile! What about Giorgio's? Determined as I was to feign unconsciousness, I nearly gave myself away with a snort of indignation.

'A German speaker we could find,' said the nun, Sister Serafina, as I now knew her to be, 'amongst our foreign music students. I believe we have a postulant studying with us at present from a convent in Bavaria. I'll send someone with a message to Sister Angelica, and ask her to send her down here.' She clicked her fingers, one of the women escorting the bier approached, and was dispatched. 'But English, no, we have no one. The English are a nation of heretics.'

I wanted to rear up and correct this assumption. Sister, my family holds to the true faith! My father rose — ineffectually, and he all but bankrupted his family in the process, but never the less he *rose* — for Rome, and James Stuart, against Hanoverian George. But I knew that if I attempted to get to my hobbled feet I would very likely be overcome by dizziness and nausea, and I didn't suppose I would receive any sympathy from this formidable *religiosa*.

The old priest took a more generous view. 'He does speak and understand some Italian, though not perhaps Venetian. He answered my questions readily enough. I confess even I find Giorgio hard to follow when he's excited, and of course Nardo has no roof to his mouth.' So saying, the old fellow bent his aged back to examine me more closely. A gnarled finger poked about under my bloody neck cloth. His swollen finger joints smelt strongly of wintergreen. I feared I might sneeze.

'Yes!' he exclaimed. 'See, he is of the Faith! He wears a crucifix. Protestants, I understand, disdain them.'

'That doesn't excuse his sending Sonia to her Maker, if that's what he did.' The Infirmarian wasn't impressed by the crudely worked silver image of our Lord on the cross that my mother had forced on me before I left for Italy. A tough old bird, this Sister Serafina.

'The kitchen women tell me his hands were wet with blood,' she added.

'Indeed, but his nose was bleeding. He had fallen, or so he said, getting out of the barge, and set it bleeding again. And, to my mind, though I know little of such things, the girl had been in the water some hours. There was no sign of blood on her, when they lifted her out. He claims to know nothing of her. He told me he was attacked by two groups of ruffians last night, and that he fell into the barge, where he remained, sleeping off the effects of his beating, until this morning.'

'I shall maintain an open mind, Don Salva, until we hear how he answers the Watch. I understand from Sister Domenica that Sonia's bed had not been slept in, and no one had seen her this morning, or sent her out on any errand. So it's possible that she was killed last night, and almost certainly not just now, when this fellow was discovered. He might have killed her in a drunken frenzy last night, of course. There were certainly groups of drunken people about,' she sighed. 'I was woken several times between the Offices. *Carnevale*, of course, and these foreigners are easily led into drinking much more than they are used to, and behaving in ways they never would at home — and our own citizens hardly set them a good example. Perhaps he was wondering how he might dispose of her more effectively when Giorgio and Nardo seized him? But let the Watch deal with him. I have made it clear, I hope, to our kitchen staff, that it is not for us to administer justice. His breathing seems regular enough, we can safely leave him for the moment. I'd better see how they're getting on with laying that poor child out,' she added, turning to walk away towards the other end of the room, from whence soft rustlings suggested that a small army of lay workers was busy removing Sonia's sodden clothing, and preparing to dress her in a clean dry shroud. The old priest stayed a further moment, peering down at me thoughtfully, whilst stroking his bony chin. Then he too pottered off, out of my line of vision.

Before he could have taken many steps however, there were fresh sounds from the doorway. Young women's voices and the patter of leather soles on stone. I opened my good eye again to see the newcomers.

Robes billowing round her portly form, Sister Serafina came hurrying back to intercept them, exclaiming, 'Paola, Marta!'

Red dresses, and the taller girl, who also had reddish hair, carried a violin by its neck. So these two were part of the celebrated choir and orchestra, of whom I had heard, even in far off Lancashire. Young and slender in contrast to Sister Serafina. Comely too, though I was in a poor state to appreciate their charms.

'Sister Angelica said you wanted me,' the girl with the violin gasped. She stared across at the group around the bier, and her eyes widened in shock. 'Oh, Sister, is it — *Sonia?*' her face drained of colour, and she began to tremble. The nun and the shorter, dark haired girl, stepped hastily towards her, seizing an elbow each.

Sister Serafina was probably well used to dealing with young women in fainting fits, but even her bracing approach didn't help. The girl's knees buckled, and she subsided onto the floor.

Her companion appeared not nearly so afflicted by the tragedy. Her concern for her friend was real enough, but nevertheless I noticed that her dark eyes flitted towards the bier with a certain startled interest.

'Our Lady have mercy, I've left the hartshorn in the dispensary!' exclaimed Sister Serafina, letting go.

'Shall I go and get it?' inquired the dark girl.

'Do, Marta. One of the Sisters will give it to you. Put that fiddle somewhere safe before you go. Don't worry about *him*, he's well bound and can't hurt her,' she added, nodding in my direction. The girl, Marta, seemed to notice me for the first time, also lying on the floor, but after sending a puzzled glance in my direction, she scurried away. Sister Serafina stood watching the swooning girl for a moment, but then returned to the bier. I continued to feign unconsciousness, one eye open for her return, but the young woman, Paola, was already coming out of her faint. Presently she sat up, and she too, noticed me for the first time.

'Who are you?' she demanded.

I struggled to a sitting position, hitching my shoulder up against the stone step, despite my tightly bound wrists and ankles. 'I am inno —' I began. It seemed vitally important that she should understand this, yet the Italian word *innocente* was impossible. It had become difficult to talk at all through my now much swollen lips. Before I could try again, a party of rough-looking individuals, led by my arch enemy, Giorgio, came barging into the vestry.

'*Ecco!* The foreigner. See, he's knocked another to the ground!' the imbecile yelled, pointing at the girl, who was sitting splay-legged on the floor. They crowded round me. Four big garlic-scented, greasy haired individuals carrying cudgels. I recognised the garlic breath... and the cudgels. I had bruises all over my body to prove this, although I hadn't seen their owners in daylight before. My second set of attackers of the night before had been members of the Watch. I hadn't imagined my heart could sink any lower.

'Oh, him!' To my surprise, the biggest of these brutes recognised me. 'One o' them foreign artists. We come across him last night,' he sniffed, 'thought you'd got another for us, Giorgio, but this here's just an incidental. Already been knocked about by the Greeks before we ran into him.'

At the sound of men's voices, Sister Serafina and Don Salvatore had come hurrying back, and the lay workers, too, left their task, and pattered over to listen in. Soon I was surrounded by another crowd, which included a small, grubby white dog, which one of the watchmen had brought along. He planted his smelly rump against my thigh, and began a serious assault on his fleas. Sister Serafina took a moment to haul Paola, to her feet.

'Greeks?' quavered Don Salvatore, against a background of shocked faces. I knew that Venetians regard all Greeks as treacherous, for having failed to help defend Venetian territory against the Turks.

'Murdering bastards!' spat the captain of this bunch of uglies, failing to observe Sister Serafina's disapproval.

'If you'd let us have a look at the dead wench, Ma'am?' he inquired of her, 'I'll show you what most likely happened to her.'

Sister Serafina, glancing at Paola, who had begun to regain her colour, but was now rapidly losing it again, frowned. I could see she was calculating whether to send her right away, but her friend had not returned and evidently she did not trust her not to faint again. After a quick glance around the vestry, she marched the girl over to a bench against the furthest wall.

Although the Captain of the Watch seemed willing to discount me as a murderer, Giorgio and Nardo were not about to give me up. Or perhaps they thought I would be eager to view the corpse with everyone else. At any rate, as the scandalised bevy of lay women parted to let the watchmen stride across to the bier, they took hold of me under my armpits and dragged me roughly along; adding many bruises to my shins, and causing my split lip to bleed again. They dumped me in a seated position against a pillar, and stood one either side of me, gawping at the proceedings, as though they had paid good money to attend a public entertainment.

Such, I fear, is human nature. I'm told it is quite the thing in London now to attend the dissection of corpses by fashionable surgeons, and my father's grooms like nothing better than to ride to Preston and see a public hanging. So it was with these people, given the opportunity to gape at a body dead by violence. Those docile lay sisters, heads bowed meekly, or so I'd thought, looked on avidly, sharp eyes glancing from the dead girl to the Captain of the Watch, eager for grisly details.

Needless to say, the big lout was enjoying all this attention, pushing the poor girl's sodden hair roughly aside to expose a bruised, depressed area above her right ear, and a cut on her left temple. Alive, they wouldn't have permitted him to touch her, but in death no one uttered a word of protest. I wanted to shout out, but could not, lest it be seen as a sign of guilty knowledge. Did no one care for this poor dead creature? I had only seen her once, and I doubted that I should have liked her much, but she had been so alive. Did no one grieve at her death? One person did, surely? The girl with the red hair. I glanced over my shoulder to where she sat, some distance away, forlorn on her bench, a young woman who had forgotten her handkerchief, and was having to wipe her eyes and nose on her sleeve. She stared back at me, brow creased, as though I was a riddle-me-ree she could not solve. The rest of them gazed at the corpse like eager spectators at a play.

The Watch Captain made sure he had the full attention of his audience, took a deep breath, and tucked his thumbs into the armholes of his filthy leather waistcoat. Here was a man with a Theory he intended to expound.

'What happened,' he assured us, 'was this,' and he began to recite in a wooden fashion, as though from a report already composed for his superiors, whoever they might be.

'Late last night, acting on information received, concerning a fracas at Zenotti's tavern, we proceeded there, to find a brawl in progress and a young fellow, a boat builder by profession, dead of a knife wound. We attempted to arrest the culprits, but they broke away from us. A band of Greek sailors they was, from that ship that's tied up on the *riva*, the *A'o Paraskava*. She's out of Corfu with Venetian Officers, but the crew's a parcel of lousy Greeks.' He made as if to spit again, but this time he spotted Sister Serafina's expression.

'We gave chase, and two of them split off from the rest. They certainly could run, lily-livered cowards! Got away, and stole a boat that was tied up by your laundry.'

He then indicated me, hunched against my column, 'We ran into *him*, staggering about on the pathway. Reckon they'd beaten him up.

Mebbe the boat they took was his? And this young woman, she must'a got in their way, and got the same. Bashed over the head, see, here?' he indicated the larger wound, a livid contusion which had barely broken the skin, 'and shoved in the canal, where she drowned, if she weren't already dead. Sad. But we've got them murdering bastards, don't you worry. Went aboard the *Paraskava* at first light. Blood on their clothes still, from the fellow they'd knifed. *They* won't be crossing back across the *Ponte dei Sosperi*.'

The Bridge of Sighs. Even an ignorant foreigner like myself knew what that meant. Those who are thrown into Venice's main prison have to cross this graceful limestone-clad bridge on their way to the dungeons. Few cross back. An icy sensation travelled down my spine, which didn't come from the stonework I was leaning against. If those harridans from the kitchens had prevailed, *I* might be the one crossing that bridge. I supposed I should be grateful to this oaf. What I should *not* do, was point out that his precious Theory was all humbug. Sonia was not the girl who had peered out from the laundry. That one, I could swear, had a long, thin face. Sonia's cheeks, even in death, were plump. I didn't believe the Greeks had killed her. Although I had been stunned by that first attack, I hadn't lost consciousness. I knew they had fled immediately in the boat. Also, it now occurred to me, on the word of the Watch Captain himself, if they had been armed, it was with knives, not blunt instruments. And who, minutes afterwards, had come rushing along the footpath, cudgelling anyone who got in their way? After I received the blows to the head, and the fall which finally knocked me out, Sonia must have come out of the orphanage building — or walked back along the footpath from a late night excursion. Perhaps the other young woman had been looking out for her, waiting to let her in? Small wonder this so-called guardian of the law wanted to pin the blame on the Greeks. In all likelihood he had killed her himself, knocking her out of the way, and leaving her to drown. No one else present had any reason to question his recital.

'So this young man had nothing to do with it?' queried the priest, nodding in my direction. *Thank you, Father.*

'I'd say not,' agreed the Captain of the Watch, magnanimously, 'though you may want to ask yerselves, was *he* the reason the young woman was outside of these premises at midnight?' At this baseless insinuation, fury swelled in my bosom, but even if I could have framed sentences, I dared not challenge him. I found it infuriating to be so helpless, so unable to express myself in words these people would understand, but there it was. Lack of fluency in the Italian language, let alone the Venetian dialect, reduced me to cowardice.

'*That* we will certainly inquire into,' said Sister Serafina, giving me a sharp glance. 'Giorgio, you may show the gentlemen of the Watch out, then go to your duties. We must prepare poor Sonia for burial. Speculating about how she met her death cannot restore her to life.'

Rather reluctantly, I thought, the men of the Watch trooped out, taking their dog, but not all his fleas, with them. Perhaps they had been hoping to be offered refreshments. Then, eyeing me with fierce disapproval — if not a murderer, then a vile seducer! — the lay workers reluctantly returned to their task.

The Infirmarian turned her attention to me.

'Well, young man, do you understand what we have been saying?'

'If you speak slowly, Sister.'

'You know that you are not, after all, accused of killing the girl? And you heard what the Watch Captain said? *Had* you arranged to meet Sonia for some purpose?'

'No, Sister. I swear it before God Himself!'

This declaration failed to impress her as much as I hoped.

Chapter 6

In which Paola receives good news and bad

    I shall always feel that I should have said something. But I didn't know Sonia was dead, that she might have been dying, even while I was spinning falsehoods to Mother Prioress up on the roof. My only comfort is, that even if I had spoken, it would probably have been too late to save her. It wasn't like her to miss our rattle tattle, but one of the little girls might have come down with a fever, and she had to stay with her. Or one of the senior commoners who patrol their dormitories could have ordered her to stitch a torn pinafore. There were many reasons, I well knew, that might have prevented her from coming. I didn't want to get her into trouble by asking someone why she hadn't kept our rendezvous. She would be in enough of that already, as I supposed, for missing chapel.

    As choristers, our day begins with singing Prime, the first Office of the day, after which we partake of bread rolls dipped in bowls of milky coffee in the refectory. Then we go to the practice rooms to warm up, play scales, or practice particular pieces under the instruction of our section leaders. That day began no differently from any other, except that Chiaretta took the violins that morning; Barbara had sent word she had a migraine. This was unusual, I couldn't remember an occasion when Barbara had missed practice pleading ill health, although she often looked tired and strained, and perhaps particularly so, I thought, of late. As for me, I wasn't so concerned about Sonia that I failed to sense the excitement in the air. Today we would be told what pieces Sister Angelica had decided were suitable for the party (she claims to consult people, but who dares challenge her choice?).

    But, when the practice hour was over, and we made our way to the music salon, she wasn't there. Audible, however, as we stepped into that quiet wood-panelled room, were certain wheezing and scratching sounds, coming through an open door from the small side room where the copyists work. Peeping in, we found Don Antonio seated at their work table, dipping a goose quill into the inkwell, and covering sheets of manuscript paper with a salvo of notes.

'Make ready with your instruments, you string players,' he growled, as we crowded into the doorway, 'I have a new piece for you to play at this party the Foscas are giving, and we have no time to lose if you're to do me credit.'

Then seeing our surprised expressions, because Sister Angelica had indicated that the music for the party was just a chore, and therefore of no interest to Don Antonio, he added, 'Signor Dall'Olgio is still suffering shockingly with his gout, but by a lucky chance, the rehearsal at the opera house is cancelled, so I find myself free. *This* is a simple little violin concerto, a mere morsel,' he declared, his pen scratching a fusillade of complications, so that ink flew everywhere, spotting his wig and Albetta's gown, 'which I have just this moment conceived,' he left off scribbling and pointed with his quill, 'in which *you*, Paola Rossa, will play the solo!'

A dry cough interrupted him. 'I'm afraid I cannot permit that,' said Sister Angelica, as the crowd in the doorway parted to let her through. 'Paola's recent behaviour has not merited such an honour.'

At this promise of a solo, I'm sorry to say any thought of Sonia flew from my head, and my heart soared up like a singing bird, but now here came Sister Angelica with a crossbow to shoot me down.

'Nonsense, woman!' grunted the *maestro*, taking up a little bag of white sand, and shaking some onto the wet manuscript. 'The way to keep these young women free of sin is to keep them busy. If she's to master this by tomorrow, I guarantee she'll have no time for foolishness.'

'She'll never manage to learn it in so short a time,' sniffed Sister A, and seeing how the army of crochets and quavers fell over themselves as they rushed up and down the stave and across each page, I feared she might be right. 'In any case, nothing new is needed for these people, at such short notice. *You* know well enough, Don Antonio, that the guests will gossip and chatter throughout the whole performance!'

Don Antonio wagged his goose quill at her. 'But Sister, *I* shall be there, and our hostess will expect something new from my pen. And if, as you say, the guests are chattering, Paola's lack of experience will pass unnoticed. How are these young women to gain confidence, if we don't put them on their mettle?'

Now we had the truth of it! Don Antonio had received his *carta*, a personal invitation to the celebrations. (Perchance he had cancelled that opera rehearsal himself?). Signora Margarita Fosca, the birthday girl, would be hoping he had written something in her honour. Perhaps, too, he knew she had a recently deceased aunt, for whom she might commission a Mass, if the birthday offering pleased her? That disastrous opera season in Ferrara had emptied my self-appointed kinsman's coffers.

'Very well, if you insist,' Sister Angelica acquiesced, purse-mouthed, 'but don't blame me if the silly chit makes a mess of it.'

'We must get to work, or the whole concert will be a disaster. Shoo, girls, shoo!' wheezed our old music master, driving us all before him as he hobbled into the music salon to take the rehearsal.

I was sent to sit in the alcove where the instruments are stored to study my solo, quaking with a mixture of fear and elation. I had played solo parts before, but only during services, tucked away behind the grille, which is somehow less alarming, since no one sees you except your fellow choristers. Though they, of course, are far from sparing in their criticisms afterwards. The thought of standing up to play in full view of a fashionable, prattling audience — my knees weakened at the thought, but I was determined to justify Don Antonio's faith in me. Could I learn the part? I was pretty confident, now I'd had a short time to study it, that I could, because, although I would never admit this to cynical Marta or anyone else, it wasn't particularly original. In truth it resembled many other pieces Don Antonio had written over the years. *My* task would be to make it sound lively and inventive, so that Signora Margarita would believe it newly minted in her honour.

Sitting with my fingers stuffed in my ears so that I could concentrate on the score, I wasn't immediately aware of a tempest brewing. It was only when Maria-Regina came barging past me, laid her trumpet on the shelf, and took up a double bass, that I realised that half the orchestra was leaving. *What in the name of all the saints?* I removed my fingers from my ears to discover what was going on. Maria-Regina obliged me by muttering, as she pushed past again, 'Strings only. Don Antonio's dismissed the brass and woodwind sections, *they* won't be needed at the party!'

Strings only! No woodwind, no brass, no timpani? Those girls who regularly play in more than one section, like Maria-Regina, were making haste to seize an alternative instrument. Poor Marta, her instruments are woodwind and voice. I looked across, and saw her standing by the door, her face flushed with chagrin, biting her lip, and wondering, I think, whether to add an appeal to Sister Angelica, to those of Carolina and Ambrosina, but it was clearly useless. Sister A had already made it plain that she disliked the party scheme, and would have preferred that none of us went. And although she could, and did, bully most of our music teachers, she had never succeeded in bending Don Antonio to her will. It would be fruitless, furthermore, for her to ask the Prioress to overrule him, when he was to be the Foscas' invited guest. I watched as Marta scowled, turned on her heel, and trailed out of the room.

As for Don Antonio, he simply ignored the fuss his announcement had created, waiting with his scores spread out in front of him, for the room to clear and the strings to be ready to play. Soon he called me to join them. We played, or at least began, a piece we had all played many times before, the first movement, the *allegro* from his *Four Seasons*. It was February, after all; there were signs that spring was on its way to Venice, and besides, people who are not knowledgeable about music like to hear familiar pieces, to which the ladies can tap their fans, and the gentlemen their feet. Which was no doubt why Don Antonio had chosen it. Barbara, who is gifted with all string instruments, was to lead on the night of the party. Sister Angelica must have convinced her that it was her duty to do so. But since there was no Barbara this morning, Don Antonio called Giulietta forward to substitute for her. Poor Giulietta was so nervous at being the focus of this sudden attention that she played badly.

Don Antonio decided to be exasperated. 'Where *is* everyone today? We have several empty chairs. Barbara pleads a headache? *I* have a headache! I was kept late at the Opera last night, and the damp night air affects my chest, but I am here, taking this rehearsal. I do not let minor ailments keep me from my work! And what of our young persons from distant lands? Our postulants, our *core spese*? Their convents have paid good money to have them study with us. *Hmm?* Sister Angelica, I trust you have made it clear to them that they should attend *all* rehearsals?' It was true, Sisters Helga and Juanita were nowhere to be seen.

Sister Angelica had retired to sit at the side of the salon, and was turning the pages of the solo part she was so certain I would fail to learn. Before she could respond to this malicious thrust, a nervous commoner scuttled crab-like into the room, and to her side, whispering urgently. What she said caused Sister Angelica's expression to darken. I suppose she was having a tiresome morning. Barbara was being difficult. Don Antonio was being wilful beyond permission; had altered her carefully laid plans, and rewarded me with a solo against her wishes. Now he was daring to insinuate that she was shirking her duties! Exasperated, she turned on me.

'Paola! Go to the chapel at once. Report to Sister Serafina. You'll find her in the vestry. I apologise, Don Antonio, on behalf of the *Coro*, for these tiresome interruptions, but I fear *I* am quite powerless to prevent them.' She flashed me a look of such malevolence, that I could believe she was blaming me for all the morning's vexations.

Clutching my violin, I walked through the line of players like one of those automatons the buskers set in motion on the *riva*, to entertain the Carnival crowds. (Sometimes we contrive to watch, from the upper windows). I *think* I curtsied to Don Antonio. Somehow I left the room.

'What's happened, girl?' A loud whisper met me from a window embrasure. Marta was hanging about in the corridor, too angry and disappointed at being excluded to go meekly to one of the practice rooms and play scales. 'Did Don Antonio change his mind, and give the solo to someone else?'

'No, one of the commoners just came. I'm to go to Sister Serafina in the chapel. I'm in trouble, judging from the way Sister Angelica spoke, though I can't think what I've done!' Even as I said this, I knew, or I thought I did. The Prioress. She must have spoken to Sister Serafina about last night. But why Sister Serafina? I could only think Mother Prioress still wondered if I had been contemplating suicide, and wanted her to give me one of her herbal remedies against melancholy.

'Ha,' said Marta, 'I saw Spotty Cristina come scurrying by, puffed up with importance, and out of breath from walking too fast. Shall I come with you?'

'Marta, you're welcome to come,' I was glad we were friends again after yesterday's quarrel, 'but it's my trouble, not yours. I think I can guess what it's about. You did warn me not to go up on the *terrazzo*!'

After Compline we had gone straight to our dormitory, where prayers followed by silence are the rule. There hadn't been an opportunity to tell her, or anyone else, of my adventures on the roof.

'I'm sorry,' I whispered, 'about Don Antonio, not allowing the woodwinds to play.'

Marta pulled a face. 'And after I went to the trouble of sewing that new collar. And you know how I loathe any kind of needlework!'

We hurried to the chapel, me still clutching my fiddle, not talking because we're not supposed to talk in the corridors. In the entrance hall, a group of the younger commoners were polishing the dark wooden panelling with lavender-scented beeswax under the critical eye of Sister Domenica. It crossed my mind to wonder why Sister Serafina wanted to see me in the vestry rather than in the dispensary upstairs.

As we made our way there, I was deciding what I would say. She would want to know why I had gone up to the roof yesterday evening. If I had the headache and bellyache, as I'd told Mother Prioress, why hadn't I gone to the infirmary after supper, for a compress of lemon balm, and a hot stone, which she would have been happy to dispense? I am not afraid of Sister Serafina, not really, for I know that beneath that formidable exterior she hides a heart of gold, but as a little child I was terrified of all the nuns, and a summons to account for myself still makes me feel five years old once more. My head was so full of how I might explain myself that I hurried into the vestry, Marta at my heels, without stopping to ask myself why there were so many of the lay staff gathered there. *Crowding round a bier.*

On which a figure lay, clothes sodden and clinging to her plump form, wet hair spread across the wooden slats. One of the lay sisters was engaged in gently closing her eyelids. Sister Serafina herself stood by, head bowed, fingering her rosary, but hearing our approach she looked up, and her face registered shock and surprise. Then she came hurrying to towards us, almost running, robes flying about her in her haste, her arms wide as though she might gather us both into a protective embrace.

'Paola, Marta! Oh, my dears, why ever did she send *you* two down here? We aren't ready for you. I asked for the *Bavarian* girl — Helga is she called? — in case we needed someone who can speak German. Although in fact I don't think it will be necessary. I was going to have her tidied up and made ready, and *then* send for you, and break it gently.'

I was staring over her shoulder, seeing but not believing. The girl on the bier. Black hair, from which water still dripped, cheeks no longer rosy in death. Another of the women was now passing a strip of linen under her jaw to close her mouth, concealing her unevenly spaced teeth.

'Sonia? She's *dead?*' I asked, although I knew it must be so. Then, as if all my blood was draining from my head to my feet, I began to sway, no longer able to see clearly, unable to breathe. My elbows were seized, my violin was eased out of my grasp. I heard Sister Serafina urging me to take a deep breath. Then darkness overcame me.

Chapter 7

Paola reflects on her earliest years, and questions Harry

Maybe you are wondering why I was so fond of Sonia? Anyone, Marta for instance, will tell you I should have put aside my childish attachment to her, that we really had nothing in common except that we had grown up together, and clung to one another when we were tiny, like two trailing plants on a shady windowsill, trying to hold one another up to the light. We were growing up in a world full of inexplicable happenings, ruled over by brisk, impersonal adults.

It had so happened that, at two or three days old, both Sonia and I were handed over to the Pietà on the same day. We weren't twins, or even related, but because we were so close in age, I think we thought of ourselves as sisters. Even then, I must have had pale skin, and a few tufts of ginger hair, and Sonia would have been rounder, plumper, olive-skinned and dark-eyed. I expect we were healthy little things, screaming for our mothers' breasts. Within an orphanage run by nuns, no breasts are available. So they did what the Pietà always does, they farmed us out: in our case, to a wet nurse in the nearby *Castello* district who had just lost twin boys, which was both lucky and unlucky for Sonia and me. Lucky because the poor woman kept us, fed us, and probably did her best to love us, for six months. But unlucky, because after a difficult birth and the loss of her own babies, our demands wore her out, and she fell into despondency. Her husband, the greengrocer, stuffed the pair of us, head to tail, into a cucumber crate, and brought us back, declaring he'd had enough of our wailing, his wife's weeping, and the money the Pietà paid wasn't sufficient for the trouble. So, from six months, we became two of the youngest residents of the Pietà at that time, and in that, I think, we were lucky too, although if we had been told so, we wouldn't have believed it. Perhaps because of one of the regular epidemics of marsh fever on the mainland, no one tried to find us a another foster home. There are frequently more babies handed in than there are wet nurses available in Venice, so many children are sent out to the Veneto, to be boarded by the peasant farmers there. The Pietà normally keeps only those obviously unlikely to survive their first few weeks, and those where something is known, about their parentage, which makes Mother Prioress feel it would be inadvisable to lose sight of them. Some very important people are kind enough to inquire about their illegitimate daughters, and have even been known to demand to see them. From a distance. The Governors pay the peasants on the mainland a small sum for a child's keep until the age of ten, with the hope that their adoptive family will grow fond enough to keep them, although many arrive back as their tenth birthday approaches. Then it's straight to the laundry, the lace workshop, or the kitchen. A few little ones may impress the village priest with sweet singing voices, or nimble fingers on the penny whistle, and then the Governors arrange for the child's early return, but I wonder how many are lost for ever?

'Drowned, falling into some Veneto drainage ditch before their second birthday,' Marta asserted, when once I mused on this, 'or sent to feed scraps to the pigs, who ate the child instead. What do the Governors care? One less to keep.'

Sonia and I escaped those fates, but alternately scolded and petted. We never knew, when we were small, whether a summons from one of the nuns would mean punishment, or being stuffed into our Sunday gowns and walked through the city, collecting alms, and kindly gifts of gingerbread.

That morning I was sad, angry and embarrassed, all at the same time. Sad and angry because the friend of my infancy was dead, and embarrassed by my faint; coming to with my skirts rucked up, and my worst pair of stockings, darned and streaked with dye, on display. I swear the laundry girls boil all our things together, just for spite. And it made it worse that the strange young man should be there. It turned out he was in no position to sneer at me, or my lamentable stockings. At first everyone seemed sure that he had killed Sonia, having been found near her body, bemused and bloody. Our two boatmen were boasting that they'd captured him, and trussed him up like a bundle of washing.

When the Watch Captain wanted to examine Sonia's injuries, Sister Serafina made me sit apart, where thankfully I couldn't see what he did. The only other person not craning his neck was the young man. He looked as if he felt as bad as I, and maybe worse, because of his hurts. His mouth was swollen, and one eye was closed.

I prayed for it to be over. Closing my eyes, I saw Sonia's dead face. My violin was lying on a shelf where Marta had put it, but I couldn't have gone back to the rehearsal, even if Sister Angelica had come in person to order me back.

To steady my roiling stomach, I stared at the young man. Marta had gone for hartshorn. The lay sister who works in the dispensary is very deaf. Sonia says — no. Don't think about that. All the girls will want to hear how this young man looked, even if it turns out he *is* a murderer. Sunlight was cutting through the morning haze, streaming through the windows. A stray beam glanced in beneath a looped curtain, and gave him a temporary halo. Surely Our Lord wouldn't allow a murderer a halo? Fair hair, his own, tied with a bedraggled black ribbon. Evidently he disdained wigs. Eyes? I couldn't tell. His face was bruised, but in other circumstances, I would have thought it pleasant, if not precisely handsome. The undamaged side of his mouth had a good tempered lift. Medium height, only a little taller than me. Clothes? Shabby. He had long fingers. He could have been a musician with that broad span, but I heard the Watch Captain say he was an artist. As soon as the examination was over, Sister Serafina sent everyone about their business. Even Don Salvatore scuttled into the chapel before she could ask why he wasn't already there, praying for Sonia's soul. If she hadn't been distracted by my faint, I'm certain she would have sent them packing sooner.

Then, arms folded across her ample bosom, she turned her attention to the young man. I strained to overhear. She was telling him that the Watch believed him innocent. Presently she bent and snipped his bonds, and he rose, shakily, to his feet.

'I had *seen* her,' I heard him say, 'but only — .'

He was interrupted when one of the commoners, a pasty-faced girl with a crop of spots on her chin, came lolloping into the vestry. Sister Serafina turned automatically to rebuke her, but she was in a panic.

'Sister, quickly!' she gasped, 'An accident! Alina was carrying a jug of boiling water, and she collided with two of the little ones! Marta Rovigo's pouring jugs of cold water over them, but they're screaming with the pain.'

'Scalded!' Sister Serafina threw up her hands. 'Who in the world entrusted that half-witted Alina with boiling water?'

The girl, Cristina, began to stammer a reply, but was shushed. 'Never mind, I'd better come.' Sister Serafina's shrewd eyes fastened on me.

'Paola? You're feeling better? We owe this young man an apology. Our people thought he might have killed Sonia, but it seems he too was attacked. Will you escort him through to Don Salva in the chapel? When I return I want to speak to him.' She eyed me intently, anxious that I understood her underlying message, which was: 'I wouldn't normally leave you alone with a man, especially this one, of whom I know little. I'm trusting you, Paola.' I suppose, too, that she thought the distraction would prevent me from dwelling on what had happened. Sonia. *Dead.*

'This way, Signore.' There was no time to feel bashful. I must be resolute. I'd heard him admit to having seen Sonia. I was determined to ask some questions of my own. 'Your name, Signore?'

For a moment he said nothing, but continued rubbing his chaffed wrists.

'*Grazier, Signorina,*' he pronounced, carefully, 'I am sorry. I understand the young woman was your friend. My name is Harry. Nobody in Italy can say my last name.' His Italian was heavily accented, but I understood him.

'You are visiting from the German states?' On concert evenings, choristers are expected to make polite conversation with the Governors' guests. We all receive instruction on how to ask the right questions.

There was a pause while he translated. 'No, from England. I am a painter.' I must have looked surprised. He smiled, and obviously wished he hadn't, because his mouth hurt. 'I'm *trying* to be a painter.' There was a rueful glint in his good eye. 'You have some fine paintings in your chapel? I've learned much, during my travels, from the great artists here in Italy.' He glanced doubtfully at the Virgin on the vestry wall. A rich benefactor wished her onto us, but I didn't want to waste time explaining that. Sister Serafina might soon return.

I led Harry into the chapel. I was too embarrassed to tell him the true reason for my surprise. Many English *milords* visit Venice, wishing to see our beautiful floating city, and having already heard of Don Antonio, and our choir and orchestra. Once they are settled into their well-appointed lodgings, they send their tutors out to purchase tickets for one of our concerts. These visitors are rich young men, in velvet coats and highly polished boots, travelling for their health, or their education. Often, they lounge on their chairs throughout the concert, bored, or stare at us rudely through quizzing glasses, as though we're some strange species. Giraffes, or antelopes perhaps? Or perhaps they are simply amazed at what the daughters of whores can do? I didn't like to say to this Signor Harry that I hadn't known there *were* any poor Englishmen. Even the *milords'* servants aren't so threadbare as he appeared to be. But though his shirt was bloodstained, and his breeches torn, he wasn't a servant. Despite the indignities he had suffered, I thought he would be perfectly at home amongst the *milords*. Where, therefore, I wondered, could he have encountered Sonia?

Inside the chapel, Don Salvatore was standing in the doorway to the *riva*, barring the way to someone who wanted to come inside. I had no alternative but to continue making polite conversation.

Harry, despite the swellings around his eyes, looked around with interest. 'Your chapel isn't normally open to sightseers? I'm grateful, Signorina, but sorry I should see it as a result of such a sad event.'

'I'll hand you over to Don Salva, our chaplain, in a moment,' I promised him. '*He* can tell you everything about our history, ever since the orphanage was founded in 1346.' We stood side by side in awkward silence for a moment. I had so much I wanted to ask, but how to frame such very *impolite* questions?

'You sing and play for services here, Signorina? You must be proud of it.' (He was better practised than I at polite conversation).

His accent was strange, but I found, as with listening to an unfamiliar piece of music, I was beginning to catch the tune. He spoke Italian better than most foreigners do. Nobody outside Venice can be expected to speak our Venetian dialect.

'I'm afraid I hardly notice, seeing it every day,' I admitted. 'Anyway, it's going to be knocked down and enlarged.'

'Knocked down?' He looked horrified.

'Oh, the new chapel will be very fine, with decorations far grander than these. Don Antonio showed us the plans. Of course *he* doesn't mind how it looks, he's just concerned about the acoustics.'

'Don Antonio Vivaldi? You're one of his pupils? Is he very formidable?'

I smiled. 'If we haven't practiced, he's terrible. We quake!'

'That Sister Serafina had *me* quaking,' he said, glancing back towards the vestry. 'Did she say she was coming back?'

'Certainly. She wants to know what happened. To Sonia. And so do I!' My heart was beating fast at my temerity, but we had moved on from polite conversation now. 'She was like my sister almost, since we were babies. If something terrible happened to your sister, wouldn't you want to know?'

He looked at me for a long moment. I thought he hadn't understood, but then he said, sounding rueful, 'Would it be wrong if we sat down? I find I'm somewhat fatigued.'

Sister Serafina certainly hadn't intended me to do more than take him straight to Don Salva, but it wouldn't be courteous to abandon him, and anyway we were in the House of God, where surely nobody could suspect us of wrongdoing? Folding chairs were stacked against the walls. We took two, and settled ourselves close to one of the side altars.

'Usually you have to pay for these,' I told him.

'So I hear,' he grimaced. 'An annual subscription just to be seated during Mass. One of your concerts is way beyond my means. I was warned that Venice would beggar me. I'm only surprised there isn't a tax on breathing the air!' We sat facing one another. The only male person I had ever been alone with before was some old music master, smelling of snuff, peppermints, and embrocation. Harry's eyes were blue. I could have stretched out and touched his arm, and I could imagine the sniggers from girls like Maria-Regina and Carolina when — *if* — I told them. Then shame swept over me. I shouldn't be noticing the colour of his eyes with my friend lying dead in the next room.

'Tell me how you came to meet Sonia,' I demanded.

He shook his head slightly, wincing, 'As I explained to your Sister Serafina, I never *met* her. I only saw your friend once before. It was sheer misfortune that it was I who found her in the canal. Yesterday, whilst I was sketching on the *riva* around noon, I saw her talking to a man by the fish stalls.' He swept a hand towards the open door, where Don Salva was still fending off the determined intruder. A finely dressed lady, a *turista*. He was speaking to her in Italian, urging her to come to Mass or to a concert, if she wanted to see inside the building.

'Your friend obviously knew this man,' Harry continued.

'You didn't see her later, last night?'

'No,' he glanced round, nervously, but the sound was only Don Salvatore, closing the door. Walking in our direction, he paused to pick up something which had evidently fallen from the side altar dedicated to San Stefano, and rolled into the shadows at the base of a column. 'Don't believe that swine of a Watch Captain,' Harry continued, lowering his voice, 'those sailors didn't kill her.'

'How can you know that, if they knocked you unconscious?'

'*They* only stunned me. The rest of my injuries were courtesy of those fine fellows of the Watch!' He was beginning to sound irritated. 'Your friend must have gone out during the evening,' he went on. 'I caught a glimpse of a woman — a lay sister? She opened the laundry door and peered around, as if she was waiting for someone, perhaps your friend? Those damned Watchmen! I really believe *they* killed her. If she was in their way, as I was, when they were running after the sailors. I was lucky, I suppose.'

What he was suggesting was impossible. I said, 'None of us are allowed out at night!'

'No? This Sonia spoke angrily to the young fellow I saw her with. A lover's quarrel? She might have persuaded someone to let her out to make things up with him?'

Sonia, with a lover? *Sonia, so fat and so plain!* Yesterday, I would have laughed. Could Sonia possibly have met someone on one of her shopping expeditions....?

'Sister Porteress locks up at nightfall. No one else has keys,' I ploughed on. 'Sonia goes — went — out in the daytime, running errands, but she never mentioned meeting... *anyone*.' This Harry couldn't be expected to understand how strictly rules are applied here in the Pietà. I recalled the letter she had mentioned. Had it been a request to meet? Had she somehow let herself out of the building to meet this man, instead of keeping her rendezvous with me? But why, when she had said she wanted me to help her decipher it? Harry and I frowned at one another, both of us baffled and dismayed.

'*Momento*!' He patted his pockets, 'I sketched them!' He unfolded a piece of paper and smoothed the creases on his knee. He held it out, and there she was! Sonia, with a marketing basket under her arm, the one Sister Porteress keeps in her office by the front door, and a hulking young man, as stout as Sonia, but taller. If the sketch was a true record, and I felt certain it was, Sonia wasn't afraid of him. How often I had seen her wagging her finger like that, in real or pretended anger, at little girls pushing in the line, or flicking bread pellets at each other in the refectory? The pencil strokes were quick and sure.

'May *I* see?' Don Salvatore had arrived, silently, at Harry's shoulder.

'Do you know him, Father? I drew this yesterday, just before noon, and now I understand she is the girl who — is dead. She seemed to be annoyed, exasperated, I think, with this fellow. When she left, he came and asked me to forget I'd seen them. In particular, he wanted me to refrain from mentioning it to — what did he say? — an old man with a tassel on his hat. In fact, he insisted on giving me a few coins...'

'To help you forget?' Don Salvatore gave his wheezy old man's chuckle. Harry flushed. 'Don't worry my son,' he patted his shoulder, 'it isn't a *mortal* sin to accept a small bribe. *Hmm*, this is he?'

Vaguely, he started looking around for a place to lodge the candlestick he had picked up from the floor. To hurry him along, I stretched out my hand to take it from him. Then he rooted out a pair of spectacles from inside his dusty cassock, and balanced them on his nose. He peered closely at Harry's sketch.

'You can certainly catch a likeness, young man! I know our good Sister Serafina isn't happy that we've got to the bottom of what happened to Sonia, and that means Mother Prioress, and the Governors, who value her opinion, won't be satisfied either. *Yeees*. I shall look out for this individual as I go about. *And* the old fellow with the tasselled cap. He might be a foreigner, a Greek or a Slovene perhaps?'

'*This* fellow had an accent,' said Harry, growing animated, 'and he wore a strange coat made of sheepskin. I've never seen a Venetian wearing such a...peculiar garment.'

The pair of them were getting excited, and I thought, ruefully, that they would both have more chance than I to seek out Sonia's acquaintance, being able to walk freely around Venice, as I am not.

I asked Harry, greatly daring, 'Could I keep your drawing for a while, please? To show to the girls here, those who work in the laundry and the kitchens? *They* might know who he is.'

Harry looked doubtful. 'I'd want it back,' he stated. 'I was rather pleased with it, and intending to use it.' He broke off, perhaps wondering if it might be thought indelicate to paint the portrait of someone newly murdered.

'When you've shown it to the commoners, you'll return it, won't you, Paola?' Don Salva promised on my behalf. 'If you go now, child,' he added, 'you'll have time to show it around before your afternoon rehearsal. Don Antonio is taking it, is he not?'

Child. To Don Salva, we're all children — of God, naturally. I knew I was being chased away, like a little girl caught hanging about the privies after the lesson bell had sounded. I didn't want to go. I had more questions for Harry, for example, about the coins the young man had given him. Were they gold, like the one I'd seen in Sonia's hand? But Don Salva was right, Sister Angelica would be sending someone to fetch me, which would be humiliating. I stood up, ready to thank Harry, but Don Salva was inviting him to Sister Porteress' office, and promising that he could wash after his ordeal, and have coffee, and they walked away together without a backward glance.

So much for you, Paola, I thought. Perhaps he *is* the next best thing to a *milord*, in spite of his shabbiness, and of course he knows, everybody in the wide world knows, that you're the unwanted child of some Venetian light skirt. Just for a moment I'd hoped that Harry might help me to find out what happened to Sonia. As it was, I had achieved nothing with my clumsy questioning. But I wasn't about to give up. I had the drawing, and inside the Pietà I could question anyone I liked. And I fully intended to.

It was almost time for lunch, although the thought of eating brought back my nausea. However, the lunch hour would be a good time to catch those who knew Sonia best. I had almost reached the refectory before I realised I was still clutching the candlestick. No time to go back. I felt like hurling the thing to the ground, but instead I tossed it into a laundry hamper by the door. It was just a brass candlestick; heavy, ugly, in need a good polish before it was put back in its place.

Chapter 8

Harry is entertained by Don Salvatore, and offered an unexpected commission

Women fall over themselves to coddle clergymen; I have observed this in my own Lancashire neighbourhood, as well as here in Venice. No sooner had Don Salvatore escorted me from the chapel to the Porteress's office beside the front door, than a plump lass bustled in with coffee, and fresh-out-of-the-oven honey and almond pastries. They smelt ambrosial.

'We heard you've a visitor, Father,' she chirped, as Don Salva seized a pastry, 'so we doubled your order.' News certainly travelled in this place.

It had been a relief to wash the blood from my face and hands in a well-appointed privy next to the Porteress's office. I was surprised at first, that an all-female institution had one set aside for the male sex, but then reflected that all the Governors and the visiting music teachers were men. My shirt, unfortunately, was beyond rescue, and quite unfit for polite company, but there was nothing I could do about that.

Settled onto chairs, with refreshments before us, the old priest set himself to inform and entertain me. When we first entered he had seen my eyes travel towards a contraption like a wooden drum, set into the wall.

'That's how our girls arrive,' he told me. 'Not all, but many. That's the *scafetta*. In other parts of Italy I understand they call it the *rotura*,'

I translated these words. The shelf. The roundabout. Don Salvatore droned on.

'In closed convents,' he explained, 'they use them to communicate with the outside world. Messages and goods can be passed back and forth without worldly contacts disturbing the life of prayer. But this, of course,' he waved a blue veined hand to take in the whole building, 'is an orphanage. If a woman has a baby it's inconvenient to keep, that's where she leaves it. Step across. Give it a spin.'

I would have preferred to snaffle a pastry. I was light-headed with hunger and fatigue, but this old man had rescued me, so I obliged him. At the lightest touch, the drum turned, exposing its interior, like a wedge cut from a cheese. Inside was a basket. Don Salvatore looked mildly surprised.

'If it's a child, they usually ring the bell,' he remarked, through a shower of pastry crumbs. I lifted the basket out, and showed him the contents.

'Hah, spinach. Somebody assuaging a bad conscience. They do it with the best of intentions, but there isn't enough to be useful. I dare say the nuns will have it served with their supper. The girl can take it when she comes for the tray.'

'Doesn't the Porteress take in deliveries?' I asked, curious, remembering that I had seen a sour faced woman open the door to Sonia. The quantities needed to feed the inmates of this place would surely keep the bell perpetually jangling. Which might explain her sourness.

'Gracious, no. All the regular deliveries go straight from the delivery boat to the kitchen,' he mumbled, chasing a dribble of honey with his tongue. 'Just the conscience offerings in the *scafetta*. And babies. Some mothers, mind you — the brazen ones — come to the door to hand the baby over. Shawls, and doeskin booties, and lists of instructions as long as your arm! "My husband's guessed she's not his!"' he mimicked. 'And the little ones with hare lips, or fingers and toes missing. Delivered like a parcel of cast offs by some haughty maidservant! Happens in wealthy families as well as poor ones. To my mind there's too much intermarrying amongst the nobility. I've noted it, over the years, too close kinship leads to deformities in the children.'

I stood a moment, examining the *scafetta*. It spun easily on its axis. Would it be possible for someone — an adult — to get in and out of the building by means of this contraption? Certainly not a solid wench like Sonia! A small child might wriggle through it, but an adult, no. So, I reasoned, human nature being what it is, and with the sounds of carnival merrymaking drifting in through the windows, the livelier young women here have no doubt explored other options. Young Paola had seemed so certain that all the doors were locked at sundown, and disinclined to believe that I had seen someone open the laundry door. She had not said, 'You must have been all about in your head,' but knowing I had been knocked unconscious, I suppose it was a reasonable thing for her to think. However, I was certain it was no hallucination. So what had I seen? Evidence of young women going out on a spree? And had the dead girl been one of them?

I recalled myself to the present, realising that Don Salva was speaking. He waved towards the jug of coffee. 'Help yourself, young man, don't wait on ceremony!'

I had noted that his hands displayed a slight tremor, so I poured for both of us, and helped myself to a pastry. There were still a few left.

My new friend sipped and chuckled. 'Sister Porteress's job is an interesting one, she never knows when that bell jangles, whether it's baby or a bunch of greens! She won't allow fish, though. Especially in hot weather! She's told all the fisher folk, if they want to donate, take it to the kitchen. There are women working there late and early, preparing vegetables and so forth, so there's usually someone to take it in.'

Well here, perhaps was my answer? Could it have been the kitchen door? Had the young woman I had seen been charged with taking in a late grocery order? But I was sure I hadn't been mistaken. It had been one of the two doors to the laundry, and there had been something extremely furtive about the manner in which she had peered out.

I ate carefully, favouring my sore mouth, trying to avoid letting honey run down my chin. My host had very few teeth, and consumed his pastries by sucking them in, and mashing them with his gums. Not pleasant to watch. His insights into orphanage life were interesting however. Harking back to what he had said about the Porteress, I phrased a careful question.

'If someone regularly donates, say someone working late, a gondolier perhaps, who likes to demonstrate his piety by supporting the orphanage? It would be the kitchen he'd go to? I ask because last night, just before I was attacked, a young woman opened the *laundry* door. I know it was the laundry because they brought me through there this morning. Big double doors. She opened one of them a fraction, and looked out. I thought she was a nun, but I realize now that it was probably a lay sister. Or a commoner? The light wasn't good, but she held a candle, and I saw she wore a white head covering. I told that young woman, Signorina Paola, just now, that I thought this person might be looking out for Sonia, returning from wherever she'd been.'

The old man looked troubled by this. 'Might have been, although she had no business to, whoever she was! The doors are locked at sundown, and everyone who lives on the premises should be inside. The Prioress is extremely strict about it. I myself have a key to the parish door, so I can come and go to the chapel, but no one else can — or should — be able to enter or leave the building without permission.'

This confirmed what young Paola had said; so no sop for my curiosity there. The old man drifted off into thoughts of his own, but presently he remarked, 'That drawing of yours. Could that fellow have had something to do with her... demise? We don't often have one of our girls run out on us. The Sisters keep them well under control, and once they're grown, if they want to marry, or leave to take a job in a private household, the Prioress is happy to arrange it. Plenty of openings — housework, laundry, looking after children. We get offers of situations in the best households in Venice,' he boasted. 'They're well trained, our girls, Sister Domenica sees to that.'

With coffee and pastries inside me, I was beginning to feel human again. But resentful. On my own behalf, naturally, because of the rough treatment I'd received, and the bruises I could feel developing all over my body, but strangely, since I hadn't known the girl, on behalf of Sonia. What right had this old fellow to sit at his ease, munching the *dolce*, while that poor lass lay dead? *And* that cool young lady, Paola, had taken my drawing. Before I could muster words to protest, this old fellow had encouraged her to make off with it. I'd had plans for that sketch; would I ever see it again? I didn't see myself ringing the bell in a day or two, asking had Signorina Paola finished with it. There was something about the way she'd folded it, and tucked it down inside her clothing, that suggested that she didn't intend to show it to the senior nuns, or whoever the people in charge here were, and if they caught her with it, what then? I allowed my mind to wander. The old priest droned on, not seeming to notice that he no longer had my full attention. Perhaps he was just glad to have a man for company in this house packed full of women. That terrifying nun, Sister Serafina! I couldn't imagine having a cosy gossip with her. And presumably there were others like her.

I could feel my eyelids beginning to droop. Safe from attack, and with food inside me, there was a strong danger that I was about to fall asleep. I pulled myself back to wakefulness with a start. As thanks for my rescue, the least I could do was show an interest in this place, obviously so dear to his heart. He was talking about the nuns.

'...is run by just five Sisters,' he was saying, 'and even *they* are what we call Tertiaries—' He paused, and bit cheerfully into the last pastry with his two remaining front teeth. 'They have chosen to serve their Order in this way, rather than entering a closed community.' He ticked them off on his gnarled and sticky old fingers, 'Sister Serafina you've met, she's girls' health and general welfare, and also second in command to Mother Prioress. Sister Angelica supervises the music department. Very strict, that one! The *Coro*, that's our choir and orchestra — you've heard of them? — is a huge responsibility. That's why I interrupted your talk with Paola. Time was getting on, and neither she nor I would have heard the last of it, if she was late for a rehearsal. She's one of our promising violinists. They have an important engagement tomorrow I understand. A concert to celebrate the name day of the wife of one of our most generous benefactors, Signor Fosca.' He slid me a glance, checking if I was suitably impressed.

'Then we have Sister Domenica, who supervises the kitchens, laundry and lace making workshops. Sister Teodora is in charge of general education. And last but not least by any means, Sister Benedetta, responsible for religious instruction ….. Splendid women, all absolutely dedicated!'

Drowsily, I considered that, having met Sister Serafina, I wasn't surprised. Five of her could probably run the whole Venetian empire in an emergency.

'Plenty of backup, of course, from an army of lay sisters, and the girls and women themselves,' the old priest assured me.

'And the unfortunate Sonia? What will they do, if, as you implied, they are dissatisfied with the Watch Captain's verdict?'

He looked at me oddly. 'A matter for the Prioress, and the Governors,' he murmured. He was embarrassed now, having caught himself being too free with the family secrets to an unknown foreigner, who might not be so innocent as he made himself out to be.

There followed a lull in our conversation. I supposed I had outstayed my welcome, and should thank him for taking my part, and for the refreshments, and leave. Or should I? Sister Serafina had said she would return, and she was a woman one somehow instinctively obeyed. Her wishes seemed to occur to Don Salvatore too.

'Sister Serafina was hoping for a further talk with you?'
'So she said, but...'

He nodded. 'So many children. Accidents happen, and at the most inconvenient moments. However,' Whatever he was about to say was interrupted by Sister Serafina herself.

She swept into the room and thrust a ceramic pot into my hand, saying brusquely, 'Here's tincture of comfrey, Signore, to make a compress for your bruises. Come back tomorrow for a phial of lavender oil. We need to decant more, it being the end of winter. Those little girls aren't badly scalded,' she told Don Salvatore, ignoring my stammered thanks. 'Praise be to God, Marta Rovigo had doused them thoroughly in cold water. A flibbertigibbet, that one, but on this occasion she employed some common sense. You might guess it was Bella and Maddelena. Those two attract trouble as flowers attract bees! Of course they were running in the corridor, although they deny it, and Alina was too slow-witted to move out of their way.'

'Signore,' she turned her attention back to me, 'I understand you are an artist?' Before I could answer, she turned to Don Salvatore again, 'Have you thought that he might help us with the wall paintings?'

The old man looked startled for a moment, and then turned to me with renewed enthusiasm, 'A capital thought! How like our excellent Sister Serafina to think of it. You know, young man — I overheard Paola explaining to you — that our chapel is to be rebuilt?'

I nodded. 'That seems tragic. Lovely things will be lost.'

'Alas, that is so, but the chapel is far too small for our present needs. They tell me the new decorative scheme will be superb. Signor Tiepolo has promised us something splendid for the ceiling, once he finishes his current commission for the Carmelites. But much, as you say, will be lost. The fresci, in particular. Fresco doesn't last well in Venice, yet they were painted with great devotion, and paid for by pious men and women of former generations. So, we've been considering getting someone to make a record of them. A series of *drawings*. Engravings, I understand, are much too costly. Would you be interested in attempting something like that?'

Sister Serafina hadn't sat down. Evidently she was too busy with her invalids just now to question me further. Instead, she paused, hand on the door frame, to hear my answer. If I was in the chapel, drawing, her narrowed eyes informed me, she could seek me out in her own good time.

Well! The inmates of this venerable institution had roughed me up, accused me of murder, and still half suspected me of debauching Sonia. Now they wanted to employ me. My pride said no, but pride wasn't contributing anything towards my board and lodgings. Until I encountered the young fellow in the sheepskin coat, hunger had been setting up camp in my belly. His carelessly tossed coins had fed me for a day or so, but were now almost gone. Copying, I reminded myself, was nothing to be ashamed of. This was, after all, how the great ones taught their apprentices. 'Sit here, boy. Take this piece of charcoal. Copy that! And don't bother me until you have it to perfection!'

Old Don Salvatore might have few teeth, but he had his eyesight. He had certainly noted the deplorable state of my attire after five months of living on dreams.

'The Prioress would, of course, want to see samples of your work,' he added, dangling hope before my eyes, and then seeming to snatch it back, 'but having seen your drawing, I'm sure you are equal to the task. Come tomorrow, early, and we'll decide where you might start.'

No one else was offering me the faintest sniff of paid employment. An inner voice did whisper that having vowed, on fleeing England, to have no further dealings with females, accepting work in a seminary where the young women sing and play like angels might be unwise. I ignored it.

When I entered the chapel next morning, laden with my drawing board, and fresh sketching materials scrounged from a couple of artist acquaintances, my new employer, Don Salvatore, wasn't immediately visible. Sonia, however, was. I have never felt comfortable in the presence of the dead, but I already knew from my recent wanderings through Italy, that in any church, in any town or village, one was liable to find the departed lying at ease in an open casket, waiting for a stream of friends and neighbours to call in, and wish them well in the next life. Certainly her presence did not inhibit anyone else who had reason to pass through the chapel that morning. She was laid out neatly in an open coffin before the main altar. Someone had placed sprays of tender new leaves from some sheltered garden around her face to disguise the bruising. I hadn't expected to find myself working alongside a corpse, but was in no position to refuse.

When, presently, the old priest appeared, he led me to the far end of the aisle, and to the South wall. 'I thought perhaps you might begin here,' he remarked, tucking his hands into the sleeves of his robe — the morning was chill — as we gazed at the ruined wall painting before us.

'You can make out what this represents?'

'Certainly, Father, the Annunciation.' It must have been very fine once. Now most of the lower half of it was missing. Gabriel and Mary had only their heads and upper arms, the rest of the plaster was crumbling from the brickwork, eaten away over the centuries by the damp salty air, and the bitter winter cold. It had been a source of wonder to me, until an acquaintance had explained the cruel effects of damp in this city built on water, that the Venetians did not take better care of their treasures.

'This was a fine specimen, or so I'm told,' the old priest said, 'but fresco is not Venice's glory. Our wretched climate, alas. You have visited Firenze? And seen what they have in the churches and the grand *palazzi* there? You have? Ah, we cannot match those. Our paintings in oils on wood and canvas though — Bellini, Giorgione, Tizziano! Magnificent! Perhaps you have seen some of their great altarpieces? *San Zaccaria? The Frari?* Glorious, are they not? Glorious! *These* old things are falling to pieces.' He stabbed with a bony finger at the feathers of Gabriel's wing, and another chunk of plaster fell away from the lower edge. I took a sharp in breath, irritated by his casual vandalism, but held my peace. This was to be my first paying commission. I couldn't afford to upset him. Those feathers had been exquisitely rendered by some painter of a bygone age, and I was fortunate indeed to be seeing them, before they were lost for ever.

'Let me be sure I understand what the Prioress wants, Father. She wants a record of these paintings, *all* of them?' Now that I looked around, I saw that this would be quite a task. Although they were in a ruinous state, their once jewel bright colours grown dingy, darkened by damp, candle grease and smoke, they covered most of the lower walls of the chapel. Perhaps as much as two weeks' employment for me, if I secured the commission.

Don Salvatore looked doubtful for a moment, and I wondered if he was going to cancel the project, but he could have been adjusting, once again, to my deplorable accent.

'Perhaps if you were to begin with a few sketches? Then I could show them to the Prioress, and she could give her opinion?'

'Just sketches, not detailed drawings?' I was anxious to be clear. Otherwise I could see myself doing a great deal of work, for which I was unlikely to be paid.

'I think... sketches, outline drawings. Isn't that what you artists call them? A record of the subjects, with sufficient detail to make them easily recognisable? Perhaps just one or two from this New Testament cycle to show Mother Prioress? Could you perhaps manage the Annunciation and the Nativity in the course of today? Then we'll find out if she wants you to add colour and additional detail.'

If the Prioress was going to demand colour and detail, I would need to beg for some payment in advance. My purse was close to empty, and I had already borrowed as many materials as I decently could. How I was going to repay people was a mystery. However, time enough to worry about that when this powerful, but so far invisible, lady had approved my sketches.

'What of these parts that have fallen away, Father? Would you want me to indicate — roughly — some idea of what must have been there? *Here*, for instance,' I pointed, 'the line of Gabriel's wings must have swept down towards this corner, and the lily, the Madonna's lily, *here* in the centre, must have stood in a vase of some kind. Look, you can see part of the rim? Would you want me to sketch that in?'

The old man was bemused, stroking his chin. He was a priest, not an artist. I was asking him about things he did not fully understand.

'Perhaps a few lines to *indicate* what was there? I will leave it to your judgment, my son. And now I must go, and abandon you to your work. I have promised to meet with Sister Benedetta. Two new infants admitted yesterday, twins! — to be baptised later today. They are said to be weakly, and we haven't yet chosen names, so the good Sister and I must consult her book of the Lives of the Saints. I will speak to someone from the kitchen too, about bringing you some food.'

With this latter promise, which I must say raised my spirits — at least I wasn't to go hungry — he shuffled away.

Leaving me alone in the empty chapel, with a murdered girl. But there was nothing to be gained by being morbid. I must try to take her presence as much for granted as everyone else did.

I commandeered two of the folding chairs which Paola had shown me the previous day, and wedged one against a pillar, and with my board propped against it, began to rough out a preparatory sketch. Gabriel on the left, stretched out his hand; the Virgin, on the right, shrank back. Two figures, a young man and woman, confronting one another. As Sonia and Sheepskin-coat had done, in the sketch I had made of them on the quayside. Except that, in my drawing, it had been she who bent towards him, while he shrank back from her accusing finger. I wondered how my chorister friend, Paola, was getting on with her task of showing it around, hoping someone in the kitchen or the laundry of this place could put a name to Sheepskin-coat.

Chapter 9

In which Harry is interrogated by the Prioress, and finds himself acquiring further unexpected duties

It is impossible, I have found, to guess the age of a nun, unless she be either very young or very old. A woman I got to know during my time in Rome, expressed the opinion that this is because their habits conceal everything above the brow and below the chin. I think she felt this gave them an unfair advantage, once they were no longer young, over the rest of their sex. There is another view that attributes their smooth unlined features to the serenity they have found in Religion. This may be true of those Orders for whom daily life is a constant round of prayer and contemplation, but surely cannot be so for those who have been persuaded that their vocation lies in the training of adolescent girls? I have no idea how old the Prioress might be, but my impression, as she swept into the chapel, later that morning, flanked by a cohort of Sisters, was of an active lady of formidable intelligence. Her face, for some reason, she kept partially veiled. Her voice was melodious.

'Signor Harry? Good morning! We have been discussing you at our morning Chapter. May we see what you have done so far?'

I handed her my drawing board, but to my surprise, after the briefest of glances, she passed it straight to one of the accompanying nuns, a thin, vague looking Sister, who reminded me strongly of an aunt of my mother's, long dead, who had her maid continually on her knees picking up spilled beads and lost handkerchiefs.

'Sister Benedetta is a better judge of such skills than I,' the Prioress remarked. I thought she smiled, but her mouth was half hidden. Sister Benedetta took my sketch and wandered into the aisle, where a strand of sharp morning light illuminated the page. Sister Serafina, the one I recognised, took a step forward, as though to follow her, but then did not. Evidently she too trusted the vague one in matters of artistic merit.

'I do beg your pardon,' the Prioress continued, 'I must introduce you! You are already acquainted with Sister Serafina of course. These are Sister Domenica, Sister Angelica, and Sister Teodora.' All three ladies frowned.

Sister Domenica was solidly built, a muscular woman who could probably heave bundles of laundry around with ease. Don Salvatore had said she was in charge of domestic training, and she reminded me of our cook at home, stout, competent, undoubtedly able to demonstrate any skills the girls she trained might need. Her eyes were kindly although her frown was preoccupied. She had probably left a cookery class with something on the boil. Sister Teodora was slight and olive skinned; her frown was meditative, as though she was thinking up a challenging arithmetic test for her young pupils. Sister Angelica, Don Salva had told me, was in charge of the Music Department. She was tall, bony, and grim of visage. *Her* frown was surprisingly personal, and disagreeable. She was disliking me on sight. If my contract to complete the drawings depended on her approval, I wouldn't get it.

Sister Benedetta turned from her inspection of my sketch, her placid face radiant.

'This is a sign from Heaven, Mother Prioress — Gabriella and Maria-Beata! I must tell Don Salvatore at once!' she announced. Now *I* was frowning, unable to imagine what she was talking about. But evidently the Prioress was used to her.

'Ah! Names for the twins? Yes, very suitable Sister,' she agreed, 'but should we pay this young man to make drawings of the wall paintings?'

Sister Benedetta blinked, glanced back at the sketch, looked at me as though she had just this moment been told of my existence, blinked again, and said, 'Oh... I think so, Ma'donna. He has some skill. And is perhaps not *too* expensive?'

'Very well, Signore! Come to me at the end of the day and we will discuss payment. Perhaps you will need a little in advance for your materials?' I bowed to the Prioress, agreeing the deal, and relieved that there was to be 'a little in advance.'

'Broken your fast, Signore?' Sister Domenica had a deep, almost masculine voice. Her eyes twinkled. 'I'll send someone to you with rolls and coffee.' This was a pleasant surprise, for me anyway. Sister Angelica's frown deepened.

Then the Prioress, and Sisters Teodora and Angelica, made their reverences before Sonia's coffin, and left. Sisters Serafina and Domenica stayed some minutes, I could hear them discussing the funeral arrangements. Sister Benedetta had hurried away to find Don Salvatore and tell him the good news. Thanks to my sketch of the Annunciation she had found suitable names for those unchristened babes. Names which, if they survived, they would probably grow up detesting, but for which, happily, they would never know I was responsible.

I settled down to work on the Nativity. I had considerable difficulty with the camel. The medieval artist had certainly never set eyes on one, and I myself had seen one only once, in the Tower Menagerie, on a visit to London in my boyhood. Strangely, I found it much more difficult to copy something poorly executed (without making it still worse) than the work of one of the great masters.

Half an hour passed, and a lumpish girl, wearing an oversized white apron over a dark coloured stuff gown, sidled into the chapel, carrying a plate of bread rolls and a mug of milky coffee. She was careful not to meet my eye, but dumped these at the base of one of the columns and fled. I concluded that this was the promised breakfast, but was unable to decide whether it was myself she found so alarming, or the dead Sonia. No matter, the food was welcome. I wolfed it down. The morning wore on. From time to time I was conscious of young women's voices, and giggles and scuffling above me behind the choir screen, but I did not look up, immersed in my tussle with the camel. At twelve noon, a cloudburst of singing showered down. The choir, praising God in a chapel empty but for Sonia and myself.

I didn't hear Sister Serafina's return until she was almost at my side, carrying a tray of hot food. Lunch time already.

'Well, how does it go?' she demanded. Her voice was deep, but pleasant. I wondered if she had once been a singer herself. I held out the drawing board for her to see, but she waved it away. 'Oh, Sister Benedetta says you can *draw*. She has a good eye for that kind of thing. But how long is it going to take you? Too long, I suppose, if that's all you've managed this morning. One young man in a female orphanage causes more *schiamazzo* than a wolf sniffing round a sheep fold! I've brought your lunch, because two of the commoners were pulling each other's hair out over which of them should carry it to you. And those silly chits in the *Coro* have done precious little practising this morning, making excuses to run upstairs and peep at you from the singing gallery! I was foolish to suggest this to Don

Salva, but I had to hold on to you somehow. Venice is a big city, you could be off doing your sketching in some other *siestière*, where the Watch don't know your face. I can't leave this place and come chasing after you.'

'Sister, I *did not* murder the girl!'

She nodded her head slowly. 'I'm inclined to accept your word on that. But you know more than I do. So I need you. You witnessed this meeting she had with a man.'

'You've seen my drawing?'

'Heard about it. You gave it to Paola Rossa, and she has it tucked into her bodice, and shows it to those girls who knew Sonia best, asking do they know him? So far without result, my informant tells me.'

'Sister,' I said, stung, 'I wasn't trying to hide anything. At first, when they brought me here, I was confused and in pain from the beating I'd received. I thought of the drawing only later. I didn't ask Signorina Paola to keep it from you. She was distressed at losing her friend—'

Sister Serafina turned slightly, and looked towards the coffin, standing lonely before the altar. 'And she wants to know, *who, and why, and how?* Of course. The questions we all ask, of the good Lord Himself, when a terrible thing like this happens.' She lowered herself onto the chair I had been using as a prop for my drawing board.

'It must surely have been accidental? Who could possibly hate Sonia?' She spread her hands. 'A very *dull* girl. And she knew it, poor child. Paola and Marta were her friends all through their school days, but she didn't have their talent, and she resented her supposed inferior status. As many of our girls do, no matter how often we tell them that each one is precious in the eyes of Our Lord; that each has her role to play in upholding our community. Sonia wanted to be important and special. We hoped we were helping her, by giving her responsibility for teaching some of the little ones; trusting her to run errands for us.' She glanced at the tray of rapidly cooling food I had laid beside me on the marble slabs. 'Oh, do in Heaven's name, *eat*, before it goes cold!'

The words were in a different language, but she sounded so like Bessie, the tough-as-whipcord Pennine farmer's daughter who had been our nursemaid, and who had ruled over my brother, my sisters and myself throughout our childhood, that a wave of homesickness assailed me. I lifted the plate of food onto my knee and dug in, using a hunk of bread as a scoop. It was *polenta*, a thick corn meal porridge which tastes well enough, but whose texture I dislike. I knew however, I must eat and be thankful, as I would have been for one of Bessie's greasy hotpots. Sister Serafina sat and watched me. From inside her sleeve came the rhythmic click of her rosary beads. Presently, she spoke again.

'Would you know him, this young fellow whose portrait you drew, if you saw him again?'

'Yes, Sister,' I mumbled, my mouth full of *polenta*, 'I'm sure I would.'

'Good. Then will you stop him, find out his name — and if possible, bring him to me? I want to talk with him.'

I set my empty plate down, translating, inside my head, what she had just said. That he might be understandably reluctant, or that I might be too craven to attempt a citizen's arrest — yes, she seriously expected me to accost Sheepskin Coat and bring him here, did not enter her mind. No doubt this was how things worked here, within the orphanage, under her wide-reaching aegis. Word came to her of bad behaviour — she had admitted to me that she had her network of informants. The suspects would be summonsed, and they would come, docile as lambs. I framed the phrases I wanted with difficulty.

'Sister, he was a big ox of a fellow. If he should prove unwilling, I couldn't force him.'

She seemed surprised. 'Why should he be unwilling, if he is innocent of any wrong doing? He knew Sonia, that much seems certain. Surely he'll want to help establish what happened to her?'

I began to understand why my mother, who is nothing if not devout, has confessed to finding those in Holy Orders annoying. Unworldliness grates.

'Sister, it feels very threatening to be accused, or even suspected, of killing someone.' In broken sentences I tried to make her understand that here, in Venice, I had found people suspicious of foreigners. Yesterday, when the boatmen dragged me into this building, I had really believed I would be arrested, thrown into prison, even hanged, just because I wasn't Venetian.

'This man, I know nothing about him, but from his accent, his clothing, I would guess he's of foreign origin.'

'There you are,' she replied. 'I knew you could help me. Useful to know that much. I will have it followed up' She nodded, satisfied.

'You know someone in State Security?' I said it without thinking. How could a nun know a secret policeman? But there is no doubt that the Venetian state employs many such, and even a nun has relatives. The glint in her eye told me that she read me like an easy finger exercise for a child of seven.

'Mother Prioress, young man! The Prioress of the Pietà is an important person in this city, she has connections,' she began, but interrupted herself, and looked round. This woman's hearing would have confounded a bat. A figure hovered uncertainly behind a column.

'Yes, Paola, what is it?

'Excuse me, Sister, I wanted to return something to the Signore.' The girl was flustered, out of breath, with bright spots on both cheeks which went ill with her reddish hair. No doubt she'd run down to the chapel from wherever she should have been at this hour, my drawing in her hand, waiting for a moment to slip it to me. She had advanced too far before realising that Sister Serafina was there before her. The nun held out her hand.

'So this is it. The drawing, about which I have heard so much.' She held it at arms' length, studying it long sightedly. Paola stood beside her, breathing heavily, her fingers twisting in and out of the folds of her gown. I wanted to say, 'At ease, little sister, she can't eat you!' but I didn't know how to phrase that in Italian, and it might be false reassurance. Sister Serafina wouldn't eat the girl, but she could almost certainly blight her life.

'A good likeness,' the nun said, 'of poor Sonia, that is. So we must suppose it is a good likeness of the youth too.' I grunted agreement. I was proud of that sketch. 'Why was she angry with him? Did he try to molest her?'

'Not that I saw, Sister. I don't know what he said to her. I wasn't close enough to hear.'

'Have any of the girls any idea who he is?' she demanded of Paola. 'I hear you've been running around, asking. What do they say?'

'They don't know him, Sister.'

It came out as a whisper. I was disappointed in Paola. Yesterday, talking with her on her own, she had seemed distressed by her friend's strange death, but lively and intelligent, eager to do something about it. A pleasant young woman, I had found myself wishing I could know her better, in happier circumstances. Now, I would have liked to say, 'Head up, don't let this woman bully you!' but I suppose it was ingrained. The girl had been scared of getting on the wrong side of Sister Serafina since she toddled her first baby steps. The nun studied the drawing again. 'He looks familiar, I feel I should know him. Someone who delivers things here? You asked everyone? The kitchen? I doubt if the lace makers would recognise him. Poor things, their eyes suffer so. The laundry?'

Paola had been nodding her head to all of these until the last.

'I asked *some* of the girls from the laundry,' she began, doubtfully, 'but Signora Amelia wouldn't let me ask the others. She said they were too busy to leave their work.'

'You can hardly dispute *that*,' responded the nun, tartly. 'They earn far more money for us, with their laundry work, than do you choristers who think such a lot of yourselves. However, they may be less occupied now that the morning rush is over. Did Signora Amelia look at it herself? No? Then you must go back. She keeps a sharp eye on all who pass by outside the laundry. Here, take it. Run, no, *don't* run. I'm for ever telling girls not to run, I expect they'll engrave it on the brass plate on my coffin — and ask her now.'

Before I could remind them that this was my property, Paola shot us both an anguished look, took the drawing, and scurried away. Possibly some of the anguish was for me, because she knew I wanted my drawing back, but more likely it was the thought of an encounter with Signora Amelia. If she was the old hag with the jackdaw, who had urged my ill-treatment with such relish the previous day, I could understand. Why was I visited by a strange feeling that I had in some way let Paola down? Had she expected me to take charge of the situation? Offer to take up a sword on her behalf, and to go and interrogate the old woman in the laundry? I told myself I was foolish, oversensitive, seeing an obligation where there was none. Just because letting girls down is what I have had the misfortune to be good at. I spared a thought for Lydia, back at home in England. Plump, blonde Lydia with her pink-and-white complexion, lisping engagingly through her pearly teeth. Lydy, my mother's cousin's daughter, whom my family had confidently expected I would marry. Her father, Cousin George, headed a thriving business. I, as the younger son of a family in financial straits, could hardly consider myself too toplofty to marry into trade. Especially when the prize was not only a good stipend, but plenty of free time to pursue my foolish ambition to be a painter, and the mutual approbation of our families. And, of course, useful connections which might bring suitors for my poor sisters. They told me I broke Lydy's heart. Perhaps I did. I'm sure I broke theirs. And my mother's. Though not, despite his financial embarrassments, my father's.

I can and do, ridicule my father's Jacobite sympathies and his business failings, but I don't deny that he, too, has a conscience. We spoke of it only once, as we rode out of Lancaster, after a family visit. A visit during which I had been expected to ask my charming coz a certain question, but had failed to do so.

Father had reigned in his horse as we breasted a hill, and looked back over Morecambe bay. One of Cousin George's three masted barques was floating forward on the tide, heading out of the mouth of the river Lune under cloud-flecked skies, for the hot sun of Africa.

'Can't bring yourself to line your pockets with money got that way?' he asked.

'No, Papa. I've always been fond of Lydy. But money got from human misery sticks in my craw. If Cousin George were in any other trade but the getting of slaves — '

'I understand,' replied my father, sadly patting pockets I knew to be empty. 'The womenfolk will be upset though. What will you do?'

'Make myself scarce? The Tour? I don't say the *Grand* Tour, because I don't expect you to pay for it. I want to see Italy. Draw and paint in Italy! And if I can't make money out of my pictures, I'll think again, find some trade that doesn't create such a stink in my nostrils.'

'Romantic ideals, my boy,' sighed my father. 'I had 'em too, when I was your age. Not sure if I could have starved for 'em in some filthy foreign garret though, *or* passed up the chance of a lovely chit like Lydia.'

We said no more, though when we reached home my mother and sisters said a great deal. Six weeks later I took ship for Bordeaux, and thence made my way across France and over the mountains into Italy. Now here I was, a free man with a clear conscience, earning a livelihood of sorts, preparing sketches of a soon-to-be demolished chapel. But failing to prevent a girl from being murdered whilst I slept. Unable to protect another from being browbeaten by a nun. I seemed to be unusually accident prone around young women.

'Don't worry about your precious drawing. I'll ensure she brings it back,' commented Sister Serafina, who had no doubt had long practice as a mind reader.

I glanced towards the coffin. 'Perhaps Signorina Paola's friend's death seems harder today than yesterday?'

'Perhaps, but there are other things. She's playing tomorrow night, the *Coro* have an engagement, so she's anxious about that. Inevitably, some of the others are jealous. A solo — she's something of a favourite with Don Antonio — *and* a private interview with a young man, yourself, yesterday. Nothing remains secret in this place for long! No doubt they're teasing her to death. Don't worry about her. Paola must learn to stand up for herself. She'll have little chance of holding her place as a soloist in our orchestra if she doesn't,' and with this harsh, but probably clear-sighted, assessment of Paola's chances, she hauled herself to her feet. 'I'll send someone for your tray,' she remarked over her shoulder, 'but don't waste time talking to any of the girls. We can only afford to pay you for a week or two, and we'd like to get our money's worth.' She nodded her head towards the coffin again. 'We've an unexpected funeral to pay for. There are few trees in Venice, and money certainly doesn't grow on them.'

Chapter 10

In which Paola steels herself to visit Signora Amelia, and learns a little more

Serve me right for telling Sister Serafina a lie. She demanded to know how I was getting on with questioning people. Someone — there are a dozen sly tattle-tales in this place — must have told her. What did she expect? A miracle? I'd been practicing my solo for the coming party, so I'd had hardly any time, and absolutely no success. When she asked if I'd shown the picture to *everyone* in the laundry, I knew she'd guessed I hadn't. 'Did you ask Signora Amelia? She knows everyone in Venice.' I wanted to howl. I hate that place, I really do. The truth was, I'd crept to the laundry door after Prime, and spoken to Marina and Sylvia, who will occasionally deign to speak to a chorister with whom they once shared a schoolroom bench, but as soon as I heard Signora Amelia screeching across the washtubs, I fled. I didn't wait to ask if I could show Harry's drawing to the other girls, reasoning that if Marina and Sylvia didn't know the man, no one would. Now I'd been caught out like a naughty little girl who has skimped her task, and ordered to tackle the old witch herself.

Best therefore, I reasoned woefully, to get it over with. I'd already spent two hours between Prime and Terce on my solo, and Marta, whom I'd conscripted to listen to it for the second hour, had turned peevish on me, and said if she had to hear it again before lunch she would certainly scream. I couldn't blame her. I was ready to scream myself.

When I was little, I had a weak bladder, and used to wet myself. I would be sobbing and shaking from head to foot as I traipsed that long stone-flagged corridor, the smell of rotten eggs growing stronger in my nostrils with every step. Sonia used to come with me and hold my hand. I used to think how kind she was; she never jeered at my mortification like the other little girls. As soon as someone noticed the shameful pool on the schoolroom floor, she would seize my hand, and come along to protect me from my doom. When I was five years old I truly believed that Signora Amelia was a witch. This time she really *would* thrust me head first into a tub of boiling water as she threatened, for wetting myself yet again. If Sonia hadn't been there to save me. Not even she could rescue me from being shouted at, and roughly stripped of my urine-soaked gown and under-shift. *That* had to be endured, as did the long wait, stark-naked on the cold winter flagstones, whilst Signora Amelia grumbled about me to the young women who sat at a table checking off the customers' laundry lists, until one of them took pity, and went through to the ironing room to find me a fresh set of clothes. Sonia couldn't prevent *that* humiliation, but at the time I gave her credit for rescuing me from being boiled, or thrust into one of the 'stoves' and smoked alive over the brimstone burners the laundresses use to clean silk gowns for rich ladies. She used to gaze earnestly up at Signora Amelia, and lisp, 'Can I see your birdies?' Signora Amelia fell for it every time. And so did I. It was years before I realised that Sonia had seen these trips to the laundry as a fine excuse to get out of lessons.

'See my birdies, is it?' the old woman would crow, thrusting her wart encrusted nose into Sonia's chubby face. 'Come with me, *bambina*, come along with me,' and off they would go, through the double doors onto the walkway, escaping from the sulphur fumes, to where Signora Amelia's jackdaw, Gino, her linnets, Carlo and Lina, and the tiny goldfinch, Tito, squawked and whistled in their wicker cages, hung against the wall. Not that I ever saw them, since naked as the day my mother dumped me on the *scafetta*, I could not follow. Nor did I wish to. From listening to the laundry girls' *rattle tatt*le, I discovered that Signora Amelia had named them after her husband and children, who had died in some mysterious and dreadful way, for which she blamed the Pietà nuns. In spite of this, she had insisted they employ her, since she, too, was now an orphan, without kin to support her. Signora Amelia, so the girls said, believed her birds were inhabited by the souls of her dead family. Are you surprised that I was frightened of her? The nuns themselves were terrifying to a tiny girl, and Signora Amelia was someone even they were afraid to cross!

As I grew older, thanks be to the Blessed Virgin and Santa Paola, I no longer wet myself, and so Signora Amelia and I rarely met, and I came to understand that in truth she had no special hatred of me. There was barely anyone in the place for whom she had a good word. Sonia was one of the few who earned her qualified favour. I knew, as Sister Serafina must, that she kept a watchful eye on everyone who passed by the laundry doors. She was rumoured to be able to name anyone in our Castello district, and to know something discreditable about all of them. Since she had *liked* Sonia, might she be willing to study Signor Harry's drawing? I took a deep breath, reminding myself that I was no longer that little girl in disgrace, and pushed open the door.

The dispatch room, a large whitewashed chamber opening directly onto the canal, where incoming and outgoing bundles of laundry are checked, was empty, except for two girls seated at a table. They glanced up, noted my red gown, then one licked her pencil, and both bent their white coifed heads over their lists, determined to ignore me. All the commoners believe that we choristers have far too high an opinion of ourselves, and the girls who work in the laundry resent us more than the rest. And with some justification. No one in Venice cleans silk more expertly than they, and since gowns made of silk from the East have become so fashionable amongst the ladies of the nobility, they can barely keep pace with the demand. I believe they charge high prices too, bringing in a tidy income for the Pietà. *They* insist, however, that we get all the praise and attention from those outside the Pietà's walls, while their industry is taken for granted.

Today, examples of their work hung around the walls, airing, to banish the rotten egg smell created by the cleaning process, before they could be returned to their owners. Gorgeous yellow, red, and turquoise ruffled gowns, some with pearl encrusted bands around the hem, peeped out from under their protective paper wrappers. Once, on one of our infant visits here, Signora Amelia had taken one of the gowns out of its wrapper to show to Sonia; (not me, I was chastised as a 'dirty wretch') a shimmering confection of apple green gauze, with exquisite silver-thread embroidery across the bodice. Such a dress as surely only a *contessa* might wear. I had longed to stretch out my hand and caress one of its folds. How might it feel to be a fine lady wearing such a gown? Today, remembering, I might have dared do it, just to annoy those rude girls, but I didn't have time. I needed to get back to my solo. I cleared my throat to demand attention. Two heads were grudgingly raised, but before I could speak, the door to the ironing room jerked open, releasing a cloud of hot steam, which swirled into the colder atmosphere of the dispatch room, bringing with it a frightened young girl. Her arms were full of freshly ironed sheets, and behind her, urging her along with thwacks on the buttocks with her walking cane, Signora Amelia.

'On the table in the *dispatch* room, girl!' she screeched, 'Holy Madonna, grant me strength!' The girl was Alina, the little dimwit who had spilled scalding water over two school children yesterday. Clearly the kitchen had had enough of her, and she had been reassigned to the laundry. Not a joyous outcome for Alina, but providentially for her, Signora Amelia now turned on me.

'And what would *you* want? Don't tell me you've wet them flannel under drawers they've started issuing to you lot to wear to Prime on cold mornings?' the old crone demanded, grinning evilly, and waggling the tip of her cane in my face. That one forgets nothing. Even after thirteen years. I felt a flare of pure anger colour my cheeks. The two checkers smirked behind their hands.

'Sister Serafina sent me, Signora.' I willed myself to ignore her taunts. 'It's about Sonia. You remember Sonia? The girl — the one who's dead?'

'Course I remember her, why wouldn't I remember her?' she lowered the cane, her snaggle-toothed grin fading. 'Saw her most days, didn't I? What does her Sistership want?'

'She wants to know if you recognise this man.' I thrust the drawing towards her. She squinted at it, but didn't take it from me. Her head turned slowly from side to side, denying, but I saw her crooked shoulders stiffen.

'Come out on the walkway,' she mumbled, 'light's poor in here. Can't make it out.' A lie. The light was excellent. Sunlight streamed in through high windows, designed to aid the checkers' quest for spots and stains. The eyes of the two girls at the table were bright with curiosity, and Alina's mouth gaped open. I followed Signora Amelia outside.

By the jackdaw's cage she halted, and began fishing in the pocket of her apron, pulling out broken segments of an orange, which she began to push through the wickerwork. The jackdaw, Gino, watched, but made no move.

'All right, girl, show me,' she demanded, wiping her hands on her apron. I handed her Signor Harry's drawing, and she studied it. Over her shoulder the bright eye of the jackdaw peered too.

'S' her brother, ain't it?' The jackdaw let out a squawk, apparently agreeing.

'Her brother?' I repeated, stupidly. 'Sonia had a brother?'

'O' course she did. Most prob'ly *you've* got one some place if you knew where to look. Twins they was, as I recall. Knew her mother, years ago, she was a friend o' mine, in a manner of speaking. Took up with a foreigner, silly bitch. 'Housekeeper' I don't think! And the twins was the result. *He* wouldn't let her keep the girl, so she ended up here, but they kept the lad, seeing as how he could be trained up to help in the business. Seen him about, now and then. No mistaking them gappy teeth, they got those from Luisa, the mother. *She's* dead too, poor jade, or so I heard, a few months back. *You* drew this, Signorina Fancy Drawers?'

'No, the artist drew it,' I replied, without thinking. I was taken aback to discover that Sonia had a brother, and also, until recently, a mother. 'Did she know? About her mother and her brother?'

The old woman wasn't listening to me. Her angry eyes bored into the drawing again. Then she seemed to realise what I had said.

'Artist? That foreign feller with the yeller hair? Him that found her? Drunk as a lord, he must 'a been, to go sleeping in the barge. *I* still reckon t'was him did for Sonia. If he didn't, what's he doing with a drawing of her? Making out he never went near her. Oh, I know what them *buffoni* of the Watch told the nuns, but you'll never get me to believe he wasn't in it somehow. Greeks, Slovenes, English, where's the difference? Nasty foreign scum, the lot of 'em! And Sister Serafina swallowed his lies. But then she would, wouldn't she? Any devil with a handsome face can get round them dried up old sticks, what's never had a man of their own. Wasn't it them sent a dying man to stay in my house, saying, "The poor feller's just exhausted with travelling, riding like he has, all the way from Rome, with messages from the Holy Father?" Rome!' she spat the word. 'And wasn't he dead of the smallpox within three days, and my husband and children within the fortnight? And what have I left to comfort me in me old age? My old jackdaw here, and my linnets, and my little goldfinch, and a parcel of lazy, useless girls to train up, that don't know how to iron their own shifts! Ain't that the shame of it, Gino, me old *carissimo*?' The jackdaw, who had been taking quite an interest in our proceedings until she addressed him directly, shuffled on his perch and turned his back, tail feathers drooping. Evidently he wasn't brave enough to challenge her prejudice against anyone who wasn't Venetian. Neither was I. Cowards, the pair of us.

'Sonia knew — about her brother?' I ventured, dreading another tirade.

'O' course, you silly wench. This picture tells you that!' The old woman tapped the drawing with forefinger red and swollen from many emersions in water. 'Daresay he'd made himself known since their mother died, getting round her mebbe, to come and keep house for them. But here she's giving him the go-by, and good for her!' she added, admiringly, 'I reckon she'd have gone in the end though, blood being thicker than water. Full of secrets she was, these last few weeks. Making up her mind to go, I'll warrant!'

My eyes smarted with tears, and I turned away. Fortunately, Signora Amelia was still intent on the drawing. Sonia had been full of secrets, and I hadn't known. Once, we had told each other everything. She'd promised to meet me on the *terrazzo*, but she never came. It was my fault we had grown apart. Oh, I could make excuses, I had so many Masses to sing, rehearsals to attend, parts to learn — and our paths had crossed rarely, for all we lived under the same roof. Yet we'd once been so close. Two little girls with our heads together, planning mischief, dreaming of a time when we would be all grown up, and wonderful things might happen. Now, for Sonia, they never would.

'Funeral's the day after tomorrow, ain't it?' the old washer-woman broke into my thoughts. 'But what do you care, off partying with the rest tomorrow, I suppose?'

'All the string section have to go. Signor Fosca has hired us to play.'

'With your little playmate lying dead! You should be ashamed o' yourself,' she jeered.

Would she have let any of the laundry girls leave their work if someone they were fond of died? No, of course she wouldn't. Fortunately, before I betrayed my anger with a retort, Gino let out a great screech and flapped his wings, startling us both.

'Oh, it's *him*!' muttered Signora Amelia, as a masculine figure hobbled towards us along the walkway, leaning heavily on a stick. 'The Reverend-I-can't-sing-mass-'cos me-asthma's-that-bad! Don't stop 'im running around like a headless chicken, making these Godless stage shows of his!'

'*Bon Giorno*, Signora Amelia! What are *you* doing out here, kinswoman Rossa, when you should be practising your piece, *hmm*?'

Don Antonio Vivaldi, pottering round to give a lesson, and dropping me straight in the *zuppe*. Next time she saw me, Signora

Amelia would demand to know since when was I his kinswoman? I wouldn't put it past her to start some rumour that I really was a by-blow of the Vivaldi clan, or worse, that *I* thought I was. More likely the latter, since to her all we choristers are stuck-up madams who don't know our proper station in life. Don Antonio beamed at us both, quite unaware that he was being tactless.

'Sister Serafina sent me on an errand, Sir,' I murmured, bobbing a curtsey, but he was busy greeting the birds. 'And how is my old friend Gino, this morning? And Carlo? And Lina? And dear little Tito.' This last to the goldfinch, which seemed to recognise him, and opened its tiny beak to sing a clear cadence to the sky.

'Do ye' hear that? This little fellow has more music in his soul than anyone in Venice! Sister *Serafina* sent you on an errand, Paola, *hmm*? And what did Sister *Angelica* have to say to that? No doubt she'll have severe looks for both of us, because *I* should be giving a lesson to that tiresome young novice from Bavaria, Sister Helga. She has already complained to both Sister Angelica *and* Mother Prioress about me. But on such a fine morning I could *not* face her! A mechanical wonder she is, no doubt, but no more delicacy in her bowing than if she was using one of Signora Amelia's scrub-brushes. Why, this little bird trills with more expression! So, is your errand done, girl? Good, you shall be my alibi, and I yours. Let us go indoors and I'll hear how you are faring with that new piece of mine.'

Glad to escape Signora Amelia, I followed him. I knew now who the young man in Harry's drawing was, but how could I set about finding him? And did he have anything to do with Sonia's death?

The drawing I kept in my hand, not liking to stop to tuck it safely in my bodice whilst walking alongside Don Antonio, so of course he saw that I was carrying something.

'What's this, *written* instructions from Sister Serafina? This must have been a most complicated errand?' he enquired, raising an eyebrow. He was being inquisitive, it was none of his business, but he had taught me since I was ten, so I showed him the drawing.

'Sonia was a friend. Since we were babies,' I explained.

'Humph, not *Coro*. Never heard anything of her but her name.' He glanced at the drawing. 'I've seen the lad though, round and about the district.'

'The young man... the artist, who is working in the chapel, drew this.'

'Did he now? And gave it to you?' Don Antonio frowned. 'Don Salva told me you two had met. Paola... I hope you will not form... too close an attachment to that young fellow. I have no proof that he is anything other than an excellent young man, but... you have a great talent, girl. Don't allow yourself to be distracted. We need you here, at the Pietà. Indeed, I have a feeling we are going to need you a great deal. Ah,' he paused, rubbing the sharp bridge of his great nose, looking at me gravely, and, I thought, a little embarrassed, 'but who am I to advise you? Go, girl, fetch your fiddle, and let me hear that piece of mine. Time is running away from us!'

Don Antonio did not see her, but I did. As we traversed the main hallway and made for one of the practice rooms, I caught sight of Sister Helga descending the stairs, Sister Juanita, as ever, at her side. Seeing us, her face flushed in indignation. Sister Angelica would shortly be hearing another complaint about a missed lesson. I wondered whether I ought to try to warn Don Antonio, but didn't have the courage to do so. We all knew he needed the money the Pietà was paying him. Too many grumbles, especially from one of the foreign pupils whose convent was paying for her instruction, and the governors would be terminating his engagement.

Chapter 11

Harry, through his foolish tendency to curiosity, finds himself further embroiled in the affairs of the orphanage

Contrary to the doubts I had expressed to Sister Serafina, I was soon to meet up with Sheepskin coat. Having spent the day sketching the Annunciation and the Nativity to the best of my ability, I packed my materials away and went to consult Don Salvatore. Where would I find the Prioress at this hour, to show her my work? He would, he said, take me to her.

'Gentlemen,' he scrutinised me doubtfully, probably unsure whether an artist merited that title, 'are not encouraged to walk about the building unescorted. Some of our young women can be rather — excitable. Particularly in the company,' he added, unexpectedly, 'of young men as well favoured as yourself. Those bruises of yours, I see, are fading nicely. Sister Serafina's tinctures are remarkably effective. To me,' he added wryly, 'the girls pay no more attention than they would to a table or a chair. Which, as I am their confessor, is just as well.'

We walked down corridors through which I must have passed the day before, but I had then been in no case to note my surroundings. Reaching the wood panelled entrance hall, we were met with a surprising scene. Two young women in dark habits, and the white muslin veils of novices (I was beginning to grasp the meaning of the different styles of dress to be seen around the Pietà) were arguing with Sister Domenica, a woman I wouldn't have cared to cross myself. With them, looking uncomfortable, was a red gowned chorister, a dark haired young woman some years senior to my young friend, Paola. I had the impression that the argument was none of her making, and she wished she was anywhere but in their company.

'We do not steal!' the stouter of the two novices was blustering. 'This we never would! A man to the door came. Your Porteress from her post was gone. He dropped the bag to the floor, and away went. So, having nothing else to do, Maestro Vivaldi having forgotten my lesson *once again*, we pick it up!'

'Sister Helga,' replied Sister Domenica, dryly, 'I am not accusing you. I merely asked you what you have there, and where you are going with it?'

'*Barbara* here suggested we take it to the nun's parlour, to see what it is,' the other novice chipped in. 'It contains some coins, that is certain.'

'And with it, I observe, a note, Sister Juanita. People often leave a donation here without stopping to explain themselves.' She glanced at the chorister. 'Barbara, surely you know that?' The young woman, Barbara, flushed pink and shook her head, but whether she was denying that she knew it, or merely seeking to disassociate herself from the whole affair, was unclear. Juanita reluctantly handed over bag and note. Sister Domenica glanced at it, but looked up as Don Salvatore and I approached.

'This is welcome,' she remarked, addressing Don Salva.. 'Money to pay for Sonia's burial Mass, and the family will provide wood for the coffin.' She turned again to the two novices and their companion. 'This man, what did he look like? The Prioress would naturally like to speak to Sonia's relatives before the funeral.'

'Just a man. My vows, I most seriously take. At him, I do not look.'

'He was young. Quite stout,' shrugged her skinny companion, disinterested. 'Helga is right. We did not come here to look at men, we came to study music.'

She flashed a venomous glance in my direction, which I felt was uncalled for. *I* wasn't stopping her from studying music. She wasn't studying music now; she was skulking in the hallway, picking up things that didn't belong to her. She hadn't been studying music when I saw her last. If it had been her? She certainly bore a resemblance to the young woman I had seen peering round the laundry door at midnight. The one with the long thin face, whom I had supposed must be a friend of Sonia's. Or was Sonia perhaps a go-between? Was this, 'we are not interested in men' just a pose? A go-between role might explain Sonia's less than affectionate relationship with Sheepskin Coat. I hadn't thought this Juanita (if it was indeed she) could have seen me well enough in the darkness beyond the reach of her candle flame, to recognise me, but I could imagine no other explanation for this flash of animosity. She and this Sister Helga were clearly very interested in the note and the bag of coins. Had they been waiting in the hallway, knowing it would arrive?

I wondered if I could persuade Sister Domenica to tell me what the note contained. It was none of my business of course, except that her colleague, Sister Serafina, had urged me to find Sheepskin coat, and 'young and stout' certainly described him.

'Sister, could this be — ?' I began, but she shook the palm of her hand before my face in a strange shushing gesture. Not so strange to me. Bessie, our nursemaid, had used it, when one of we children had been about to blurt out something better left unsaid.

'I'm pleased to have caught *you*, Signor Harry,' she said, firmly changing the subject, 'because I want your help. You know that some of the girls of the *Coro* are going to Signor Fosca's house tomorrow evening? No? I thought the whole place was abuzz with it. I wondered,' she frowned at Helga, Juanita, and Barbara. 'Ladies, I won't keep you. *I* will ensure the Prioress receives the money and the note.' She waited, pointedly, until the three of them moved out of earshot, 'if you would be willing to perform a small service for us? One of our boatmen, Giorgio, has sent word he is laid up with some bilious complaint, and although Nardo can handle the barge on his own, he needs someone to steady the instruments. The cellos and basses are too cumbersome for the girls to carry through the streets, which, as you must have noticed, are extremely crowded at this season. Mother Prioress has agreed a small remuneration.' Seeing my bafflement, she went on. 'I'm sure an able bodied young man like yourself, being an artist, and therefore a person of sensitivity — will understand that musical instruments should be handled with respect. Will you do this for us?'

I raised an eyebrow. Yesterday I was a murderer. An evil foreigner. Now I was promoted to odd job man, a useful fellow to have about the place when the laundry man went down with gut-rot (which I considered well deserved for the way he had treated me) Was it only yesterday? It seemed like a lifetime. I was fast learning too, not to be too proud to accept small sums of money. The payment she mentioned would relieve my landlord's anxieties, but I had never handled musical instruments in my life.

'How many instruments, Sister?'

'Two of each. Four large instruments.'

'And all that is required is that I travel in the barge and steady them?'

'And stay at the Fosca's house until the girls have played, and accompany Nardo on the return journey.' She coughed, embarrassed, 'I don't like to send any of the girls in the boat with Nardo. He is not to be trusted around young women when his brother isn't there to check him. The Foscas will, I'm sure, give you both supper.'

In the servants' hall. How surprised my haughty English relatives would be to find me reduced to this. Or perhaps not, remembering the gloomy predictions they had made on my departure. However, I had heard a good deal about the gorgeous *palazzi* in which wealthy Venetians lived. Surely I would find an opportunity to peek into the Fosca's *piano nobile*? And, in the midst of a noisy celebration, I might find chance for a word with Signorina Paola, who had not yet returned my drawing. Don Salva and Sister Serafina had both mentioned that she would be playing. She must have shown the sketch to a good many people by now, including the old laundry woman, and I was interested to hear what, if anything, she had discovered.

'Very well, Sister. Tomorrow evening, at what time?'

The following evening, after a long day at the drawing board (the Prioress having been pleased to approve my preliminary sketches) I reported for duty. The instruments were lying on their sides in the dispatch room of the laundry. Two strapping young women in red gowns were guarding them, and being harassed for being under her feet, by the old hellcat, Signora Amelia. Her scowl told me her opinion of *me* had not changed. When I explained that I was appointed to travel with the instruments, the big-boned chorister with the bold eyes sighed with relief.

'Holy Madonna be praised!' she exclaimed. Now we can lay 'em back to back in the bottom of the boat, pass a canvas over 'em, and tie 'em down with this coil of washing line the Signora has been so *generous* as to loan us. *Pace*, Signora, we're getting 'em loaded, and out of your bloody way, now!'

'Curb your mouth, Maria-Regina!' snapped the old woman, brandishing her walking cane round the girl's ears. 'A fine one *you* are for the *Coro*. Foul-mouthed as your whore of a mother, Bianca Molin was. Always knew she'd come to a bad end, and so she did, and so will you, mark my words. Get yourselves out of here, the lot of you!'

With this delightful blessing, we carried the cellos and basses out, loaded them, and tied them down. Nardo, to my surprise, showed me no animosity, seemingly having quite forgotten the citizen's arrest he had performed on me so recently. He was a great brute of a fellow, whose vacant, watery eyes rested longingly on the plump posteriors of the two choristers as they bent over to secure their instruments, but he made no move to molest them. I fancied this Maria-Regina would have elbowed him overboard if he had tried. The two girls then leapt ashore, displaying a good deal of their sturdy legs in darned stockings. Hooting with laughter, and shouting who-knew-what ribaldries, they waved us off.

Nardo might be a lack-wit, but he knew how to propel the flat bottomed barge through the water with easy, fluent strokes, and we made steady progress out of the *rio*, and north and westwards into the mouth of the Grand Canal. The sun had gone down, leaving apple green and lemon trails of cloud across the Western sky. Darkness fell quickly, as it does in these Southern climes. Nardo had placed partly used altar candles in glass jars in the prow and stern of the barge, to signal our presence to other boats. Away from the sheltered backwater, I began to understand why my assistance was necessary. The wind had risen as the light faded, and the Adriatic, its meagre tide on the turn, slapped choppy wavelets against the boat, causing it to rock. I sat to one side with my hands on the highest points of the covered instruments, although in fact the girls had secured them well, and they barely shifted beneath their canvas shroud.

I had no idea where Ca'Fosca, to which we were headed, might be, but just as some dullard of a jehu would know his way about the more obscure streets of London, so this fellow, Nardo, seemed to have a map of every canal in Venice inside his noddle. I found myself considering him, in the light of what Sister Domenica had said. He was not to be trusted to keep his hands to himself around young women. He had shown little emotion when Sonia's body was discovered, it was his brother who had done most of the shouting. Then I chided myself. Poor fellow, with no roof to his mouth, very likely no woman would look at him twice. This did not mean he was a murderer. On the other hand, it did not mean that he was not.

Presently we turned aside from the Grand Canal into a minor waterway, and then into another and another. I became disorientated, with no idea of our whereabouts, but in the shelter of the tall buildings, the waves calmed, and my responsibilities lessened. The barge sighed through treacle dark waters smelling of mud and rotting wood, beneath the high cliff faces of marble and mosaic-clad palaces, and under stone bridges lit by flickering lanterns encased in wrought-iron cages. An occasional sleek black gondola slid by, unlit, the passengers, if any, hidden within the lacquered *felze*. We, in our turn, skimmed past many beautiful buildings, whose history I should like to have known, their carved and crenulated rooflines silhouetted against the darkening sky. Atop one such building, perhaps a church, perhaps the *scuola* of some important guild, the statue of a saint stood, outlined against the evening glow of the heavens, holding up one of his marble arms to bless those of us below. Mirroring this, Gondoliers raised hands in salute as we passed, grunting harsh greetings. One of them was singing, a sweet, lilting melody, which echoed from the walls of the chasm through which he was propelling his boat, making one think him a small choir, rather than one man alone. Around one corner we suddenly came upon a carnival procession, lantern bearers to the fore, men and women dressed like living *Punchinellos*, in yellow, scarlet and green, their faces hidden beneath feathered masks, following one another; shouting, singing, and trying to keep time to a shaky dance rhythm played on a squealing fiddle. Then, just as quickly, we had passed around the bulk of another building, onto a quiet backwater, and the sound was muffled, lost. Above us, for a brief moment, I saw a beautiful painted face peer down from a lighted lattice, and then retreat, its owner slamming the casement shut. No gorgeous Venetian courtesan would waste more than a passing glance on such as Nardo and myself. Somehow they can sense when a man is penniless, and of no importance. For a moment, I felt dejected, excluded from the wild exuberant Venice that is *carnevale,* a lone Englishman, stuffy and dull, with nothing at all in his pockets, except what he could earn running tiresome errands for the pious ladies of the Pietà.

At the next bridge, however, I was surprised to be hailed. 'Eh! 'Arry! Where you'se going, my friend?' It was Luca, monkey-faced would-be actor, and my fellow lodger. We were passing close to the opera house where he was somewhat intermittently employed.

'Earning my bread!' I called up, as we passed beneath him. He ran down the steps, and as we emerged, jumped aboard. Nardo made no protest about the arrival of an extra passenger.

'*This* is part of your work?' he enquired, as, puzzled as well he might be, he settled himself in the bottom of the boat. The night before, buoyed up on the Prioress's approval of my sketches, I had returned to our dismal lodgings, and announced that it was my turn to stand the bill at our favoured tavern. There, seated by a warm fire, and full of roast guinea fowl with chestnut stuffing, I had treated him to description of my splendid commission to draw for the Pietà, and mayhap, somewhat bosky by the end of the evening, boasted that I had those nuns eating out of my hand. Now I had to confess that the opposite was, in fact, the case.

'A little extra task they have found for me. Alas, for little payment, these Pietà ladies aren't liberal with their funds,' I admitted, ruefully, 'but if you care to help, I might manage to secure you a free supper.' Luca pronounced himself at my service for the evening.

'Nothing for me at *San Angelo* tonight,' he explained. 'No performance. The Signorina Girò is singing at a private party, and old Vivaldi is going along to hold her hand.'

'Well, I know for a fact that old Vivaldi, as you call him, is due at the Fosca's place, where the young women of the Pietà are to play these instruments.' I patted them, proprietarily. 'Could this be the same event?'

Luca began to tell me why he thought this unlikely, but we were immediately distracted by shouting from a bridge ahead. On it, an old man was performing a strange dance, waving his arms above his head, at the same time bawling out a tuneless ditty, whilst a younger fellow, who must surely be his son, urged him to stop being a fool, or so I supposed, although it was impossible to make out words. Nardo, grasping that this was a drunkard who might fall off the bridge (for like many Venetian bridges it had no guard rail) on top of us, rested his oars, and we waited for the old fellow to heed his son. He was making passes to snatch hold of his father's coat, and haul him down. Meanwhile our boat drifted closer, and I recognised the younger man. He was Sheepskin coat — and yes, sure enough, the old fellow with him had a tassel to his hat.

Startled, I was unwise enough to call out, 'Hoy! You! I must speak to you!' Hearing my voice rising from the water, but unable to see me in the shadows (it was now fully dark) he peered down, letting go of his father's sleeve. The old man, suddenly free, jerked away, over balanced, yelled, and fell into the canal with a prodigious splash.

'See what you have done!' howled the son, 'Papa cannot swim!'

'The water's not deep!' called, Luca, who was lounging in the stern, laughing at this crazy pair. 'Tell the old fool to stand up!'

'But he is drunk!' exclaimed the son, as though we might not have guessed this. 'He cannot right himself!'

Since the fault was partly mine, I stood up to survey the situation. The old man was floating with his head below water, and his heels to the sky. He wore strange baggy breeches like a Turcoman, and in the folds of these, air was evidently trapped, keeping him from sinking entirely, and from time to time he raised his head and spewed out a fountain of filthy water. It was as much as I could do not to join Luca, doubled up in mirth. Instead, I urged Nardo to heave to and lend me an oar, which he was somewhat loath to do. Then we scrambled out of the boat, and tried to persuade the drowning drunkard to catch hold of it, so that we could drag him on to dry land. It took three of us, the son, Luca and myself, to haul the old fool out, so heavy did his wet clothing prove, and by the time we had done so, we too were sopping wet, and covered in reeking slime from the sides of the canal. We even rescued his hat, although the tassel was a sorry rat's tail. It was unfortunate that I had donned my last clean shirt in honour of my visit to Ca'Fosca.

'I must speak to you!' I gasped to the son, breathless from our exertions. 'Though you may have heard it...bad news, from the Pietà, I'm afraid.'

'Our Sonia?' he hissed back, 'We heard — the old woman from the laundry, Signora Amelia, told some person from our street. I took money to the nuns yesterday, for her funeral. That's why Papa here's drunk himself senseless. Hearing she's dead, and what it's costing to bury her. He never bothered with her when she was alive,' he remarked, bitterly, gazing down at his supine parent, 'but now she's dead, he says he's determined on vengeance — as though *this* is anyway to go about it! I must get him home, or he will catch his death!'

I doubted this. If he was a habitual drunkard, and his mottled and veined nose told their own tale, water wouldn't kill the old man. He lay like a stranded fish in the pool of light from the flickering lantern on the bridge, spewing up the canal, and making no attempt to rise, but now and then singing a snatch of song. Something had become clear to me, however, when the son said, 'Our Sonia?' just as humble folk back home might speak of a family member. Who could this fellow be but Sonia's brother? I asked him, and he confirmed it.

'What were you two quarrelling about, that day I saw you on the *riva?*' I asked, curious to hear what he would say. He looked at me, hurt, and to my alarm (I am after all an Englishman) I thought I saw tears gather on his lashes, though it might have been the reflection from the beam of the lantern on the bridge.

'You are not imagining that *I* killed my sister? We were twins you know? There was no quarrel. Not on my part. She had heard... well, the truth is I had begged her to come and live with us, and keep house, but that old witch in the laundry had told her bad things about Papa. How he used to beat our mother, how he took Sonia away when we were only a few days old, and put her on the *scafetta*. Sonia was angry. She said I was trying to cheat her, saying we wanted her home, when all we wanted was a drudge. But Papa didn't even know. I hadn't told him. I thought, if I persuaded her to come, once she was there, looking after the house, Papa would consent to it, and I'd see to it he didn't ill-treat her.'

'Ah. I see,' I said, and I did. Sheepskin coat might genuinely want his sister home, but Papa would only accept her as a servant he did not have to pay. However, I found I believed in this brother of hers. His plan to invite her to join the household without first informing Papa might have been foolish, but surely he would not kill her if she refused? Not numbering murderers amongst my close acquaintances, I cannot say what I expected, but someone who made such strenuous efforts to rescue his dreadful old father, and who spoke of 'our Sonia' and his determination to protect her, as though her loss had genuinely distressed him, seemed unlikely (to my way of thinking) to be a homicidal monster.

'He'll do,' he assured me, casting a considering glance at his father, who now showed signs of trying to rise. 'I'll walk him home briskly.' Probably this was not the first time Papa had taken a tumble into a canal, and this incident had shown me how easily it could happen. With my suspicions of the brother abated, perhaps, after all, the unfortunate girl *had* simply slipped and fallen, hitting her head as she fell? If she had stumbled out of the way of rushing on-comers on the narrow walkway? Perhaps I should even exonerate the men of the Watch? An explanation seemed frustratingly far off.

The son pulled the old man upright, none too gently, and began to march him away. Once on his feet, the old fellow spewed one last mouthful, and began to sing again. 'Heyyy!' I called to their retreating backs, suddenly realising what I had forgotten to ask. 'What's your naaame?' My voice echoed back off the blind walls of a neighbouring *palazzo*.

'Fredianoooo!' the man I'd christened Sheepskin coat called over his shoulder.

'Where do you liiive?' I shouted, but they disappeared around a bend in the canal.

'*I* know where they live,' remarked Luca, who had stood hugging his arms across his chest against the cold throughout my interrogation, 'if you really wish to know? The old man's the timber merchant, isn't he? Størje, his name is. Slovenian fellow. Lives down by the Arsenal. I've been there a few times, to get timber for flats for the opera house. Mean old bugger, when he's sober. Treats his son like dirt. What d'you want him for? If you're hoping for cheap off cuts for your painting, forget it. That old swine won't sell anything cheap.'

'*I* don't want him or his goods at any price,' I replied, 'but one of the nuns asked me to find the son. And she'll certainly want to speak to the father as well. That poor girl I told you about, the one whose body I found in the canal — is evidently his daughter.'

'Could well be, from what I've heard of him,' Luca shrugged, his comical face wry. 'Sort of thing that stingy miser would do. Dump his daughter in an orphanage, so he didn't have the expense of feeding and clothing her. They say the son's a bastard, fathered on some woman who kept house for him. It's well known, he's a wife and six children in Koper. Goes over and pays them a visit now and then, whenever he needs to increase his timber stocks. You heard the son say he resents paying out for her burying — although no one could get wood for the coffin cheaper than he can — and he's out for vengeance. You'd best warn the nuns I've heard old Størje can be nasty if he has a grievance.'

I shrugged. All I could do was pass on the information, and my impressions of Sonia's family, to Sister Serafina, to make of it what she would.

'Now, w-h-hat about us?' Luca demanded, his teeth chattering. 'I'm w-wet to my skin!'

There was nothing useful we *could* do, but climb back into the boat, and urge the dumb Nardo to proceed. As we sailed on through the darkness, stars now glinting overhead, I fell to musing on what I had heard. As the person who found her body and had been accused of killing her, even if I was now exonerated, I still felt a personal interest in discovering what had happened to her. Yes, it was true, in the noisy turmoil that is carnival in Venice, such an accident could happen easily enough. A crowd of drunken people rush by, a girl is pushed aside, and falls to her death. But somehow I could not quite convince myself that this was what had happened. The woman I had seen looking out of the laundry door. She was not Sonia. But might Sonia have been waiting there, with her, to be told that the way was clear for whatever errand she was to embark on? Or was it possible that Sonia been killed inside the building, and the watcher was waiting for an opportunity to put the corpse outside? Could such a thing happen in that quiet, well ordered place? I found myself wanting very much to talk with Signorina Paola, and hear what if anything she had discovered.

'Now what?' demanded Luca, as Nardo turned the boat in under the water gate of an ancient merchant's house. We had arrived at our destination, dirty, smelly, and dishevelled. And late. We were, of course, deeply unpopular.

Chapter 12

In which Paola sets out for her first party, and endures several uncomfortable experiences

Once a wearying day devoted to rehearsals, on top of our normal commitment to sing in chapel at the appointed hours, was over, I tried once more to sneak the drawing back to Signor Harry. I found his sketching materials neatly piled on a corner of the chancel step, but he had already left for the day. He would be displeased, since I knew he hadn't wanted to lend it to me in the first place. Then I took time, which in truth I did not have, to struggle to light a votive candle, which I placed next to Sonia's coffin, and knelt for a moment to whisper a prayer for her. It was the least I could do, leaving the friend of my childhood here alone. The coffin had been sealed. Tomorrow she would be committed to the ground in the old, overcrowded burial place beyond the shipyards. As I rose to my feet to leave, someone opened the door from the vestry, causing all the candle flames in the chapel flicker and bend in the draught. I turned, startled, but it was only Sister Juanita, the Spanish novice, on her own for once, without Sister Helga. She looked surprised to see me, as though she had not expected to find anyone there. 'I come to make prayers,' she remarked, and veered away towards one of the side chapels. Evidently the prayers she intended to make were not for Sonia.

I hurried to the dormitory to scramble into my concert gown. Marta, rather grudgingly, since she was still feeling her disappointment at being excluded from the evening, had offered to dress my hair. She is neat handed, and with a few deft flicks of her wrist, and a pin or two, can fix a topknot which will stay in place. I've tried to copy her many times, but I've never mastered it.

I found her perched on my bed, with Carolina beside her. 'Paola, trust you to be late! I've done Albetta and Lucrezia already; they're dressed and gone down.'

'Sorry!' I gasped, dropping my day gown round my ankles. 'I went to light a candle — for Sonia.'

'Ha! You've heard what they're saying?' demanded Carolina,

'about your precious Sonia?'

'It might not be true!' cautioned Marta, rising, and seizing hold of the back of my shift, forcing me to sit down, so that she could begin combing out my hair. 'You know as well as I do, Carolina, how those commoners love to gossip.'

'What are they saying?' I don't much care for Carolina, though generally we manage to rub along. Never mind the commoners, no one enjoys spreading spiteful rumours more than she.

'Claudia and Dora were sure it's true. Sonia was always poking her nose into other people's business. Well, you know she was! And she wasn't above telling tales if it suited her. Or threatening that she would.'

Marta dragged the comb through my hair. 'They're saying she must have threatened to tell someone's pet secret. And that person lost her temper and hit her. Hard enough to kill her? That's just malicious rubbish, Caro!'

'Claudi thinks it's true. She says Sonia must have asked for money, to keep mum. She says Sonia *did* ask girls for money — or trinkets, or a handkerchief, anything they had to give. She apparently told someone she wanted to leave this place, and needed money, and she didn't see why people shouldn't pay her if they didn't want their secrets broadcast.'

'What secrets?' I was glad Marta was standing up for Sonia, disbelieving this spiteful tittle-tattle, but my heart was strangely heavy, remembering that gold coin she had so hastily returned to her pocket. Remembering too, when we were younger, that Sonia had made a habit of threatening to 'tell' about childish crimes, in order to exact a slice of apple, or a handful of raisins, from other little girls, in return for holding her tongue.

Carolina lounged back, elbows supporting her on the bed, watching, whilst Marta twisted my hair up on top of my head.

'What secrets could anyone here have that they'd pay Sonia to keep quiet about? And if they *did*, where would they get the money?' Marta demanded. 'I can't imagine anyone going to Mother Prioress, and saying "Please, give me something from my savings account?" She would ask what they wanted it for.'

We Pietà girls each have our own savings account, but it isn't disbursed lightly. It's money put aside from our earnings as musicians, laundresses, or whatever. A dowry, in case we should marry, or, as the nuns hope, take vows.

Carolina shrugged. 'You'd be surprised. Some of those foreign novices have money of their own. They're supposed to hand it to the nuns for safe keeping while they're here, but I've heard they often keep some back to pay the commoners in charge of the housekeeping for little luxuries, like having a fire in their rooms, or extra butter with their breakfast rolls. And there are the day students, those girls who come here for music lessons. Some of *them* must have money, judging by the way they dress, fancy scarves and gloves, bracelets and embroidered handkerchiefs' This was an oft expressed grievance of Carolina's; her resentment of these daughters of wealthy townspeople, whose parents paid to have them taught music. Well, to be truthful, we all envied them more than a little.

'Nonsense!' Marta wasn't having any of it, twisting my hair so tightly on the crown of my head that that I could feel my eyelids begin to stretch. 'However nosey Sonia was, she couldn't have found out any secrets about the day students. How would she? She never saw them, she was working with the schoolchildren all day. *Or* the novices. They're so busy demonstrating how holy they are, and finding fault with everyone else. And the rest of us don't have money to give. *Or* any terrible secrets.'

I let them argue, saying nothing. I didn't *want* to believe it. I would have liked to defend Sonia as stoutly as Marta, but I couldn't. I didn't understand how she could have found out anything so awful, so secret, that anybody would give her money or valuables to keep it quiet, but I *had* seen that gold coin. I hadn't imagined it. What sort of secret was worth a gold coin? A very big secret, surely? Much larger than those for which Sonia might have won that handful of prettily coloured buttons. Buttons some commoner would have been glad to sew in an inconspicuous place on her dull work gown. Just to have. Something no one else here had. And that string of beads. Broken, dropped perhaps by a fishmonger's wife on the chapel floor during Mass, but treasure to a young orphan. We have so few possessions. But I kept coming back to the gold coin. Surely nobody would kill for handful of buttons or a broken string of beads, however loath they were to have their secrets spread abroad? But it was beginning to seem that Sonia had made someone so angry, so afraid, that they had done so. And if it was someone here, how had her body come to be found outside in the canal? Marta drove the pins across my scalp so hard that I squealed.

'There! That won't come adrift. Climb into your gown and I'll fasten you up. Hurry, you're late already. Sister Angelica would be glad to go without you!'

Sister Angelica said nothing about my tardiness, because I arrived in the middle of a heated argument she and Sister Benedetta were having with the two foreign novices, Helga and Juanita (whose prayers had evidently not detained her long) whilst the rest of the *Coro* stood around with their mouths hanging open. My head being full of Carolina's revelations, I didn't immediately grasp what the argument was about. Surprisingly, it seemed Sister Benedetta was going into combat, while Sister Angelica merely stood by, grim faced.

'You haven't understood how important our governors are!' Sister Benedetta was declaring, her normally pale face pink with agitation. I don't believe I had ever seen Sister B so worked up, except perhaps that time when Maria-Regina and Carolina hid one of the store room kittens in her book cupboard, and it kept mewing pathetically all through her lesson on the Early Fathers of the Church. She made them both stay behind and copy out a long passage from a bestiary, which they didn't enjoy one bit, although the little cat did well out of it, and can still be found, curled on a pile of missals in Sister Benedetta's classroom, purring contentedly.

'I *know* this is not how they order things in your convent,' she was telling Sister Helga, 'but here, we do things differently. Our governors are all very important men in this city, and they give their valuable time — *and*, I may say, generous donations of money — to this orphanage, and in return, Mother Prioress tries to accede to any reasonable requests...'

'But this is not just that of which we complain, Helga and I,' Sister Juanita, interrupted. 'We are agreed, that such a frivolous occasion is unsuitable. But that you should drag Barbara from her sick bed! This is most wrong! You can see that she is still unwell.'

'Barbara is the leader of our orchestra. She is one of our most accomplished players,' Sister Angelica broke in, 'and unless she is seriously indisposed... and she assures me she is much better... it is her duty as a member of the *Coro* to carry out the engagement. Signor Fosca's wife is her Patroness. She has always taken a keen interest in her career. They will expect her to be present. You both know, Sisters, because I have told you so, that I do not myself relish this type of affair, but I accept Mother Prioress's ruling on these matters, and I think we have heard quite enough of your views on the subject. Now that *Paola* has finally honoured us with her presence, I believe we should be on our way.'

Despite the finality of this statement, Juanita seemed inclined to continue arguing, although Barbara did not appear to be particularly grateful for her concern, insisting (although none of them were actually listening to her) that she would do well enough, and that a walk in the fresh air was just what she was in need of. I was quite surprised to hear Sister Benedetta arguing so forcefully in favour of the party. As our teacher of religion I would have expected her to share Sister Helga's disapproval, but here she was, insisting that the evening 'would most probably be delightful; the Foscas were so *very* well meaning. 'After all', she explained, 'it *is* carnival, and although, of course we do not participate in *that*, we shall soon be celebrating the solemn austerity of Lent. And before that is upon us, I do think the dear girls deserve a small treat.'

'Sister Teodora offered to come!' Albetta, who was standing next to me, whispered in my ear, 'but Sister Benedetta outranks her! And Sister Angelica can't stand Sister Teodora, because she's always butting in to tell them how they did things when she was with the Order in Rome. She chose Sister B, so naturally Sister B has to support her!'

Our departure was then slightly further delayed because Mother Prioress herself arrived to wish us well, bringing with her Don Salvatore to pronounce a blessing. Evidently once we had been blessed, the matter was regarded as closed, and the two novices retired, defeated.

The great front door was thrown open. Dressed in our Sunday gowns and a variety of hand-me-down cloaks, we stared out, dismayed. The night was pitch black, with a stiff breeze blowing off the lagoon. In the Grand Canal basin, one or two lanterns bobbed in the prows of fishing smacks, and the occasional passing gondola rose and fell on the swell. Were we really going to walk to the Foscas' house, situated beyond *San Marco*, in this wild darkness? Those girls who enjoy creating a fuss clung to one another, squealing, and declaring they were frightened. Sister Angelica soon put a stop to this nonsense, ordering us to each take a partner, and line up behind Sister Benedetta and herself. We violins and violas were each carrying our instruments. The cellos and double basses were being conveyed to Signor Fosca's house in the barge, whilst their owners walked with the rest of us. There was no danger, Sister Angelica insisted, Signor Fosca's menservants were waiting to accompany us. Like meek schoolchildren, we did as we were told.

The Fosca menservants carried flambeaux, which flared and guttered in the wind. These would light our way and discourage drunken ner-do-wells. I noticed that the man walking closest to me had a long knife in his belt. He evidently felt less confident of our safety than Sister Angelica. My partner was Albetta, whom I like well enough, but she was sulking, wishing she could walk with Maria-Regina, who had chosen her fellow bass player, Giovanna, instead. Albetta grumbled that the Foscas were miserly, not to have sent boats for us, but I was too absorbed in my thoughts to pay her much heed. Sister Angelica urged us to walk briskly and waste no time in prattle, but most people ignored this prohibition, and there was little she could do about it, since she wanted to keep the group moving, rather than waste time stopping to reprimand the guilty ones.

Attending a fashionable party the night before my childhood friend was to be buried must strike you as unfeeling, and I would have given much to have it otherwise, but as I had told Signora Amelia, I had no choice. Signor Ugo Fosca, the Chairman of our Governing body, is a very rich man, and if he desired the *Coro* to play at his wife's birthday party, it would indeed have been difficult for the Prioress to refuse. No one knows better than Mother Prioress how much we depend on the support of our wealthy patrons, and no doubt she had in mind the expense of the repairs needed to Lucrezia's cello; the leak in the roof above the lace workshop when the wind comes from the North, and the fabric for new night-gowns, urgently required in the infants' dormitory.

It was on my conscience that I hadn't managed to return the drawing to Harry, let alone speak to him of what I had discovered. I'd caught glimpses of him each time we sang in chapel, below us, fair hair tied neatly back with a fresh ribbon, his head bent over his drawing board. It seemed everyone knew that as a way of apologising for suspecting him of killing Sonia, Mother Prioress had arranged for him to copy the wall paintings in the chapel. Anything unusual that happens within the walls of our orphanage home goes around like wildfire. The more brazen spirits — Maria-Regina and Carolina, for two — peeped through the metal grille at him, wiggling their fingers through the holes, scuffling and giggling to attract his attention, until Sister Angelica spotted them. Harry never looked up, for which I was glad. I had already endured sly winks and sniggers from those who knew I'd spoken with him. *How* did they know? I'd hardly mentioned him, even to Marta.

As today had worn on, too, those members of the *Coro* who were not to perform at the party had worked themselves up into a fine state of discontent, encouraged by Helga and Juanita, who had contributed to the bad atmosphere by declaring that their non-attendance at rehearsals was in protest. It was sinful, they claimed, to take part in something as worldly and indulgent as a party to honour a rich, spoilt woman.

'My Mother Superior, *never* would such a thing permit!' Sister Helga had announced. It was small wonder that Sister Angelica was even more short tempered than usual. At one moment I thought she was going to slap Cecilia, for day dreaming and losing her place in the score for a third time.

To begin with, our walk went smoothly. Our seaward end of the *riva deghli Schiavonni* was largely deserted. The fish sellers had packed up for the night, and the wind, swirling in from the open expanse of the *bacino*, was discouraging buskers and carnival merrymakers. We were passing the Doge's palace, its pink tiles faded to grey in the darkness, before we met the first bands of revellers. A thin crescent moon sailed amongst the racing clouds over the white marble dome of the *Salute* across the water, and a few stars sparkled overhead.

Below, we were now in the midst of *Carnevale*, our Venetian festival between Christmas and Lent. Noisy parties of men and women in fancy costumes, their faces hidden behind masks and plumed headdresses, were making their way to gambling parties and routs. Many of the men wore those long-beaked masks they call *Medico della peste*. When we were small, one of the lay sisters used to frighten us into good behaviour by telling us that these were the old plague doctors, come to take disobedient children down to Hell, and we more than half believed her. Now, I think they cause their wearers to resemble sinister predatory birds, but it still makes me uneasy to see them. Those beaks lend themselves to being poked into bodices between female breasts, and their wearers were taking full advantage of this. Meeting what they thought was a dark-cloaked religious procession, headed by nuns, called for ribald comments, and since their identities were hidden, there was nothing these roisterers dared not say — or do. One prankster, spurred on by his comrades, even darted up to the girls at the back of the line and attempted to lift their skirts. There was nothing the nuns could do about it, except urge us to keep moving and hope we wouldn't understand the rude jests they were calling after us. I saw Sister Angelica clench her teeth, but Sister Benedetta marched on cheerfully, perhaps taking comfort from her belief that her most revered female saints would have ignored such vulgarity, as they walked to glorious martyrdom. One wag, asked by another where all these nuns were going, replied, 'Reckon someone's smoked them out of their nest. They're swarming, like bees. We'll find 'em all up at the top of the *campanile* tomorrow, clinging to the bell rope!'

Both Sisters would have been horrified if they had stopped to look behind, and realised that we understood our tormentors well enough, and there was much eye-rolling, blushes and giggles. Maria-Regina and Giovanna pulled faces, and stuck out their tongues. The Fosca menservants ignored most of the revellers' sallies, but if they moved in too closely on our party with those beaks, they found the flaming torches thrust into their faces. The air soon reeked of burning tar, mixed with paint and glue, and there were howls of rage, as elaborately decorated masks and headdresses were spoiled.

However, as our procession crossed the Piazza, crowded at this hour, it was obvious that nothing could keep the surging masses of sightseers and partygoers at a distance. A group of young men in bright turbans, and slippers with turned up toes, called out in a strange tongue, made exaggerated bows, and then threw rotten oranges after us. Drunken men reeled out of the dark, stinking of wine and sweat. They buffeted their way through our line, attempting, as they did so, to fumble with our cloaks, grab at our breasts and pinch our bottoms. Naked flames would suddenly flare in our eyes, and there were shouts and curses for our ears, and gusts of wine fumes and garlic in our nostrils. Someone in our crocodile, confused and out of step in the smoke-filled darkness, trod on my heel. My shoe came off, skittering away across the paving stones. Automatically, I limped after it. Without it, how could I play my solo? In my stocking feet? Clutching my violin case like a shield, I dodged through the mass of humanity, receiving painful elbow jabs, and a heavy-booted foot on my instep. Then, just as I reached my shoe, it was snatched up.

A little bandy-legged old fellow held it above his head, cackling with glee. The long tassel on his hat swung to and fro as he capered, keeping the shoe just beyond my grasp. Puzzlingly, he seemed to have been taking a swim. His clothes were dripping wet.

'Yours for kiss, lady!' he screeched in a strange foreign accent. Other men in the crowd surged closer to see what the fuss was about, pressing up against me, pinching me, breathing down my neck.

'No, *please*!' I sobbed, but the old man whirled away out of reach. Despairing, and numb with fright, I stood clutching my fiddle, flinching as the bottom pinching continued, and male voices whispered lewd suggestions in my ears.

Then, after what seemed like an age, although it was probably less than a minute, I smelt burning tar, and the strong hands of one of the Foscas' men pulled my tormentors away, knocking their heads together as he did so. At the same time, a stout young man dove into the crowd, seized the old fellow, and recaptured the shoe. He fought his way back, and thrust it at me.

'*Scusi, Signorina*!' he gasped, 'Papa is flown with wine, he means no harm!' Then the swirling crowd swallowed him. Idiotically, I stared after him. I hadn't recognised him in the smoky torch-lit dimness of the Piazza, but as he thrust the shoe into my hand, I saw his wide, gapped-toothed mouth. The man in Harry's portrait, Sonia's brother!

I called after him, but he was gone, and I, like a fool, had not thought to ask Signora Amelia his name.

I was escorted back to the file. My protector said nothing, but his silent disapproval made his opinion of my rash behaviour clear. Our crocodile was now passing out of the north east corner of the Piazza. No one else seemed to have missed me except Albetta, who squeaked with relief.

'I thought you'd be raped and murdered!'

Breathless and thoroughly shaken, I did not reply. We turned into an alley which led us to yet another of Venice's four hundred bridges. On this one, two young men in velvet coats and elaborate waistcoats stood, blocking the pathway. If the nuns were expecting the menservants to push these sprigs of fashion out of the way, they were mistaken. The servants drew to a polite standstill, whilst the elder sprig bowed low, addressing us.

'Good evening, Sisters. Young ladies! Marco Fosca at your service. This is my brother, Bruno. We're here to guide you to our father's house.'

He made such an elegant leg, and grinned so engagingly, that I noticed Sister Benedetta had to force herself to keep a straight face. Sister Angelica was not amused. She inclined her head politely, but her chilly expression was intended to let them know their escort was unwelcome.

'I thank you,' she said. 'But your father sent servants to accompany us, as you see, and I understand we are now near to your home?' I was close enough in the line to hear her murmur to Sister Benedetta, 'Our good Prioress means well, but you see now why I was unenthusiastic about this engagement? She can have no idea how unruly people are during Carnival. And now we'll have to keep these young puppies of Fosca's in check, who will lead the girls into all kinds of foolishness if they get the chance.'

She indicated, with another dip of her head, that we would proceed, and the two Fosca brothers stood aside to let her pass, but then fell in alongside us, down a still narrower alleyway, Marco asking us our names, and what instruments did we play, and was Sister Angelica the old dragon she seemed? Bruno, the younger brother, said nothing, but his eyes roamed over us, trying to see our faces, and brushing up against our bodies in the narrow space, which made me, for one, after my recent experience in the Piazza, ready to scream. The servants, used to the young master, ignored this.

Fortunately for Sister Angelica's peace of mind, we were indeed close to *Ca'Fosca*, which now came into sight, adorned with red and gold banners in honour of the occasion, its upper windows ablaze with light. And here was Signor Fosca himself, hurrying forward accompanied by a servant with a lantern on a pole, to lead us through a side-gate into a courtyard garden, sweet with the scent of crushed winter-hardy herbs, rosemary and southernwood, and up a wide marble exterior staircase, adorned with carved marble lions' heads, to a receiving room. Here, he presented us to his wife.

'Make yourselves completely at home! Leave your cloaks and instruments, and feel free to retire here if the heat and the crush is too overwhelming,' our hostess cried, throwing open the door to a richly decorated side-room. So delighted was Signora Margarita Fosca to be welcoming her dear young ladies of the Pietà, that she condescended so far as to show us the room herself, rather than leaving this duty to a maid.

'They *say* Fosca's family are recorded in the *libro d'oro*,' I heard Sister Angelica murmur, looking around grimly at the overwhelming decorative scheme of red velvet, gold damask, and banks of wall mirrors, in the small salon set aside for us. 'But I understand *she* is from a *merchant* family in Bergamo.' Sister Benedetta folded her hands in her sleeves and adopted an expression of radiant piety, probably imagining dear, *dear* Santa Chiara surrounded by similar extravagance, turning her back on wealth for a life of holy austerity.

There are, believe me, no crystal chandeliers, no velvet, no damask, and certainly no wall mirrors, anywhere within the walls of the Pietà. Fascinated, most of the *Coro* rushed to look at their reflections. Soon, nearly everyone was peering at herself, tugging at her hairpins, twitching at her lace collar, borrowing her friend's comb, and pinching her cheeks to give them colour. I was not of their number. My experiences in the Piazza had left me shaken and nauseous, and I was glad to subside onto an fragile gilt chair and breathe deeply. Thankfully, for I would not have liked to have to explain my agitation, everyone else was too much occupied with this opportunity to study her own appearance to notice.

'Girls!' said Sister Angelica, awfully, 'Come away from those mirrors *immediately*. I will not have you behaving like... like wantons! You are here to give a concert, not flaunt yourselves like a lot of ill-bred *hussies*. Lay your cloaks neatly on this — piece of furniture, and attend to the tuning of your instruments!'

'We *are* ill bred!' muttered Maria-Regina, under her breath. 'We're in the Pietà because our mothers were no better than they ought to be. We're our mothers' daughters!'

We were to play immediately before supper. Marco Fosca soon appeared, bringing Don Antonio, to discuss with Sister Angelica how we should be seated, on a raised dais at the end of the grand salon. Whilst the seating was arranged, he suggested we choristers — chaperoned by Sister Benedetta — might like to go up on the gallery that ran around one end of the salon, and look down on the guests? He would be happy to take us there. Most of us were happy that he should, and streamed out of the door before Sister Angelica could rule otherwise. I tagged along, hoping the distraction would stop my knees from trembling before it was time to play. Sister Benedetta hurried after us, possibly feeling as Santa Marta must have done, that she would like to put her feet up, but this was her bounden duty.

Chapter 13

In which Paola excels herself in music, but is overwhelmed by subsequent happenings

'Very unsettling!' Sister Benedetta murmured to herself, as I stood beside her, looking down from the gallery onto the colourful scene below. I'm certain Sister Angelica would have ordered us back to the retiring room, but all Sister B did was close her eyes tightly, no doubt to call on the saints for protection.

The *Coro* on the other hand, was enraptured. Even I was beginning to feel less agitated, drawing in deep breaths, and gradually calming myself, as I gazed down on the Foscas' luxurious *salone*. Small groups from the *Coro* are invited, now and then, to sing in the drawing rooms of wealthy ladies, but these are decorous affairs, or so I understand from Marta, never having been chosen myself, with only the hostess and a few of her choice female friends present. The Foscas' *grand salone* stretched across the whole of the front of the house, overlooking other brilliantly lighted buildings across the canal, through arched windows framed by graceful columns shaped like twists of barley sugar. It was far more sumptuously decorated than anything *I* had ever seen, hung, as Marco Fosca was anxious to inform us, with gilded leather wall hangings, and richly patterned carpets his father had brought back from a business trip to Constantinople. These carpets, he said, were far too valuable, to be laid upon the floors for people to walk on. Huge chandeliers, blazing with wax candles (no smelly tallow here) filled the room with dazzling light and heat. Below us, fashionable people paraded to and fro, arm-in-arm, or reclined on sofas and chairs around the walls. Even at this distance we could catch the drifting scent of the ladies' perfumes. The necklines of their gowns were so shockingly low, that as Albetta remarked, (fortunately not in Sister Benedetta's hearing) 'You can practically see their belly buttons!'

On a corner of the raised platform, a young man sat strumming a mandolin and singing a popular ballad, although he was barely audible above the babble of noise as the guests exchanged greetings.

'He's my mother's sister's stepson's tutor, or some such, I forget,' drawled Marco, airily, when I ventured to ask who he was. 'The background music creates a delightful atmosphere, does it not?'

Don Antonio had emerged from his discussion with Sister Angelica, and now stood directly below us looking grouchy (perhaps the popular ballad did not appeal to him) leaning on his cane; his dusty black coat buttoned up to his chin. He was being talked *at* by a voluble young man, very spruce in fawn, whose eyes darted around the room, noting everything.

'That's Signor Goldoni,' Marco told us, 'the playwright,' he added, seeing we looked puzzled. He chuckled, 'I suppose he'll put us all in one of his plays!'

Sister Benedetta said she devoutly hoped not, but she must have been relieved that Don Antonio's immediate companion was a man. That woman sitting over there, the one with the wreath of flowers in her softly powdered hair — it *couldn't* be? But it was! Marco overheard our whispered speculations, and confirmed it. The famous Anna Girò, Don Antonio's *particular friend*, would be singing later in the evening!

'Oh, rapture!' exclaimed Albetta, who has a lovely voice herself, 'I've always wanted to hear her! She is attractive, isn't she?' she added, learning out over the gallery to get a better view, and thus exposing rather more of Albetta than was seemly. 'Not beautiful, but look how expressive her eyes are! They say her singing voice isn't all that good, but she's such a fine actress, she's acclaimed in every role. Who's the woman sitting beside her?'

'Her sister, the Signorina Paolina. She's much older and looks after her,' Lucrezia put in, confidently. I'm always astonished at the things Lucrezia contrives to know. 'She acts as her housekeeper and chaperone, and makes everything look respectable,' she added, before Marco could reply. We smothered our mirth.

'You young ladies obviously follow the musical scene in Venice closely,' he chuckled. 'I'm amazed that you manage to keep up with these things, in your restricted circumstances. My parents are tremendously keen on all aspects of the arts,' he boasted. 'They were even hoping to have Signor Francesco Guardi, the painter, here tonight, but alas, he has influenza. But with you charming young ladies to entertain us, tonight is going to be a wonderful *musical* occasion!'

I glanced at Sister Benedetta. How uncomfortable she looked! The world had been creeping into the Pietà, under the doors, through the windows, without her knowledge. Even a fifteen year old like Albetta, hardly out of the schoolroom, was gossiping about the domestic arrangements of opera singers! And this young man was flirting — *yes, flirting!* — with us, and promising we should hear Anna Girò sing. She must have been wondering how to convey this news to Sister Angelica in time to hurry us away before this deplorable spectacle took place.

But Sister Angelica had things on her mind other than preventing us from being corrupted by the sight and sound of Anna Girò. *Barbara*, she told Sister Benedetta in a shocked whisper, had suffered a *crisis*. Because of her religious feelings, and finding herself surrounded by this overwhelming luxury, she had decided she ought not to play after all.

'Now is fine time to be discovering her Vocation and renouncing the World! I knew she was uneasy about playing, but when those tiresome foreign novices made all that fuss, she insisted on coming!' hissed Sister A, exasperated. 'If she refuses to play, who will take the lead in 'Spring'?'

'Paola?' suggested Sister Benedetta, doubtfully.

'Over my dead body!' replied Sister Angelica, much to my relief. '*She* wouldn't be playing at all, if I'd had my way, but Don Antonio has a foolish weakness for redheads. But he certainly wouldn't want her hacking her way through 'Spring', which she hasn't rehearsed. *You* try to persuade Barbara, Sister! Convince her that her name saint would wish it!'

'Saint Barbara?' said Sister Benedetta, doubtfully. '*She* is to be invoked against cannon balls, and thunder and lightning.'

'Then Barbara had better invoke her. If we let Signor Fosca down in front of his guests, the whole Pietà will be dodging lightning strikes! Tell her that, Sister. And Chiaretta, you're her friend, come and see what you can do!'

After a hasty consultation with Don Antonio, they decided the solution was that I should play first. Whilst I did so, Sister Angelica would calm Barbara, take her for a walk in the fresh air away from the enervating atmosphere of the *grand salone*, and persuade her either to play the *allegro* or to lend her instrument to Chiaretta, who was leading the violas on this occasion, but would if necessary take her place. I was thrown into panic by this change of plan, for it had always been intended that we would play the allegro first (Don Antonio keeping our hostess in suspense, before relenting, and introducing her birthday offering) but Sister A would have no truck with my feeble entreaties. She ordered me to get out there, and get on with it. Even so, we had to keep our audience waiting, as it appeared that the boat carrying the basses and cellos had only just arrived, and they were sadly out of tune after travelling in the damp evening air. Giovanna murmured in my ear that 'the artist' was helping to carry them, evidently thinking I would wish to know this. I tried to look indifferent to this news, but a tiny bit of me was pleased that Harry should be here to hear me play.

The guests showed no sign of displeasure at the delay. Why should they, when they were sipping the Fosca's fine wines, nibbling the dainties that servants were passing around, and gossiping with their friends? As for Signora Margarita Fosca, she seemed positively to relish these difficulties, pressing her great hooped skirts of shot puce taffeta to her sides, and going downstairs to urge the men transporting the instruments to hurry. She was sure, she gushed to Don Antonio, that whatever we eventually played would be 'quite delightful!'

Then the guests were hushed while Don Antonio made one of his waspish little speeches, praising the Signora for her musical taste, wishing her a happy birthday, and introducing the 'special piece' he had written for the occasion. The Signora was so overcome, or so she would have had us believe, at the thought of this music, specially dedicated to herself, that she subsided onto the nearest sofa, fanning herself vigorously.

Then I found myself standing on the dais, raised above the throng, and Don Antonio was bringing his stick down with a thwack, for the piece to begin.

So much had happened. My head had been so full of Sonia's death, of Carolina's revelations, and my frightening experience in the Piazza, that picking up my bow and drawing it across the strings seemed to restore me to normality.

I have never felt any inclination to become a nun, and the religious feelings Barbara was experiencing have never touched me. Yet at the moment I stood up to play under the fierce heat of a thousand candles, for the first time I saw a little of its attraction. Within the quiet walls of a convent, surely each day would have its shape, its demands, but also its music, its profound peace, its holy order? No one there would be found dead by violence. Never in that place would lewd men inflict painful pinches. And yet ... since all music there must be for the Glory of God alone, neither, I supposed, would anyone praise you, or even express their pleasure, when you played well. I felt a pang of sadness, that Barbara, who had such great gifts, was considering taking herself away from us. From the world.

For once all the notes came sweetly. When I reached a few bars of rest, and dared to raise my eyes, the guests were standing or sitting quietly. Women were wafting exquisitely painted fans against the heat of the room, but no one was chattering, as Sister Angelica had predicted. Just inside the door to the stairs, the men who had carried the large instruments up from the canal were lounging against the wall, arms folded, listening. With a jolt of recognition I saw that one of them was indeed Signor Harry, and felt a little curl of pleasure inside me, at knowing he was there.

Nearer at hand, I noted with astonishment, a pale little woman wearing a flounced gown in a harsh shade of green, sat mopping her eyes with a handkerchief. Could my performance really be moving her to tears? My place came again, and I applied my bow, and discovered I was enjoying myself. Even Sister Angelica would have to admit I was playing well. I glanced up, to see if she was sparing me a little of her approval for once, but only Sister Benedetta hovered close by, in her role as our chaperone. Of Sister A there was no sign. She must still be outside, calming Barbara.

The piece ended on a diminuendo. For a moment there was silence, the audience unsure if there was more to come. Don Antonio turned and executed a curt little bow, then gestured for me to step down from the dais and join him, favouring me with his thin lipped smile, and a brisk pat on the shoulder. He was pleased! People began to applaud. Signora Margarita leapt to her feet, as though she was the soloist, and the applause was for her, but as she did so (perhaps to receive it, perhaps to congratulate me, who knows?) there was a sharp snapping sound, a great flare of falling light, and then an almighty smash, as one of the great chandeliers crashed to the floor. The Signora fell back on her sofa with a shriek, and fainted dead away.

Sister Benedetta assured me, later, that it was my name saint, Paola of Rome, who saved me from harm, though in the midst of my best and deepest curtsey, I was showered with shards of Murano crystal, as they shattered and bounced up off the marble floor. The chandelier had actually fallen into an open space, many feet away, but the smashed pieces flew up from the ground towards us. Instinctively, I hugged my violin to me, shielding it from flying glass particles, and thus failed to see a still lighted candle, which rolled forward, sending a flicker of flame along the hem of my gown.

It was Don Antonio, wheezing alarmingly, but with great presence of mind, who knocked it away, beating at my skirt with his stick. I suppose I should have been devastated. After all, at this moment I should have been enjoying my success, revelling in my share of the applause. Dazed, I could only think how comical it must appear. The great music *maestro*, the moment the piece was over, belabouring his soloist!

Chapter 14

In which Harry is impressed by Paola's calmness in the face of danger, gains a new acquaintance, ponders the possible guilt of another, and parries an alarming accusation

'I suppose if I put such a scene on the stage they would declare it too far-fetched. Yet it has wondrous comic potential!' chuckled the dapper fellow in the well-fitting fawn coat, surveying the confused scenes that followed the fall of the chandelier. For a moment there had been a profound silence. Then, inevitably, shrieks of fright from the ladies, and shouts of alarm and indignation from their men folk. Although nobody, in fact, had been hurt. Maids rushed to press lace trimmed handkerchiefs soaked in *sal volatile* beneath the noses of their mistresses. Luca and I were pushed aside by a band of officious Fosca servants with shovels and brooms. Somehow we found ourselves bundled into an alcove together with the gentleman in fawn, who was finding the calamity amusing. Luca dug me in the ribs. A habit of which I would like to cure him, but he is not a youth responsive to hints.

'*Signor Goldoni!*' he hissed behind this gentleman's back. '*The playwright!*' he added, reverently. Luca had alternated between this elbowing and hissing throughout the evening, as he identified people whom he considered to be 'notables' amongst the Fosca's guests. No one had seemed to mind, or even notice, that we remained in the great salon (admittedly in a shadowy corner) on completing our porters' duties. My hankering to see the style in which these wealthy Venetians lived had been fulfilled more easily than I had dared hope. The decorative scheme of their *salone* was certainly striking. Turkish carpets, and crimson velvet in excess. My mother and sisters would have pronounced it vulgar.

'Ah! I thought I recognised you!' Signor Goldoni, who evidently had good ears, raised one of the new-fangled quizzing glasses, and turned it on Luca, 'Stage hand? Bit parts? I've seen you around the theatres. But you're hired out to the Pietà for this evening? What splendid young women they are, standing there, grouped around old Vivaldi, as calm and serene as if they were in church, whilst around them chaos is enacted! I wish the old fellow would tell me his secret, so that I could use it with my actresses. That charming young creature who played the solo — her moment of triumph quite ruined! But does she weep and wail? No. She simply asks her friends to remove any bits of glass from her hair.'

I was impressed with Paola myself. Admittedly my studies of young women have been largely limited to the young ladies of our Lancashire neighbourhood; my sisters, the fair Lydia and her friends. But I fancied that any one of them, having played her well-practised piece to the company, only to be showered with broken glass instead of praise, would have treated us to strong hysterics. I found myself foolishly pleased with Signor Goldoni's compliments, as though I could take some credit for the *coro's* composed demeanour, although my entire contribution to their performance had been to carry two double basses up an awkward staircase. I told myself I must beware. After so short a time , I was beginning to think myself as a regular member of the Pieta's staff, and what was perhaps more worrying, the champion of a young woman with whom I had spoken on precisely two occasions.

Signor Fosca, the host, now rallied, and took charge. To my eyes he was a pompous little man, in a coat so full-skirted that he appeared twice the width he actually was, and wearing a lace edged cravat so high, and so stiffly starched, that it looked likely to chafe his chin raw. He soon calmed his guests however, by urging them to move through to the dining chamber whilst the room was completely cleared. The mention of refreshments instantly revived the womenfolk, including his lady wife, and the company removed themselves. One of the nuns, I recognised her as Sister Benedetta, the vague one, who had spoken in favour of my drawing abilities, now gathered the *Coro* to her, and led them, crunching over scattered glass shards, to one of the side rooms. I was surprised to see her taking charge. Where was that sour puss, Sister Angelica? She had certainly been around to reprove us for our late arrival.

The girls had left the basses and cellos propped against chairs. Were they to play again, or should we remove them? Nardo, who must know what was usual on these occasions, had contrived to disappear within minutes of our arrival. Luca, consulted, said how should he know? Without being consulted, Signor Goldoni suggested I ask Don Antonio, before briskly trotting away to join the other guests in the dining salon.

The famous composer had remained behind, muttering over his score, making pencil notes in the margins, oblivious of brooms being plied around his feet. Asking him was the obvious thing to do. My Italian was improving daily (or I should say my Venetian) and I was getting used to the idea of myself as a 'hired lackey', by no means too high in the instep to get my living fetching and carrying. It was a relief to be earning sufficient money to entrust my shirts and small clothes to a washerwoman. But how should a (currently rather grubby) porter speak to a great *maestro*? We have few servants at home, being unable to afford them. Those we have accord us very little in the way of deference. A composer, I reasoned, however famous, is still a paid employee, albeit several rungs further up the social ladder than the man who carts the instruments to and fro. I thought it unlikely that Don Antonio Vivaldi would be amused by the kind of 'North Country' bluntness I am used to from my family's old retainers. However, I never got to frame my question, because Signor Fosca reappeared, accompanied by a liveried major domo, both of them in a state of agitation.

'Don Antonio!' he lighted upon the old boy, 'you will be shocked to hear this, but my man here tells me the fall of the chandelier was not an accident! Sabotage!'

The old music master looked blank for moment, blinked, and then said, 'Indeed? I have sometimes thought lately that Venice is tired of me, but now do you tell me someone intended that contraption to fall on my head *and kill me?*'

'Well, perhaps only to cause you alarm, since it was not sufficiently close to fall on you directly. *You* tell him, Molin!'

'Alas, sir,' quavered the uniformed dogsbody, 'it appears someone interfered with the mechanism — the rope and pulley by which we raise and lower the chandelier. It is just outside the door in the passage way leading to the... er, the house of easement. And the under servants tell me few people have passed that way since the young women of the *Coro* began to play.'

'But someone must have?' demanded Fosca. 'None of my guests, surely?'

'No, sir. They think only one of the Pietà girls. And one of the nuns who went looking for her. And perhaps one of the Pietà menservants.'

One of the Pietà menservants. I had the sensation of melting ice trickling down my spine. Perhaps because I had been thinking of our servants at home, I could hear old Bessie's voice. 'Duck walked over tha' grave, lad?' It was ridiculous to assume *I* would be suspected. I have lived twenty four years in this world without being found guilty of any greater crime than breaking a young lady's heart. (I doubt that was true. Fair Lydia was probably promised to another by now). But I *had* been suspected of causing Sonia's death, and my bruises from that episode were still tender. *This* time, I reassured myself, I had a witness, Luca, who could swear I had never left the room. Thanks be to Our Lady that I had thought to invite him along!

Never the less, it was with a sinking of the spirits that I responded to Fosca's abrupt, 'Come here, you two men!' Luca flashed me a look of reproach. *Now what kind of trouble have you landed me in?* We obediently stepped forward.

'Sir, I don't *think*,' murmured the major domo, 'that these two men left the *salone* during the performance. But they must know who the third fellow is.'

'You know both these men, and can vouch for them?' Fosca ignored his steward, and directed his question at Don Antonio. We were just serving lads, to be talked about, rather than to.

'Don't *know* either of 'em!' snapped the old man, affronted. I hadn't hear him speak until now, but his scratchy old man's voice was somehow familiar. 'I imagine the nuns must have sent them over from the Pietà with the large instruments. I know this one's a painter fellow who's doing some copying work in the chapel there, and the other I'm more used to seeing lolling against a piece of scenery at the opera house. Can't think why either of 'em should want to do me harm! Or anyone else for that matter.'

'But there's a third fellow?' Fosca might be a pompous old article, but no fool. 'Who and where is he?' I was unsure whether this question was directed at Don Antonio, the major domo, or Luca and myself, but Luca took it upon himself to answer.

'The boatman, Signore. He went to the servants' quarters — I think.'

'Nardo Piccoli. That's the fellow,' agreed Don Antonio. 'You won't get a morsel of sense out of him. He's no roof to his mouth. Where's the other brother, Giorgio?'

'Down with colic, Signore.' I felt it was my turn to contribute.

'Drunk again, you mean? That explains why you two were pressed into service.' Don Antonio Vivaldi might consider himself above such matters as the day to day running of the orphanage, but he had worked there for forty years. He knew the boatmen's foibles. 'Well, I take it neither of you loosed the mechanism for the chandelier?'

'No, Signore,' I answered, 'we remained in this room, being unsure where we should go, and when we would be needed.'

The old man's eyes narrowed. 'Enjoying a free concert, and ogling the young women!' He wagged a finger at me. 'You, Signor Painter, are a disruptive influence! The girls have been running upstairs and peeping and peering at you from the singing gallery all day long. And yes, I heard from Don Salva, about the cosy chat you had with Paola. Attend to the drawings the Prioress is paying you to make, young man, and resist the urge to turn my young women's heads! Signorina Paola has some talent, and if she keeps her mind on her music she will do well. I don't want to arrive at the Pietà one morning to find she has run off with a scallywag of a painter!'

I was so taken aback at this baseless accusation that I think I stood like a mooncalf, with my mouth wide open. I dared not glance at Luca. By the gurgling sounds, I judged he was in danger of a choking fit. Even when I managed to bring the two halves of my jaw together again, I thought it wisest to say nothing. Around us, the Fosca servants continued to chase after the glass particles and smashed candles that skittered away from their brooms.

'Might this boatman wish you ill, Don Antonio? Would he do this in a fit of spite?' Fosca wasn't a man to let the matter drop.

'Can't imagine why he should,' grumbled Don Antonio. 'I dare say I have spoken sharply to him any number of times over the years, for lugging the instruments about with insufficient care, but not in recent days that I recall, and I doubt he would remember an old grudge and act on it. His brother might, but not Nardo.'

'Is he a joker?' persisted Molin, the steward. 'Would he think such a trick amusing? After all, you were not, in fact, injured. The chandelier fell well short of where you and the young woman stood to take your bows.'

A servant should not interrupt his betters, especially in a strange household (our servants at home rarely concede that we are their betters). I stood mute, though inwardly agreeing with Don Antonio's assessment of Nardo. The boatman might well take immediate offence if corrected, but I couldn't imagine him brooding over wrongs for any length of time. He did not seem even to have remembered that I was the man he had taken captive. And he surely lacked the wit for practical jokes. There was, however, Sister Domenica's observation; that he was not to be trusted around young women. Perhaps she meant only that he was apt to try to fondle them, but it might be more than that.

The duck walked over my grave again. I wondered whether Nardo might have made advances to Sonia, and when she resisted, killed her, either accidentally or in anger. He might also know that Paola had been going around the orphanage asking questions. Alarmed at what might be discovered — had I said something to Frediano in his presence tonight that aroused this dread? — might he have decided to do away with Paola? Or merely frighten her into dropping the subject? The chandelier had fallen far short of the musicians, but as it fell it had seemed to jerk outwards, as though the culprit meant it to harm. Someone should warn her.

'So we must conclude this Nardo loosed the mechanism?' demanded the host, determined to find somebody guilty of spoiling his party.

Don Antonio frowned. 'I find it hard to believe, but it is quite unthinkable that Signorina Barbara, or Sister Angelica would do such a thing, and your man seems to believe they were the only other people who went that way.'

Having been subject to her sharp tongue on the subject of our late arrival, I would have been gratified to hear that Sister Angelica had been caught stealing the soap, or rifling through her hostess's jewel casket, but I couldn't imagine her letting loose the chandelier. The *Coro* were her pride and joy; that was obvious, even to a newcomer like myself. Surely she would never do anything that might injure them? Barbara, I did not know, although I remembered that she was the young woman who had appeared so embarrassed by the activities of the two novices who had found Frediano's bag of money in the hallway, and subsequently got into an argument about it with Sister Domenica. I had also heard Maria-Regina and her comrades whispering about her as they reclaimed their instruments. She was indisposed, had been scheduled to play a particular piece, but had begged to be excused. Poor girl, if she was unwell enough to have spent the evening traipsing back and forth to the privy, she was to be pitied. *If* the Fosca servants were telling the truth — and how sure was it that they really knew who had passed along that corridor? — it did appear that the culprit must be Nardo.

'Have some of the men track him down,' Fosca ordered his steward, 'and lock him in one of the storerooms by the Watergate. We can't have him roaming the place, carrying out murderous attacks on our guests!'

Rather belatedly, but perhaps excusably in the circumstances, maids now appeared with trays of food, one for Don Antonio, and one to be shared by Luca and myself. The portions were not generous, but the wine was better than I would have expected them to serve to persons of our lowly status. Luca and I retired to a window embrasure to imbibe. Don Antonio sipped his wine, but ignored the comestibles, and continued to fuss over his scores, marking alterations, striking through passages, and scribbling copious notes in the margins. I wondered whether Paola, should she be required to play it again, would even recognise the piece. It was also coming to me where I had heard Don Antonio's grumbling tones before. He was the elderly party who had disembarked from a boat whilst I lay semi-conscious in the laundry barge, and who had complained to his female companions about the unwillingness of the boatman to take them further up the narrow *rio*. Heavens, was I suspecting *him* of killing Sonia? Surely not, because her body (I was confident) had not been dropped into the water until after his party had departed. Was it possible he, or the ladies who accompanied him (Anna Girò and her sister?) might have seen something? Or someone? Noticed whether the laundry door was open? Did I have the courage to ask him? Frankly, no, I didn't.

Chapter 15

In which Paola is rescued from an unwanted admirer, with disastrous consequences for Harry

The Foscas' servants brought us a most delicious supper, and with it, jugs of wine. The *best* wine, to which no water had been added! The *Coro* was delighted, but as we are quite unused to strong drink, the effects were — startling. After a glass and a half, my head felt light, and suddenly everyone around me was speaking loudly, with flushed cheeks, and subject to fits of giggles. Thanks be to all the saints, that I had finished with my solo! I told myself I should eat something, but although all the dishes set before us looked heavenly, I found it difficult to swallow. Sister Benedetta, bless her, should have realised we were getting fuddled, but she probably wasn't used to unwatered wine herself. Her face too, was pinker than normal, and her gentle voice unusually loud, as she reproved Giovanna for snatching a savoury from the plate, just as Albetta reached for it. When Sister Angelica returned, bringing poor Barbara, who did not seem to have benefited at all from her lengthy stroll in the courtyard, she took one look at us, and her eyes positively blazed with anger. The next serving lad who put his head around the door was ordered to 'Remove this wine, *immediately!*'

Normally, none of us would have dared to argue with Sister A, but stimulated by strong drink, Maria-Regina gave tongue.

'Hey, no! Sister, we need something to drink with these pasties!'

'Then it had better be water, Maria-Regina, or none of you will be in a fit state to play.'

'Nonsense! We're fine, aren't we girls?'

Heads were nodded enthusiastically. Emboldened by wine, and fully recovered from the shock of the falling chandelier, the *Coro* was in the mood for defiance, especially as Maria-Regina, as instigator, would garner the blame. I have never quite understood how Maria-Regina gets away with as much as she does. Sister Angelica doesn't exactly tolerate her, but even she has difficulty keeping her in line. Perhaps, as Marta once speculated, her father is some grand personage who cannot acknowledge his illegitimate daughter, but gives the Pietà a handsome donation every year. The unfortunate serving lad stood, looking petrified, with a jug in each hand.

'Very well, take those empty jugs, and bring them back *filled with water*. We will dilute the remaining wine ourselves.'

I remember thinking, a good try, Sister Angelica, but it's too late — we're all *poco ubriaco*. And of course as soon as the boy left, girls poured themselves extra glasses of the unwatered stuff, and swilled it quickly down. Voices rose higher. Albetta threw a prawn roll at Lucrezia, who collapsed in shrieks of mirth, and fell off her chair. *Someone*, I find it hard to believe it could have been *Chiaretta*, but I think it was, handed a full glass to Barbara, saying, 'Here, drink this, it will put a bit of colour in your cheeks!' I ate a crab patty, and finished my second glass (or was it my third? I'd somehow lost count) in tiny sips, but now the room seemed to be spinning. By the time the water arrived, Sister Angelica had, for the first time I can ever remember, lost control of the *Coro*.

So it wasn't surprising, when Marco Fosca knocked on the door and invited us all to come and hear Anna Girò, who was about to begin her recital in the *salone*, that girls bounced to their feet and rushed out, before Sister A could say a word. I was slow to follow, largely because I wasn't sure what would happen when I stood up. I now understood exactly what people meant when they spoke of wine 'going straight to the head.' Would the room continue to spin? Would I fall over? I must have looked as unsteady as I felt, because Marco stepped forward.

'Ha, the young lady— Paolina, is it not? — who suffered such a shock when the chandelier fell! Let me take your arm.' Which he did, and led me out into the *salone*, and across to what he told me would be a good vantage point, at the back of the room. If Sister Angelica forbade it, I didn't hear her. Nor do I know exactly how my feet took me there, since I fear my head was not on speaking terms with the rest of me.

Anna Girò was singing a Venetian folk song, something light and charming, but my head was muzzy, and I couldn't attend. Marco Fosca was still holding my arm, which I knew he ought not to be doing, so publicly. And yet I confess I was just a little flattered that he had chosen me, and not Lucrezia who is so pretty, or Albetta with her full breasts and dimples.

Like a fool, I couldn't find my tongue to protest when he said,

'Shall we step outside? A little cool air, perhaps?' and led me out of the room.

On the landing, I did try to call a halt, 'No, no we're not allowed! Your parents will think me...' but he gave no sign of hearing, and in one swift movement, lifted me off my feet and carried me down the stairs, and out under an archway to a lantern-lit landing stage that ran along one side of the *palazzo*. Lanterns, hung at intervals along the landing stage, gleamed softly, reflected again and again in the black, still waters of the canal. It was beautiful. And absolutely deserted. Even in my muddle headed state I knew that I should not be there. All the buildings (palaces, warehouses? I couldn't tell) across the water were dark, unlit except for an occasional candle flickering in a high latticed window. Someway to our left there was a bridge, but no one was crossing at this hour. We were absolutely alone.

'There! Is this not delightful, Paolina?' he said, setting me down, but still keeping a firm grasp of my waist. He pulled me close with one arm, pushing his other hand inside my bodice. Oh, no, no! I thought. *I've been through all this already in the Piazza! You don't really like me! You called me Paolina! You haven't even got my name right. I'm just a Pietà girl who's got herself a bit befuddled, and now you think I'm an easy conquest. Just a harlot's daughter, easy and willing as was her mother before her, that's what the men of Venice think of us.*

Shouting would do me no good. Behind me was the Fosca's great house, from which the sweet cadences of Anna Girò's voice barely floated above harsher voices shouting orders; the clatter of cutlery and the clash of pots. We must be close to the kitchens. No one inside the building was likely to hear me if I cried out, or leave their work to investigate if they did. Even if someone in one of the candle lit chambers across the canal did hear me, what could they do, with a wide expanse of water between us? All this rushed into my despairing mind as I tried to squirm free, but he was stronger. With a huge effort, I pulled away, but he grasped my wrists and pulled me back. This was a nightmare. I wriggled and squirmed in his grasp for what seemed like a life time. Then I heard a cough, and then a voice, from the shadowy doorway.

'Err, *permesso*, Signore? Sister Angelica sends me to inform you that Signorina Paola is now required.'

Santa Paola, Maria, Blessed Virgin, thanks be! Harry, with his strange English accent, and oddly phrased speech, come to rescue me. Part of me was hugely relieved. But another part was furious. Why did this have to happen to *me?* Why did *Harry* have to be the one to find me in this embarrassing situation? If Sister Angelica had sent him, she must have seen me being led away. *Oh, no, please no!* As these anxious reflections flashed across my mind (rapidly clearing now) Marco's grip relaxed somewhat, but he still held me by one of my wrists.

'I will bring this young woman back shortly, fellow,' he said, coldly. 'She is enjoying a breath of air. Having delivered your message, there is no need to wait around.'

'Indeed? That is not how it appeared to me!' Harry took several paces forward. In the lantern light his face was tense with anger. His hands were doubled into fists, though he kept them at his sides. I suppose Marco Fosca must have weighed up his furious expression and aggressive stance, and decided not to risk a punch on his highborn nose. Suddenly he pulled my wrist back sharply, pulling me close to him again. Generally, I think, perhaps because I *am* a red head, I've learned to contain my anger, but he had provoked me too far. I jerked my free arm back, and slapped his face. Then he hurled me from him, snarling, 'Oh, have the little whore, she isn't worth it!' I cannoned backwards into Harry, my raised elbow jabbing him in the chest. Caught off balance, he staggered back, arms flailing. Then he fell off the landing stage into the canal. I very nearly followed him, but my knees had buckled, and I sprawled heavily onto the boards.

'Oh, Harry!' I cried, uselessly. 'Please! Someone help him!' But there was no one. Marco Fosca had run swiftly up the steps and was gone.

Chapter 16

In which Harry suffers the indignity of being rescued from the deep by a lachrymose female

As I sank through the icy water my furious thought was, trust a woman to make a mess of it! She went with him, nobody forced her. I should have left her to her fate. Why can't I mind my own business? Now I shall drown. No barge to break my fall this time, and I am an indifferent swimmer. Then I knew nothing more for a space, stifled by the cold.

My body must then have floated towards the surface of its own accord, as a cork or a spar of wood might do. My head broke through the surface, rousing me to consciousness, and allowing me to suck in air for a moment, before I sank once more. This time my feet touched the bottom. The canal here was hardly more than six feet deep, although my scrabbling toes soon established that there might be many layers of mud below. I struck out, inelegantly, for the landing stage, and grasped one of the wooden piles that supported it. Raising my head, I found myself nose to nose with Paola, who was kneeling on the boards, looking down at me, and weeping.

'Signor Harry, I'm so sorry!' she sobbed, 'I didn't want to go with him! I didn't realize until too late... the wine went to my head.'

'I know, wretched girl!' I gasped, spluttering out filthy water. '*Now*, for God's sake, instead of weeping, get me out of here before I die of cold!'

'But... this landing stage doesn't seem to have any tide steps.'

'Never mind that! If I can manage to heave myself up, perhaps you... could grasp me under my arms... and pull?' I'd risked a fist fight — and Heaven knows what the Venetian punishment is for drawing the cork of a member of the upper classes — to rescue this girl. Just at that moment I could have throttled her. But first I must get out of this stinking canal. I do not say that lightly. Having disturbed the mud at the bottom, years' worth of foul putrefaction had risen to the surface with me.

Paola seemed confounded by my request. I suppose she had never touched a man's body before, let alone been required to grip hold of one. I was only asking her to grab my *clothes*, for heaven's sake! They don't teach these choir girls anything useful. But after two or three tries I managed to persuade her to take a hold under my left armpit, clutch the back of my sodden coat, and pull sufficiently hard for me to get my knee up onto the jetty, and haul myself out.

'I should never have drunk that second glass of wine — if Sister Angelica only makes me scrub out the privies I shall count myself fortunate!' she sniffled, as I finally sprawled, like a landed fish, on the boards.

I dragged off my sodden coat. Ruined! It had barely survived the attacks by the fleeing Greek sailors and the men of the Watch, but this time I saw no hope for it. I might as well cast it back into the water to join my shoes, which must be sunk in the mud at the bottom. I set about dragging off my wet stockings. Modesty forbade undressing further, lest she began to suspect I was no better than the Fosca puppy. Though why should I care what she thought? My teeth were beginning to chatter uncontrollably, and I would probably go down with a fever, caught from the vile rotting material I had inadvertently disturbed. (I must admit, on reflection, that having set out to be a hero, rescuing a maiden in distress, I was mortified to have had to ask *her* to rescue *me*).

'For Heaven's sake, girl, stop snivelling! What has this detestable Sister Angelica to say to anything?' She stared at me, tears sliding down her cheeks and running into her open mouth.

'But *you* said.... You said she'd sent you to say I was wanted?'

I had completely forgotten this. 'So I did,' I ground out, 'but I lied. Sister Angelica knows nothing about it, or so you had better hope. I happened to be behind you as you left the *salone*. I saw that you were … unsteady on your feet, and that Fosca's intentions were... not good.' I wanted to say, *dastardly*, but had no notion of the Italian word for this. 'So I followed you, and saw that he was... *troubling* you, and said what I thought might impress him.'

'Oh, thank you! For coming to my rescue. I'm sorry it went wrong. I mean, because you fell in.' Tears were replaced by a hesitant smile. 'But now I think you *were* right — about Sonia. It could have been an accident. Perhaps someone did push her, but she hit her head. When you stayed under the water just now, for what seemed like an age, I thought you must have hit your head on one of the piles. I thought you were drowned too! It's her funeral tomorrow,' she went on, chattering anxiously now, oblivious of my sodden state and furious mood. 'I'm going to pray for her, and put it all behind me, and stop worrying about whether she was getting money from people to keep secrets.'

For two pins I could have tossed the wretched girl into the water, so that she could suffer too. My wet clothes were clinging to my skin as though I was encased in ice. All I wanted to do was get away and find Luca, who might be able to beg some dry clothes for me, but this remark did pique my failing interest.

'Getting money? You mean she was....' I hunted desperately for the right words, my teeth clattering together. 'Blackmail' doesn't translate easily. 'She was extorting money...?'

'Carolina told me. I'm afraid it's probably true. She did love to know peoples' secrets. Oh, and, I must tell you, Signora Amelia says the man in your drawing is her brother ... she has a father too! I believe recognised them both in the Piazza tonight. Maybe she wanted the money in case ... Signora Amelia thinks the brother had asked her to go and keep house for them, and she would have wanted to have nice clothes, and... and to be independent.'

My whole body was shaking now. 'Yes, I know about them. Her brother's name is Frediano. I saw them earlier, and spoke to him. Luca, the friend who is here with me, knows the family. The father is a Slovenian, a timber merchant, and said to be very... unwilling to part with money. From what Luca says, Sonia would have been wise to have some money of her own. Her death *may* have been an accident. Although I ought to warn you—.'

I repeated what Sister Domenica had said about Nardo, and added that he was now suspected of loosing the chandelier. 'Which made me wonder if he might have attacked your friend. I've no proof that he did, but perhaps you should be careful?'

'*Nardo Piccoli?*' Her eyes widened. At least she had stopped blubbing. 'Oh, but he's harmless. Honestly! He pinches the laundry girls on their... Sonia says...used to say, just show him your clenched hand, and tell him you've caught a spider. He's scared silly of spiders! I can't imagine why he would loose the chandelier. He'd be too scared of upsetting Sister Angelica and Don Antonio. He dropped Lucrezia's cello a while back, you know? It's never been quite the same since. Sister Angelica wanted him sacked!'

I was pumping my arms, trying to get my blood circulating.

'I must go!' Paola jumped to her feet, suddenly panic stricken. 'They're sure to be ready to play the second piece now!' No word of concern for my likely imminent death from exposure.

'Don't worry, Signorina,' a voice broke in, and Luca wandered into view. 'I'm here to tell you. There is to be no second piece. The Sisters have informed Signor Fosca that they feel it's best if you all go home. The alarm caused by the falling chandelier, and the resulting lateness of the hour, is given out as the reason....'

Paola took to her heels and fled, only glancing back on the stairs to call back, 'Thank you for rescuing me, Signor Harry! Oh, I nearly forgot. Here is your picture!' She produced a crumpled piece of paper from her bodice, and leaned over the carved stone stair rail to hand it to me. Of all inconvenient moments, when I was soaked through, and had nowhere dry to stow it! I took it gingerly between finger and thumb, and held it well away from my wet shirt.

Luca watched Paola run lightly up the stairs. 'They do say to be careful around red headed girls,' he remarked with a knowing grin. 'What happened? You tried to kiss her, and she pushed you in?'

'No such thing!' I snarled.

'No? Shame on you, a missed an opportunity!'

'It's a long story, Luca, and I will only tell it if you go and beg some dry britches for me. If necessary, steal me a pair! Here, take this drawing before it gets ruined — though I doubt I shall ever do anything with it now. I'll go down to the boat and wrap myself in the canvas until you come!'

A torch, burning low, flickered in a sconce on the wall, lighting the Watergate beneath the house. The laundry barge was tied up where we had left it, but two gondolas had poked their long noses in beside it, their fretted prows throwing gigantic, sinister shadows on the wall, reminding me of long snouted monsters with huge teeth. Stepping across from one to another, I puzzled that there seemed to be something bulky in the bottom of our boat. I knew we had left the canvas folded, and for a moment I thought, Lord, now what, another corpse? Drawing closer, however, I heard rhythmic snoring, rising above the slapping sound of the wavelets that flowed in from the canal outside. Nardo Piccoli, for whom Fosca's servants were searching so industriously, was fast asleep in the barge. An empty wine flagon rolled gently to and fro at his head as the boat moved on the swell. Perhaps he always drank himself into a stupor on free liquor, when he found himself marooned in a wealthy household on an evening errand? The canvas, which I had grown to think of as a personal friend, was underneath him. Not knowing how drunk he was, or how aggressive he might be if woken, I stripped off, wrapped myself in a fur rug, filched from the *felze* of the nearest gondola, and sat down to await Luca's return.

He came more quickly than I had dared to hope, bringing a pair of much patched britches, a shirt, and a pair of boots. No, he hadn't asked permission, there was nobody around in the servants' quarters, and he hadn't wanted to waste time in case I caught my death. Thoughtful of him, although if the Fosca servants reported the theft... he and I might yet become acquainted with one of the doge's prison cells.

'The nuns are lining the girls up to go, and Signor Fosca, *very* apologetic about the mistake with the wine, is arranging to send them home by boat,' he reported.

'Not in this one I trust?' I said, indicating the snoring bargee. 'Can *you* handle a boat? I can't.'

'*We* won't have to row them home. Fosca's sending his own gondolas, and one of the guests has offered his. Tough for that fellow's gondoliers, who'll then have to come all the way back to take their master and his wife home. Why don't we get the instruments down here, and then pour water over this Nardo until he comes to? That is, if you don't want to tell Fosca we've found him?'

'I don't. I doubt he had anything to do with the chandelier. I'd say he filched this flagon, and came straight down here to enjoy it.'

'One of the footmen said young Master Bruno, the younger son, might be at the bottom of the chandelier business. No one has seen him all evening, and he was said to be in high dudgeon because his father wouldn't admit some of the young rips he goes about the town with.'

'What of the older son, Marco, after I rescued young Paola — or tried to?'

'So *that* was it? Haven't seen him. Licking his wounds, I daresay!'

We both hoped so. It seemed improbable he would have an opportunity to trouble Paola further, now that the nuns were rounding up their flock. Once I had donned my stolen garments (the boots pinched abominably) we made our way upstairs and collected the instruments. Anna Girò had been prevailed upon to sing arias from one of Don Antonio's successes (from *Farnace*, I believe, although I never saw any of them performed) which was no doubt pleasing to them both. Certainly she seemed to be charming her audience, and Don Antonio looked as cheerful, at the continuo, as I ever saw him. I had heard the rumours, as everyone in Venice would undoubtedly have done, that they enjoyed too close a relationship, but to me his expression suggested more an indulgent Papa to this lady, than a lover.

Whilst all eyes and ears were on Signorina Anna, we were able to creep around in the shadows without drawing too much attention to ourselves. Heaving the heavy double basses into the boat roused Nardo without our having to resort to the cold water treatment. He sat up, very bleary of eye, but, surprisingly, not incapable, and after a good deal of hauling and straining, the three of us had the instruments tied down. And would have made our departure, but for the fact that we were interrupted by loud voices, and feet thundering downstairs from within the *palazzo*. For a moment I feared that the search party was upon us, still looking to capture Nardo, but the toughs who entered were Fosca's gondoliers, charged with rowing the Pietà girls home. They were unhappy with this assignment, and said so, in coarse Venetian terms that made even Luca blink.

'I hope those girls don't suffer with seasickness,' he remarked, once we were finally on our way (drinking a whole flagon of wine did not seem to have affected Nardo's ability to navigate). 'Because those rogues intend giving them a rough ride!'

I thought, but did not say, that I hoped the Signorina Paola would be so sick she fell overboard.

Chapter 17

Paola and her comrades endure an uncomfortable journey home, and arrive to find themselves locked out

It must be that Santa Paola interceded for me once again. I escaped censure! I arrived back at the withdrawal room just at that muddlesome moment when a group of people is about to depart. Several members of the *Coro* were lined up and ready, but others were still in the privy, and yet others had forgotten their cloaks, or their instruments, or their scores (or in some cases all three) and gone back for them. So I was able to slide into the line, and pretend I had been there all the time. If I looked a little dishevelled, then so did everyone else. At least my top knot, thanks to Marta's skill, had stayed more or less in place. Happily none of the more inquisitive girls (Albetta, or Lucrezia for instance) demanded to know where I had been, and there was no sign of Marco Fosca at our departure. Praise be!

We were briefly delayed at the head of the staircase, because the little lady in green (no longer weeping) hurried up to Sister Angelica, to tell her something. Whatever it was, I thought she glanced down the line in my direction several times, and though I would ordinarily have hoped that she was telling Sister A how much she had enjoyed my playing; tonight I would have preferred it if Sister Angelica wasn't reminded of my existence.

You may be sure I chose to ride in Sister Benedetta's boat. At the very last moment, before the gondoliers pushed our boat away from the landing stage, someone detached herself from a group waiting to board Sister Angelica's boat, scuttled across, and scrambled down beside me. Hidden inside the hood of her cloak, I wasn't immediately certain who she was. Since I seldom see my fellow members of the *Coro* muffled in cloaks, all I could have said about her was that she was tall and slender. She was evidently someone who, like me, did not want to be under Sister A's all seeing eye just now, and that gave me a notion. That, and the fact that I recognised her violin case. There is a fault in the stitching of the leather, close to the carrying handle. She didn't want to talk, pulling her cloak tightly around her, and turning away, although she wasn't marvelling at the brightly lit *palazzi* as we floated by. Instead, she bent her head over the side, studying the bubbling eddies in the black waters as the gondola moved through the swell.

Well, I thought, if you don't want to be sociable, *I* needn't be. Perhaps you drank more wine than I did, and your stomach is rebelling. Better you throw up over the side, than over me, girl! I pulled my own cloak close against the wind, which was blowing colder now, whipping up choppy waves as soon we left the shelter of the backwaters for the wide expanse of the Grand Canal.

My silent companion and I were at the back of the boat. The two girls in front of me, Giovanna and Lucrezia, had their backs to us, and seemed to be half asleep, leaning against one another. Just for once, there was no one to quiz me. How rare that is! Within the orphanage I'm always surrounded by people giving instructions, querying my conduct, demanding explanations. All day I'm practising, rehearsing, playing, singing, praying. And every minute, morning and night, I'm being observed; by my friends, by my enemies, and most of all by the nuns, who examine every one of us for signs of sinful thoughts and behaviour. By the end of each day, most days, I'm so tired that I fall into bed and sleep until Sister Domenica sends someone to ring the rising bell. But tonight, just for the length of this journey across the waters; the thoroughfares of Venice, I was able to lose myself in my own thoughts.

I wondered what had become of Harry. How panic stricken I had been when he disappeared beneath the water, and I feared he would never resurface! I'd found myself weeping, because... because? Because I had thought he was gone for ever, and I'd discovered that I couldn't bear it if I never saw him again.

Oh, now, Paola, be careful! Could this be how this 'falling in love' that everyone talks about, feels? When I was little I loved Sonia, and one of the lay sisters, Sister Anna-Maria, who worked with the youngest children, and was kind to two motherless mites. That's one kind of love. Is what I feel for Harry the other sort? The kind you're supposed to feel for a man? Your betrothed. The man you hope to marry? *Well, you won't be marrying Harry, you fool, not after you pushed him into the canal, and nearly drowned him! You acted like a dithering little milksop. All right, he must realise it was an accident, but why couldn't you take a good hold of him and pull him out? He was really angry, and all you did was blather on about Sonia!*

Pietà girls *are* allowed to marry, encouraged to do so in fact, if they aren't *too* talented, and can easily be replaced. Mother Prioress and the nuns are happy to arrange it. *Arrange*, we're not encouraged to choose. Anyway, we choristers have little opportunity for choosing. Some of the commoners do. They meet butcher boys, grocery boys, bakers' rounds men, rubbish collectors and the man, and his apprentice, who kill the rats, and clear the drains. Sometimes love blossoms at the kitchen door, or over a bundle of laundry. Sister Domenica is a gruff old thing, but she has a sentimental streak, and puts in a good word with Mother Prioress, if she thinks well of the girl, and the young fellow who has taken her fancy. If *choristers* wish to marry, however, we're expected to accept the man chosen for us. Widowers with children, who want a well conducted young female to teach their daughters to sing and play. Someone who will be ready to provide a little music in the evenings, when the master comes home, tired from the glass factory, or the spice warehouse. Most of these marriages turn out happily enough, as far as I can tell. Ex-Pietà girls come to Mass at Easter or Christmastide, proudly dressed in silks and India-shawls or fur tippets, eager to show off a diamond ring, or a plump, chortling baby.

So, would I like to marry Harry? *Supposing he will ever speak to me again, after tonight?* Well, Paola, before you even *dream* of such a thing, there are at least two, *no* three — difficulties. Firstly, he doesn't seem to have any money, or he wouldn't agree to the irksome jobs the nuns keep finding for him. So the Prioress (and the Governors, because they have to sanction marriages) would never allow it. How could we live? Secondly, his home, if he has one, is in England, where for all I know he has a wife already. Thirdly, he doesn't love me in return. Well, why would he, when all I do is vex him? I've just shown myself up as a drunken little fool. I'm *not* what Marco Fosca called me, but my mother must have been, or I wouldn't be a Pietà girl, would I?

Why was I such a fool about putting my arms around him? He must think me a complete ninny. But if I'm still childish at seventeen it's because I've never had the opportunity — or the time, to grow up. Oh, Harry, my dear one! Oh, Paola, you idiot! Nothing can come of this, and well you know it. And if he will not help you find out what happened to Sonia... Hot tears of self-pity began to collect behind my eye lids. Fiercely, I blinked them away.

I was so busy having this most private conversation with myself, that I hardly noticed that we were now in the middle of the Grand Canal, and the gondoliers, for some reason, had lined up all three boats abreast. They were calling out to one another, laughing, agreeing something. The girl sitting next to me gave a little moan. Of course I had known who she was, all along. *Barbara* — the most talented musician of us all. Sister Angelica's favourite, who was feeling out of sorts even before we set out. Now she had run away from Sister A's solicitude. Or her nagging.

'They're going to race!' she whimpered, 'Oh, can't we stop them?'

Of course I understand Venetian, but we're expected to speak nicely, 'proper Italian', particularly in the *Coro,* and the Venetian the gondoliers use is almost a language in itself. Also, wrapped in my own thoughts, I just hadn't been paying attention. I looked round, at the man standing behind me in the stern. He grinned, flashing a few white teeth with blackened stumps between.

'Just a *leettle* race, Signorina! Those two boats,' he gestured, 'belonging to Signor Fosca. This one, old man Lodi, my master. His wife, she ask him to lend, take you orphan girls home. Soft hearted lady, my mistress. Fosca's men, they've challenged us! Guido and me,' he nodded to the man in the prow, 'won a race last Ascension Day. Fosca, he don't let his fellows compete. Won't give them time off to practice. We can beat 'em! Easy. You'll see.'

In one of the other boats, I could just make out Sister Angelica remonstrating, her black clad arms flung up like crow's wings, but it did not appear that the gondoliers were paying any attention to her. In our boat, Sister Benedetta sat smiling calmly, her rosary clasped loosely in her fingers. Perhaps she thought this pause was just a brief moment for prayer and reflection along the way?

'We'll just have to hold tight, Barbara,' I told my companion. 'They're going to do it, whatever we say.'

In reply, she thrust her violin case towards me, and clutched the side of the boat with both hands. 'I shall be sick again, I know I shall!' she groaned. 'I feel so ill! Oh, if only my life were over, and I could sleep in peace!'

I'm sure I stared at her in astonishment. I had never heard Barbara speak like that, she's usually so gentle, so obliging, never thinking of herself. When she speaks or acts, the nuns, even Sister Angelica, nod their heads, as if to say to the rest of us, 'There! That's how you should all conduct yourselves!'

There wasn't time to reply before one of the gondoliers yelled the command to start, and our gondola lurched forward, its silvered *ferro* glinting in the starlight, dipping, then rising high above our heads. Girls began to scream, Maria-Regina and Albetta louder than anyone of course, although their laughing faces told another story. Our gondoliers dove the great oars deep into the water, and the boat surged ahead. I glanced back at the oarsman behind us; he was grinning, matching each stroke with his comrade in the prow. A trail of white foam cut a swathe through the water behind us.

'We'll do it, Signorina!' he shouted above the sound of the waves slapping and bumping against the sides of our boat, 'Guido and me, we'll leave those mangy water rats floundering in our wash!'

I considered pleading for Barbara's stomach (she was heaving, piteously) but there was no way to make him hear me, above the yells of the *Coro*, screaming with fright or elation, according to their temperaments.

Actually, I was almost enjoying it — but quietly, in deference to Barbara — the exploding cascades of spray, white and silver in the starlight, the graceful silhouettes of palaces and churches, receding into the distance now that we were heading out into the wide open water of the *bacino*; the dancing flames of the lanterns, flickering wildly in the prow of each boat. A boat load of carnival revellers in a sailing craft cut across our bow (fortunately not closely enough for collision) going in the opposite direction. Some of the occupants were standing up, trying to dance, grasping at one another around the waist (or indeed any part of one another's bodies that could be grasped) falling over, and screaming with mirth above the sound of a badly played concertina. As they passed by, some of them hurled wine bottles into the swirling wake of their boat. One clanged and clattered against our *ferro*, and fell into the gondola, dousing the girls at the front in wine lees.

As we drew closer to the mouth of the Grand Canal, the waves grew larger, and our gondola's plunges wilder. Plumes of water began to crash in on us, and the shrieks became less joyful as gowns were soaked, and stomachs began to revolt. Even Sister Benedetta was looking anxious, as though this was a test of faith her favourite saints had forgotten to warn her about. I glanced round, to see how the other two boats were faring, and saw, peering round the braced knees of our straining gondolier, the prow of Sister Angelica's boat, close to our stern. Fosca's men were straining at their great oars, trying to benefit from the smoother waters in our wake and avoid being deluged, but they didn't seem to be gaining on us. The flame of the lamp in the prow, streaming in the wind, showed Sister Angelica to be nearly as wet and angry as Harry had been. I hastily turned my head. If she saw me smile, there would be no more solos for me.

Our two gondoliers proved to be champions indeed, and the girls in our boat began to shriek encouragement. We fairly skimmed across the *bacino*. At no point did either of the other gondolas come anywhere near to overtaking us, although the one containing Sister Angelica nosed alongside our stern as we slowed a little to make the turn towards the *riva* and home. At last, pulling into the steps up to the quay, our gondolier called down, triumphantly, 'Did I not tell you? Guido and me, no one can beat us!'

Barbara staggered to her feet the moment the boat touched the stone steps. For a moment she looked down at me and muttered, 'It was a mistake. That business with the chandelier. Nobody meant *you* any harm,' and then she leapt clumsily ashore, nearly tipping me into the water (we were not yet tied up, and the boat swung out as she jumped).

I called after her, because she had left her violin, but she didn't look back, bunching her cloak above her knees, and scurrying across the *riva* to the front door of the orphanage. I suppose she hoped to avoid everyone, and perhaps escape to her bed without a further encounter with Sister Angelica. If so, it was not to be. The front door was locked fast. She tugged on the bell rope.

'Pull harder!' someone called out. We heard the bell peeling inside, and then dying away into silence. The door remained fast.

Even the two nuns were nonplussed by this. Sister Porteress, they assured us, had known that we would be returning late, but nobody seemed entirely certain how late it actually was. Even the nuns do not own time pieces. We were all tired and cantankerous. Girls were shivering in their damp clothes; in this Barbara and I, having been at the back of the boat, were luckier, and drier, than most. Someone began to cry. Barbara sat down on the doorstep and buried her head in her hands. I set her violin down beside her, but she did not look up, let alone offer me thanks for retrieving it. I thought, I wonder, did she resent Don Antonio's giving me that solo? But Barbara had never behaved in such a way when others were given their chances; had always been kind and encouraging to the less experienced members of the *Coro*. Goodness knew, I was not so good a player all of a sudden that she needed to feel jealous. Perhaps, having made up her mind to seek the religious life, she was simply impatient: to be gone from the Pietà and all of us, with our petty triumphs and resentments.

The nuns' quarters and the dormitories are at the rear of the building, but the Porteress sleeps close to the front door. 'If I had my trumpet, I'd wake them!' grumbled Maria-Regina. This was after she had already shouted loud enough to rouse the dead, jangled the bell, thumped on the wooden drum of the *scafetta*, and hammered on the door with her fists. There was some desultory discussion as to whether it would be possible to squeeze Cecilia, who is tiny, having been prevented by some condition from birth, from growing to full adult height, in through the *scafetta*, but Sister Angelica forbade us to try it.

'Shall I go round and see if there is anyone still working in the kitchen?' I offered (since nobody seemed to have any better ideas). Sonia had once told me that the kitchen workers stayed late, supposedly preparing the next day's meals, but, actually, according to Sonia, lounging around the big scrubbed table, enjoying their rattle tattle over a glass of wine at the end of the day.

Sister A opened her mouth, possibly to tell me not to be a fool, but Sister Benedetta beamed at me.

'Paola, that's a sensible notion! I'll come with you. I can only think something *dreadful* must have happened, though I pray it is not so.'

Although I have known Sister Benedetta all my life, I have never known her well. I've sat through her religious instruction classes, year on year, and joked with the others that she knows the intimate details of the lives of every saint that ever lived — perhaps even a few that his Holiness in Rome would be hard put to recall. I couldn't ever remember her speaking to me on my own. However, as we made our way round the side of the building, and took the narrow walkway along the *rio*, she took my arm.

'Paola, dear, I'm so glad to have the opportunity to say how well I thought you played tonight. I know it can't have been easy, knowing that your friend's funeral Mass is tomorrow, but you didn't let us down, you played beautifully! Don Antonio was pleased, I know he was. I only wish Sister Angelica had been in the room to hear you. You may be sure I shall tell her! That dreadful business with the chandelier! And your dress, is it badly scorched? I'm sure someone will find you a new one if it's very much damaged. You'll want to look your best tomorrow to show your respect for Sonia.'

Believe it or not, the small triumph of my solo had by now almost faded from my mind. I was touched by her kindness. I was sure Sister Angelica would never concern herself with how I might be feeling on the eve of my friend's funeral, let alone whether I had a dress fit to wear.

Sister Benedetta may have guessed what I was thinking, because she went on, 'Sister Angelica is *so* worried about Barbara. As we all are. She has always been such a *good* girl, so gifted, so conscientious, never causing us any concern, but she's suddenly lost her way. One day she wants to give up the *Coro* and enter a convent, the next she says she wants to stay here as a lay sister and scrub floors!'

'She does seem... out of sorts. Unwell, perhaps?' I ventured, as she seemed to expect a response. 'Coming over in the boat just now, she said something about wishing her life was over. Do you think she *is* just suffering from melancholy, Sister, or has some particular thing happened to distress her?'

'I wish I knew, dear. It seems to have blown up out of nowhere. We're all at our wits end. If it was *just* a matter of being unsure whether she has a Vocation... I've spent time with her, together with Don Salvatore, but when we try to discuss it she clams up, and says she isn't ready. I noticed she chose to sit with you just now. I think she likes you, sees you as someone who might one day take her place, leading the *Coro*. Perhaps *you* can encourage her to talk about what is troubling her?'

'I wish I could,' I said, 'but I'm.. just a junior member of the orchestra. I don't feel... I don't know her very well. Chiaretta has always been her closest friend.'

I had just been thinking that perhaps Barbara had taken me in dislike, although in the past she had always been kind to me, more so than I deserved, on occasions I had been less than diligent with my music. I couldn't imagine her opening her heart to me.

'Chiaretta says she won't talk to her about it.... whatever it is,' Sister Benedetta began. At this moment we came in sight of the laundry, and saw a boat drawn up outside. Someone was lifting one of the cellos out, whilst another figure knocked on the laundry door. I jumped, hearing Harry's voice call out, and was very glad of the darkness, which hid the hot blood rushing to my cheeks. He must never know how I felt. If I let him see, I was sure he would reject me, and then how would I face the laughter and spiteful comments of the rest of the *Coro,* with whom I would have to live for years, if not for the rest of my life? This was something I could not share with anyone, not even Marta.

'Is no one answering?' Sister Benedetta enquired, as we drew level.

'Not yet,' Harry grunted, thumping the door again. 'This fellow Nardo is *ubriaco fradicio.*' (I wondered how he had learned that phrase to describe one sodden in drink?) 'In truth, Sister, I don't know how he managed to get us back here without capsizing the barge,' he went on. 'We were told to get these instruments ashore quickly, out of the damp night air. Signora Amelia promised the laundry girls would let us in.'

'*Did* she now?' Sister Benedetta peered at him, frowning in the light of the lantern his friend Luca was holding aloft. We could see Nardo Piccoli standing in the stern of the boat, eyes half closed, leaning heavily on his oar, and swaying from side to side, ready to crumple into a drunken sleep at any moment.

'Signora Amelia takes a little too much upon herself at times!' said Sister Benedetta. 'I don't believe the Prioress would be happy to hear that girls are being instructed to open doors late at night without her express permission. *However,* as it seems the Porteress is missing from her post, and we are *all* locked out, I suppose we must see if anyone here answers.' She raised her fist and knocked. We waited. Nothing happened.

'Perhaps they're in the kitchen?' I murmured. There was a small window next to the kitchen door, and I could see a light glinting within. I stepped a few feet to the right, and tapped on the narrow kitchen door. A key turned, and it swung open. One of the kitchen commoners, Annetta, peered out, a sharp paring knife in her hand. Two pop-eyed, open-mouthed laundresses peered over her shoulder. Behind them, on the table, I caught a glimpse of candles propped in makeshift holders, open wine bottles, beakers, and plates of pastries It was clear that the commoners had been having a party of their own.

'Oh, it's *you*,' Annetta grumbled. 'I thought you were going to be that madman.'

'Annetta!' snapped Sister Benedetta. 'Stop waving that knife about, you'll do someone an injury! What madman? What *is* going on?'

'An old man, Sister... he said he's Sonia's papa, and we've murdered her! That is, he said you nuns have. He knocked Sister Porteress to the ground, and made her head bleed real bad! Then he ran into the chapel, just as we were all filing in for vespers, and shouted at Mother Prioress, 'You lousy nuns have killed my daughter!'... and a lot of bad words I'd better not say. And then his son came, and dragged him away.'

'I see,' said Sister Benedetta. 'No wonder Sister Porteress didn't answer the door. Annetta, you go quickly now, and open the front door to the *Coro*, they're wet and cold. Sister Angelica is with them. Leave that knife behind! Martina and Rita, come next door and open up the laundry, as I understand Signora Amelia asked you to do. We're all tired out. It has been a difficult evening, and these young men want to leave the instruments and go home to their beds! We all do!'

The two laundresses scampered next door. Waiting on the silent walkway, I heard them struggle to lift down the great wooden bar that held the double doors in place. *Of course!* Startled, I glanced round at Harry, but he wasn't looking in my direction. He was standing patiently, his expression grim, holding a cello by the neck. I had insisted to him no one could leave the building without a key.... but anyone who had ever visited the laundry (as I had myself, a hundred times) could have realised that the double doors are not locked, but *barred*. It would take a strong person to lift the bar unaided.... but two together can do it easily enough. This must be how Sonia left that night, which chimed with what Harry said he had seen. But did she leave alive.... or dead?

Chapter 18

In which Harry attends a funeral, discovers a motive for Sonia's death, and reflects on some problems of his own

Of all the exasperating evenings! I told myself, before I slept, that I had had quite enough of the Pietà, and all who dwelt there. The sooner I finished those drawings, pocketed my fee, and moved on, the better. I rose early next morning, relieved to find I had not come down with a raging fever as a result of my ducking, but still determined to complete the job as quickly as possible.

I had completely forgotten about the funeral. Instead of drawing, I found myself standing next to Frediano Størje, as Don Salvatore's voice cracked and wavered through the Mass for the dead. Almost every member of the orphanage was present; Prioress, nuns, choristers and commoners, even the little girls from the school, in clean white pinafores, round eyed and overawed by the sad solemnity of the occasion. Only the injured Porteress was seated, her head swathed in bandages. Even old Signora Amelia stood, leaning heavily on her cane, together with Don Antonio, leaning on his, their heads bowed.

Since I could not, out of respect, continue with my drawing during the service, I attempted to skulk in the shadows. Had I remembered that they were holding the service, I would not have come at all. However, I was spotted there by Frediano, who, recognising me from our adventure of the previous day, greeted me as an old and valued acquaintance, and urged me to come forward. I could well understand his being anxious for masculine support amongst this sea of females. So, quite contrary to my expectations, and indeed my inclination, I found myself near the front of the chapel, beside the chief mourner. His father, he said, was 'too sick' this morning, by which I understood he meant too sunk in drunken stupor, to be roused.

No music was performed during the funeral Mass. No shower of golden notes floated down to us from the singing gallery. Paola, and Marta, as the dead girl's closest friends, stood a little way from us, their heads covered in fine black veiling. Marta held a handkerchief, and kept glancing at her friend to see it was needed, but each time she received a shake of the head. Once, Paola looked up, saw me, flushed beneath her thin veil, and dropped her eyes.

Then it was all over. Giorgio, Nardo (both apparently recovered) and two other men, porters borrowed from the fish market judging by the aroma that assailed our nostrils as they passed by, stepped forward and hoisted the coffin on to their shoulders, to carry it out to the barge, waiting on the *riva* in the watery sunlight. As they did so, Marta suddenly produced a tiny treble recorder from the folds of her skirt, whipped back her veil, and began to play, a simple, lilting melody. It sounded like something to accompany a children's rhyme, and indeed the schoolchildren's eyes widened in recognition, whilst Paola, who evidently hadn't been expecting this, was caught off guard, and at last dissolved into tears.

The whole congregation followed the coffin out on to the *riva*; all but the youngest children who were ushered back to their lessons. It seemed this was the custom when an inmate died. Only the priest and the male mourners, if any, would be permitted to travel to the burial place, but all Sonia's friends and teachers (and perhaps her greatest enemy?) assembled on the quayside to see her off. It was a soft grey morning with more than a hint of spring warmth in the air; an occasional gleam of sun breaking through the thinning clouds over the onion dome of San Giorgio Maggiore across the *bacino*. We stood huddled in groups, watching, as the boatmen manoeuvred the coffin into the barge. A flock of pigeons, startled by this sudden eruption of people from the chapel, flew up in panic and circled over the roof of the orphanage, eventually settling in a silvery huddle on the red tiled roof of an adjoining building.

As often happens after a funeral service, there was a lightening of the atmosphere now that the solemn ritual was at an end. The girls and women moved about; little knots formed to talk to one another, quietly. Elderly passers-by with nothing else to fill their morning paused to demand to know who the corpse was, and what she'd died of, and then stayed to mingle with the throng.

The Prioress and Sister Serafina approached, solemn in their black robes, and took Frediano aside. I could hear their murmurs of commiseration, though whether these were for his sister's death, or his misfortune in having so tiresome a parent, I could not tell.

I found myself standing beside Marta (Paola had wandered away, her face buried in the handkerchief) and asked her, for something to say, what was the tune she had played?

'Oh, it's just a children's song,' she muttered into her veil, embarrassed, 'something we all learn when first we begin on the recorder. It was the only tune Sonia ever mastered. I thought she ought to have it, as a farewell gift. I shall probably get into trouble for it.'

'I'm sorry, if so,' I said. 'I thought it a kind gesture.'

'Sister Angelica doesn't care for gestures, however kind. But I wasn't always very nice to Sonia, I don't have Paola's patient nature. I felt I owed her something.'

'Paola told me last evening that Sonia wasn't always very nice to other people. That she was in the habit of demanding money for keeping secrets?' Paola had wandered further away from us, as though she was avoiding me. True, I'd been furious with her last night, but the funeral service had recalled me to charity. She stood watching Sonia's coffin being lowered into the barge for her last journey. Marta glanced towards her, and then back to me.

'Oh, you found a chance to discuss that at the party, Signor Harry? I'm surprised, I thought, from Paola's demeanour just now, that you must have quarrelled? I'm told the party was a riot! Not by Paola, she doesn't want to talk about it. What happened? Was her solo a disaster?'

'No, she played very well. Not that I am any judge, but everyone said so.'

'And the wine flowed freely, Albetta tells me! Most of the string section have sore heads this morning!' She glanced anxiously across to Paola once more, and then dipped her head to say, softly, 'You won't be unkind to her, will you? You see, she doesn't... That is, she's lived here, in the Pietà, since babyhood. She doesn't know any other life. I was nearly ten years old when my parents died, and my uncles placed me here. At least I know *something* of the world beyond these walls. I think she likes you... by the fact that she won't talk about you, even to me... I don't want her to be hurt.'

I have to say, my heart sank. This was a complication I had not bargained for. I was, after a night's sleep, and some holy words in church, rather grudgingly prepared to forgive Paola for being such a little goose about the whole business of Marco Fosca, and my unexpected swim in the canal, but I wasn't ready to be the focus of a young woman's dreams. The whole idea was preposterous. Yes, she was an attractive girl, that I did not dispute. She was tall, and held herself well, not precisely pretty, but with fine eyes, an engaging smile, and of course, a prodigious talent for music. I could picture heads turning appreciatively, if I entered a room with such a girl on my arm. But she was not for me. Most definitely not.

'Alas, I find you friend charming,' I told Marta, 'but my family...'

'Would not accept a girl from the Pietà?'

'Would not, and could not. We are... unfortunately placed. Our family is an ancient one, but... I believe you have noble families here in Venice who have fallen on hard times and live in poverty? The *Barnabotti*? Those men I see walking about the city clad in silken rags? My family is not quite so destitute as they, since in England, unlike here, nobles are not forbidden to work, or engage in business. Indeed I must work. My father cannot afford to support me. I have an older brother, who will inherit my family's house and land, and three sisters for whom my parents are trying to raise dowries...'

'Ah, so you will work hard at your drawing and painting, and presently you will find a rich patron, and then — *then* you will come back to the Pietà, and claim Paola! I should think she will be five and thirty, and quite tired of playing the violin by then!' Marta was laughing at me. Just as well for her that she was veiled, for at that moment, Sister Angelica approached, accompanied by the fubsy faced novice, Sister Helga.

'Marta Rovigo, I think you should go and join Paola. The boat is about to leave. Surely you should be there to support her?'

Truly, that woman could draw a cloud over the brightest day. Marta scurried away to Paola's side. 'And you, young man, should you not return to your work? I would think Mother Prioress is expecting you to finish those drawings by the end of the week. Since you claim you never met Sonia, I cannot imagine why you felt the need to be present at her funeral!'

I had thought Signora Amelia an odious female, but Sister Angelica took the prize. However, even as a retort found its way to my lips — my family may be impoverished, but we don't care to be spoken to like scullions — Frediano came up to me, wanting to shake my hand, and thank me once again for saving his father from drowning. I had apparently earned his undying gratitude, although it was hard to imagine why. He was now about to board the boat to travel to the burial place, and urged me to come with him. With Sister Angelica standing by, I hastily declined, giving my work as the excuse.

To soften my refusal, I walked with him across the *riva*. Behind us, I could hear Sister Helga saying, loudly, '*Why* does the Prioress permit this young man to work in the chapel, even speak with the girls if he wishes? Such conduct my Mother Superior would *never* countenance. Yes, everyone reminds me that this is not a convent, but these young women.... their mothers were low in morals. Surely they should be doubly guarded, to keep them from the same path following? This, I think, should be an all-female establishment, and that rule most strictly kept should be!'

'It would certainly prevent a lot of giddiness,' Sister Angelica responded, grimly. 'And now, on top of everything, Mother Prioress tells me, we have a Royal Personage, a late arriving visitor to Venice for Carnival, who wants to hear the girls perform. *So* distracting for the *Coro*, when we are about to enter the Lenten period, and need to prepare the music for Easter to follow! We have nothing rehearsed, nothing prepared, but Don Antonio has had the effrontery to suggest that the girls perform *an opera* for this prince! An opera! I told Mother Prioress I think it's completely unsuitable, but she says it's a most respectful theme, and the Governors are happy for us to do it. As for the painter... *he* will take himself off once he has finished what he is being paid to do. An undesirable influence!' I had moved away, but parts of her discourse floated back to me on the salt laden morning breeze.

My old nurse, Bessie, always insisted that listeners hear no good of themselves. Once I had finished the drawings of the chapel frescos, I had fully intended to move on as soon as possible, but now (though I deny that my ears were burning) I was furious, and I'd be hanged if I would hurry away. Besides, I should like to see this Royal Personage. Not that I care two penn'oth for royalty in a general way, but it makes something to write home about. (I reflected, guiltily, that I had not done so, since I left Rome).

I walked to the edge of the quay, where the boat was just pulling away. Paola and Marta stood side by side; Marta, who was short in stature, with her arm around her taller friend's waist.

'*Arrivadeci!*' the girls called after the departing barge, '*Arrivadella! Partenza con Dio!*'

'*Que no va con Dios!*' hissed a fierce voice behind me. I swung round, astonished, to find the Spanish novice, Sister Juanita, staring out across the water, her face contorted with anger and misery. Harsh words tumbled from her lips, as though she was uttering curses on the dead girl. Then, seeing me staring, and realising that I must have overheard her, her eyes blazed, and she spat at my feet, before stalking away towards the orphanage building.

'Well! If she isn't the limit!' exclaimed Marta. Whatever did you say to her, Signor Harry?'

'Nothing at all. She wasn't speaking to me. She must have realised that I was standing close enough to overhear what she said. Clearly she didn't like Sonia. Could *she* have some secret that she wouldn't want others to know? And Sonia discovered it?'

Marta shrugged, but Paola, keeping her eyes lowered, apparently not wanting to meet mine, said, 'Maybe. You wouldn't be aware of it, Marta. It was when the string section were practising on our own that we all noticed. When she first came, Sister Juanita took a great fancy to Barbara. At first everyone thought it was just admiration, because of course Barbara *is* such a wonderful musician... and Barbara goes out of her way to be kind and helpful to anyone who is new to the *Coro*, and doesn't know our ways. But then she was hanging around her all the time.. finding excuses to touch her arms, her hair, as though, you know, she was... in *love* with her? It was embarrassing for Barbara, and we all thought she must have asked her not to do it, or asked Sister Angelica to do so, because she stopped. We're not allowed...' she explained, flushing, though her eyes were still on the ground, 'it's forbidden... if any girl develops a *passion* for another girl...'

'The nuns put a stop to it!' finished Marta. 'Do you think Sister Juanita might have *killed* Sonia? Because she has passions for other girls? Maybe Sonia saw her making up to someone else, someone other than Barbara, and demanded money from her not to tell? That would make sense, particularly if she had already been in trouble about it.'

The idea that girls might form passions for one another made me rather uncomfortable, as I suppose it would most men, although I had overheard shocked whispers at home, that this was one of the things (besides the dowry they demanded) that had discouraged my sister Maria from pursuing her enquiries about the convent in Brussels.

'She certainly seems to have found some reason to hate your friend, judging by that performance,' I replied. To me, it was as strong a motive for murder as any that had been mentioned so far. 'Presumably the nuns here will report back to Sister Juanita's convent in Spain, if her behaviour is unsatisfactory?'

What would happen then, I had no idea, but doubted that the outcome would be a happy one for Sister Juanita. 'The problem is, we don't have any proof of any of this, do we?'

'But we can look for it, can't we?' Paola was serious, meeting my eyes now, brushing her veil aside. 'Now we know... enough to ask someone the right questions. Such as, just where *was* Sister Juanita, the night Sonia... disappeared?'

'For Heaven's sake, be wary, Paola! Don't approach her directly. I have no idea what her involvement might be, but she strikes me as someone under considerable strain, and of uncertain temper.' Both girls nodded, solemnly.

'I wanted to tell you, Signor Harry,' Paola glanced around, to see who was watching us, and then said, in a rush, 'that you were right about people being able to open the laundry door. I'd forgotten — well, I never thought about it — but I noticed last night, when Martina and Rita opened up for us. There is no need for a key, only for two people to lift the bar out of its place, and pull up the floor bolts. So maybe Sonia did go out, or..' a tremor crept into her voice, 'or someone here killed her, indoors... and took her body out that way.'

I found myself shaking my head fretfully, as I watched the two of them walking back into the orphanage building. More and more I was coming to believe that someone inside the Pietà *had* killed Sonia. And to that person Paola would be a threat. I might have no plans to form a romantic attachment, but I didn't relish the idea of her putting herself in danger. That falling candelabra... perhaps it had just been the unpleasant trick on the part of Fosca's disgruntled younger son, but perhaps someone had intended to cause Paola harm.

As they left, the funeral barge was pulling away, out into the *bacino*, and as it did so, bells began to ring all over the city. San Marco, Giorgio, Zachariah, Bragora, Salute, Miracoli, chiming, calling out over the water, singing Sonia on her way to her eternal rest.

A sweet and holy sound, and I was just thinking how fitting it was, when it was interrupted by hoarse cries of anger. A bandy legged figure, his arms waving frantically, staggered towards us along the *riva*.

'Come back! My daughter! My *tepec* of a son!' he cried, and seeing me, he called out, 'You, fellow! Fetch a boat! Call a gondola! They are taking my daughter to her grave, and that great *tepec* did not wake me!' Mladan Størje had roused himself from his drunken slumbers, too late to attend his daughter's funeral.

'I regret, Sir....' I began, pacifically, there being no gondolas within hailing distance. However, he lost interest in me, having spotted the Prioress and Sister Serafina, who were about to follow the girls indoors, but who now turned to see who it was who was shouting.

'Here! You women! You nuns! You murderers!' he yelled. 'I will call a gondola and go after her, and you shall pay the gondolier! She was my daughter! Have I not paid for the coffin? You killed her... she told her brother, one of those nuns will kill me! Now you will pay for me to see her buried!'

Perhaps it would have been better if Mother Prioress had ignored him and continued on her way, but his yelling had alerted the passers-by, the fish stall holders, and a group of workmen attempting to replace the broken mast of a fishing boat drawn up against the quay, so she turned, Sister Serafina at her heels, and came towards him.

'Signor Størje, I am so sorry you missed the service, and are now too late to go with your son...'

'I am not too late! I will go! This fellow shall call me a gondola, and you will pay for it!' The ridiculous little man was jumping up and down in his rage, his fists doubled, and the tattered tassel on his hat swinging madly to and fro.

Now the workmen had lowered the mast to the ground, and were edging forward. One of the fishmongers was wiping his hands on his apron, and stepping out from behind his stall, preparing to come to Mother Prioress's aid if needed. As one with pretensions to be an English gentleman, I felt I must do no less, and stepped forward to stand at her shoulder.

'If you insist, a gondola shall be called,' agreed the Prioress.

'But you are mistaken, Signore, if you imagine we are under any obligation to pay for it,' snapped Sister Serafina.

Infuriated beyond reason, Mladan Størje lunged forward, fists at the ready. I reacted instinctively, completely without reference to the boxing lessons my brother and I had taken with the Bolton Battler our teens, shoving the old fellow roughly in the chest with the heel of my hand, and knocking him to the ground. Since he was certainly as old as my father, and probably not half so hale and hearty, I was immediately ashamed of this. However, it met with the instant approbation of our audience of old biddies, fishmongers, and ships' carpenters, who roared their approval.

'I am sorry, Ma'donna,' I apologised, 'I was afraid he was about to hit Sister Serafina.'

'I'm afraid you are right,' she agreed, looking down compassionately at the fallen enemy. He, however, was far from vanquished, and after sitting, panting and cursing, on the pavement for some moments, clambered to his feet again.

'It is an outrage!' he panted, 'my daughter was coming to keep house for me! My son had asked her, and I had agreed to it — although I was full of fear that her cooking would be just as uneatable as her mother's — and now you have killed her! You shall...' he muttered to himself, searching for a word, 'You shall *compensate* me!'

'Indeed we will not! How dare you speak so to Mother Prioress! None of us killed your daughter. None of us, I say! The Watchmen are satisfied that she was killed by some escaping Greek sailors. Be off with you! Call a gondola, and follow after your son if you want to show your poor daughter a little respect!'

I winced at this, fully expecting I might have to hit the old monster again. Sister Serafina hadn't believed the story of the Greek sailors herself, so why she thought it would satisfy Signor Størje, I couldn't imagine. But the wind seemed suddenly to have gone from his sails. 'I will go and see her buried! I paid good money to Leonello the carpenter, *figlio di puttana* that he is, to make up the coffin! And the wood! I could have got an excellent price for it, it was pine from the best forests in Slovenia,' he grumbled. 'I could have sent it up the Po river to a violin maker I do business with in Cremona, and got many sequins for it. See, there is a gondola!' he began to wave his arms, signalling frantically, and hobbling away from us towards the quayside as it drew closer.

'But you shall compensate me!' he called back, over his shoulder. 'All those girls you have, locked up in this place! Send me one to keep house for me!'

Chapter 19

In which Harry acquires a further commission for the Pietà, and shares his suspicions with the Prioress and Sister Serafina

By the evening of the next day I had completed the majority of the sketches, and was pleasantly satisfied with them. Sister Angelica's insinuation that I was neglecting my task, though unjust, had rankled, and I was determined to prove otherwise. I sought out Don Salvatore (who was snoozing in the vestry, though he insisted he was not) to accompany me as far as the Prioress's office.

I found the lady at her desk in the heart of the building, her face, as always, partially concealed. Sister Serafina was with her, but they broke off their deliberations to welcome me. Above the Prioress's head, I could not help noticing, was a fine panel painting of the Massacre of the Innocents, the first thing a child would see, when sent to her in disgrace. She saw me looking at it, and her exposed eye twinkled.

'I don't massacre them! Just a few *very* firm words are usually sufficient. It's fine picture, is it not? Giovanni Bellini. A gift from a patroness, with more than a little on her conscience, I would imagine. Do you know his work?'

'Not well enough, Ma'donna.'

'Then you must certainly study him while you have the opportunity. He is one of our great masters. You have brought me the finished drawings? Splendid! Lay them out here on the desk and let me see.' She urged me to take a seat, on a stool in the corner of the room. The one on which, I imagined, naughty girls might be made to wait, until she was ready to speak those few *very* firm words.

She gestured to Sister Serafina to join her, and together they studied my drawings, one at a time, making little comments about the subjects and murmurs of surprise and approval.

'I had not realized... the Good Samaritan. His donkey is rather delightful!'

'And here are the thieves, about to waylay the traveller, very cunningly concealed behind this rock. The chapel is so dark, and the paintings are now so dirty, that one does not see them clearly.'

'It is a great pity that they are to be destroyed,' I ventured from my naughty stool. 'If some way could be found to clean them...'

But this apparently was not possible. Even if someone could be found who had the skill to do it, they told me, the Pietà could not afford to waste money on them, when no way could be found to incorporate them into the new enlarged chapel.

'And enlarge it, we must,' the Prioress assured me. 'Already it is far too small to accommodate all those who wish to attend our concerts of sacred music. For this *next* affair,' she added, turning to Sister Serafina, 'We shall of course use the music salon. It will be a very select gathering, just His Royal Highness, his entourage, the Governors and their wives. Although how we are to be ready, I cannot conceive. Sister Angelica is furious with me for even countenancing this idea of Don Antonio's — but do you know?' she chuckled like a mischievous school girl, 'I have always longed to see one of his operas performed, and this is the nearest I shall ever get! Of course, it won't be a three hour affair, and he assures me the theme is perfectly pure and moral, and quite suitable for our young women to perform.'

'What *is* the theme?' demanded Sister Serafina. I was glad she had asked, because I was equally curious.

'Well... as I understand it, it concerns a fishing village on an island. A fishing fleet sets out, despite the warnings of a tempest to come from a wise old seer. The girls are to take the parts of the fishermen's mothers, wives and daughters, going down to the shore to look for their men folk returning when the great storm blows up. They sing and pray to the Holy Virgin, and their prayers are heard. The storm subsides and they see the fishing boats returning safely, and sing peons of praise and thanks. Nothing, so far as the content goes, so very much different from the oratorios we have always performed. I can't see anything *objectionable* in it, can you? Rather less, in truth, than in *Judith and Holofernes*, which we did a few years back. I have often thought that just because something is recorded in the Bible, it doesn't necessarily make it edifying.'

'No, indeed,' agreed Sister Serafina, dryly. 'I see no problem with the *theme*, but I foresee all kinds of other problems. There always are, when Don Antonio gets the bit between his teeth. Why is he doing all this anyway? I thought we were only paying him to teach violin this year? He seems to have taken over as Director of Music again. Is

Dall'Olgio still gout stricken? I'm sure I've sent round enough ointments and potions to cure a horse!'

The two of them seemed to have forgotten me, temporarily. Fascinated, I did not remind them of my presence.

'In agony still, his manservant tells me. *Of course* Don Antonio wants to put on a show for this Prince Ferdinand — it may lead to a commission! I think he has hopes in that geographical direction. The Emperor Charles, you know, has sent him a medal, a great honour...'

'Are we ever allowed to forget? I'm sure he wears it under his nightshirt! But did you not say this princeling is Ferdinand of Bavaria? The Holy Roman Emperor is surely in Vienna?'

'Certainly, but all these German princes are related. And all very rich. So, Don Antonio is writing a little opera for him, and wants our girls to perform it.'

'Sister Angelica hates having these things dropped on her at short notice.'

'I sympathise, because it *is* a lot of extra work, and she is such a perfectionist,' countered the Prioress. 'I've had her here in such agonies over what happened at Margarita Fosca's birthday party! As far as I can see, if Fosca hadn't given the girls too much wine, it would all have gone perfectly smoothly.'

'And if his idiot son had left the chandelier mechanism alone! Sister Beatrice in the wardrobe has had to find a new concert gown for Paola Rossa. One of the candles burned quite a sizable hole in her skirt,' replied Sister Serafina. 'Which reminds me, will there be... costumes? For this opera ? Scenery even? Like you, I have never seen an opera, but I understand they are usual?'

'Goodness, I hadn't thought of that! I suppose we should do the thing properly, if we're to do it all. They'll hardly look like fisher girls in Pietà concert gowns! Do you think Sister Domenica could set her needlework classes sewing costumes? They need not be elaborate, or even well finished, since they will surely only be seen from a distance. What do fisher girls wear, anyway?'

'Rags.'

'Well I'm sure we have enough gowns that have been darned and patched, and could find extra rags to stitch onto them. Scenery, now!' The Prioress looked up, suddenly remembering my presence.

'Have you ever painted scenery Signor Harry?'

'No, Ma'donna, but I would be willing to try.'

'You have attended the theatre? You are familiar with what is required?'

'In London, Ma'donna.' On precisely two occasions, but I did not tell her this. Like Don Antonio, I was scenting the enticing possibility of a commission. Employment for young Luca too. I would need him to help me. Carpentry is not a skill I would lay any claim to.

The Prioress sighed, 'All this will cost money, which would be better spent on new instruments and babies' nightgowns, but the Governors are determined to claim the honour of entertaining Prince Ferdinand. If we don't, he'll go to a concert at the *Mendicanti,* and that would never do! I have no idea what would be required, but if you are willing, Signore, and we paid you at the same rate as before?'

I indicated that I was willing.

'Then speak to Don Antonio and find out what he wants. Discover what the materials will cost, and where they may be obtained, and come and tell me. If the cost is not too appalling, I suppose we must purchase them.'

'All this on top of paying for Sonia's funeral,' remarked Sister Serafina. 'At least her dreadful old father provided the coffin. You haven't had any more thoughts on that subject, Signor Harry? Remembered any more details from the night she died? I saw you in conversation with Paola and Marta on the *riva* yesterday, after the Mass, and before Signor Størje put in an appearance. Do they have any further ideas about what may have happened? As you know, I still don't feel,' she added, aside to the Prioress, 'that we have found out the truth about that poor child's death. It troubles me.'

I thought carefully before I replied. I was loath to incriminate the innocent, or betray confidences, but it did seem to me that there were things the Prioress and Sister Serafina should know, and could investigate more appropriately than I, and more safely, if my suspicions had any foundation, than Paola would be able to do.

I told them about Paola's discovery that Sonia had been in the habit of asking other girls for money to keep secrets.

'So that's what Sonia was up to! Taking money and other treasures from other girls to keep her mouth shut.' Sister Serafina seemed remarkably unsurprised. 'Nobody comes running to tell me things like that, in case *I* demand to know her terrible secret! Of course, I usually know their little secrets all along, and if I feel I need to, I report them to Mother Prioress and the other nuns at our regular chapter meetings, and we decide what action to take. But most of them are such innocent peccadilloes, that no action is necessary. I had, for instance, heard the rumour that Sonia was thinking of leaving us to keep house for her father and brother, and that she was uncertain whether to do so. Now that we have met the father, I understand her doubts!'

The Prioress turned to me. 'Once a girl has left the Pietà, we rarely take them back. It would be impossible, we are housing so many already. That is why we try to insist, if they wish to leave, that they go to placements that we ourselves have approved. Sonia knew that, and she would guess we might have doubts about her returning to her family. Her father has never contacted us; offered anything towards her keep, or shown the slightest interest in her welfare since she was placed here as a baby.'

Sister Serafina nodded. 'Sonia wasn't one of our brightest inmates, but by no means a complete fool, so I imagine the money was to be her insurance, in case living with her father proved unsatisfactory, as I feel sure would have been the case. An odious man! Perhaps she and the brother had some idea of setting up house together?'

I shook my head. 'I don't know about that. I've met Frediano, and spoken to him, and he seems a pleasant enough fellow. I expect he thought he could protect his sister.' I supposed he had been trying to reassure her of this, on the occasion when I had seen them together by the market stalls.

'On two occasions now the father has made the outrageous claim that one of *us* murdered Sonia,' she continued. 'Indeed, you heard him do so, yesterday on the *riva*. He insists, from what I understand of his drunken ravings, that Sonia had told his son that 'one of the Sisters' had threatened to kill her.'

'He said so,' agreed the Prioress, 'but I'm sure the accusation was baseless, or greatly exaggerated. When a person feels threatened, it is highly likely that she will utter threats in return. It does not mean that she will carry them out. And "one of the Sisters" could mean almost anyone. A nun, a lay sister. We have only five fully professed nuns, but more than twenty lay sisters. Besides, would Frediano have been quoting her words exactly? Sonia may simply have meant someone more senior, who had authority over her.'

'Or even a novice?' I suggested, deciding to spill the beans. 'I don't like the idea of becoming one of your tale bearers, Sister

Serafina, and I am not implying that she is guilty of anything, but yesterday on the *riva*, as the coffin was leaving in the barge, I happened to overhear the Spanish novice... I believe her name is Juanita. She was watching the boat as it left, and... well, I don't know much Spanish, but I believe she was... *cursing* the dead girl.'

Sister Serafina raised her eyes to Heaven, and the Prioress gave an exasperated sigh.

'Juanita! A thorn in Sister Angelica's flesh, and therefore in mine! Her behaviour has been most unsatisfactory from the moment she arrived. Helga, too. A most tiresome, opinionated young woman! I wonder what *else* Juanita can have been doing that Sister Angelica doesn't know about?'

'Be sure, whatever it is, Sonia would have found it out!' said Sister Serafina, grimly. 'Sonia really was the most inquisitive girl that ever lived... and perhaps she died for it!'

'I'd better have Juanita in, and question her!'

I left them, satisfied that I had handed over the responsibility to those whose task it must be. I wished Juanita no ill, but from that brief encounter on the *riva*, I sensed that she was in a dangerous state of mind, and it would be better if she was challenged by the Prioress in her official capacity, rather than by Paola.

I went in search of Don Antonio. I found him amidst the sunlight and shadows of the *cortile*, bickering with Giorgio Piccoli, whilst his brother stood by, slack jawed and vacant eyed. It was to be Giorgio's job, Don Antonio was insisting, to build a temporary platform in the music salon, on which this fledgling opera would be staged. Giorgio was mutinous, having, he declared, no wood, no nails, and no time for such a chore.

'My brother and I fetch and deliver laundry, that is what we are paid to do,' he grumbled. 'Also, we stoke the fires and heat the water for the laundry. We carry heavy packages, furniture. Coffins with dead bodies in them! We convey the instruments to Fosca's place, and wherever else we are sent about the city.... but we are not stage hands! If you want this, Signore, you must bring someone from the opera house...'

At this show of defiance, Don Antonio embarked on a tirade, banging his stick on the flagstones, and making uncomplimentary remarks about the brothers' parentage and intelligence, and recalling various times when they had dropped or damaged cellos, or music stands, or on one occasion, a valuable clavier. However, noting my arrival, he paused in this recital of past crimes, gasping and wheezing.

'If you want these villains... I advise you... not to waste your breath ... as I have been doing. The Piccoli brothers are as mean a pair of idle, drunken, good for nothings...!' he ranted.

'I was looking for *you*, Signore,' I said, mildly. 'The Prioress has asked me to assist you. She thinks you will want scenery — a backdrop perhaps? — for this opera you are planning. I am at your service.'

'Ha! She has offered to pay you? Good, good! And that youth I saw you with at Fosca's place? You can get hold of him? *He*, at least, should know how to knock nails into wood.' Don Antonio was a grumpy old party, but he was shrewd enough to know when to abandon the unprofitable (Giorgio and Nardo) and press home his advantage with someone likely to prove more co-operative. He dismissed the brothers with a glare, and a flip of his hand.

'Let us leave these dolts and repair to the copyists' room, Signor Painter, where we can be seated at a table, and discuss what I have in mind.'

In a corridor near the entrance to the music salon we passed Sister Juanita. She kept her eyes demurely lowered, but I was feeling more and more certain that she was the young woman with the candle who had opened the laundry door. I had had the impression, at that time, though I would be hard pressed to say why, that she was on the lookout. Waiting for someone, who might have been Sonia, or some other person. Or was she waiting for a moment when no one was about, in order to dispose of a corpse? She was a painfully thin sallow skinned, unhealthy looking creature, surely hardly strong enough to lift that heavy bar, let alone carry out the dead Sonia? Yet if a person is desperate enough, I understand, he or she can achieve that which at another time might seem impossible.

'There is something about that young woman...' murmured Don Antonio, as we passed out of earshot. 'Something I cannot like. Plays well enough. Not inspired, but competent, but always she seems to be creeping about the place. Often I seem to encounter her where I think she has no business to be.'

'In the laundry for instance?' I risked.

'Hmm, yes, now you mention it. The night that girl was killed and you were attacked. The gondolier refused to take us on into Castello, said he was on his last run, wanted to get back to Guidecca. A girl opened the door and looked out, and I could have sworn… but come, we must get to work if my opera is to be a success!'

Chapter 20

In which Paola has to take a back seat whilst others have the chance to shine, but learns something that may lead her to those who wished Sonia ill.

Two days after Sonia's funeral, the whole *Coro* was summoned to the music salon. There we found not only Don Antonio and Sister Angelica, but also Mother Prioress. This was unusual. She rarely attends our rehearsals or interferes with the programmes of music Sister Angelica and our music teachers choose. I think we all guessed something out of the ordinary was about to happen.

And so it was. She told us that we, the *Coro* of *Santa Maria della Pietà*, were to perform our own little opera! Don Antonio had written it for us, and we would be presenting it, in just over a week's time, in the presence of His Most Royal Highness, Prince Ferdinand of Bavaria. Putting on a performance for royalty doesn't particularly excite us, once we have been members of the *Coro* for a year or two. Almost every Carnival we play a concert for some visiting royal personage or another. Last autumn we played one for — I think it was — Frederick of Saxony. But an opera! With costumes and scenery! The room buzzed like a whole orchestra of basses tuning up. Mother Prioress held up her hand until we quietened down. Then she went on to assure us, with a sharp glance in the direction of Sister Helga, that she had personally assured herself that the content of this little opera was both pious and worthy, and we need have no fears that anything 'immodest' would be asked of us.

'I'm ready for immodest!' hissed Marta in my ear. 'Just let me try!'

Mother Prioress then said that Don Antonio would explain what the opera was about, and which girls he thought would be suitable to take the solo parts. An expectant hush fell.

'It's a very simple piece,' he began. Don Antonio always thinks his pieces are very simple. Which usually means a whole feast of complications. However, he began by speaking, not about the music, but the story. He told us about a fishing community on an island, perhaps not unlike the islands we can see across the mouth of the lagoon. How the men go out fishing, to feed their families, whilst their mothers, wives, sweethearts, daughters, must stay at home and wait. And pray. A wise old seer, *Il Mopso*, lives on the island, and he warns the fishermen not to go because he sees signs in the sky, and in nature, that foretell bad weather, but their families are hungry, so they ignore him and set sail. A storm erupts, and the women run down to the shore, weeping and calling on the Blessed Virgin. The storm becomes a tempest, and all seems lost, but *Il Mopso* urges them to continue with their prayers. Then, at last, their pleas are heard and the tempest dies away. Presently they see the fishing boats on the horizon, and know that their men folk are returning safely.

'Everyone, chorus and soloists, gives praise to God on High, and that's it.' said Don Antonio.

I thought it sounded just as the Prioress had said, pious and worthy. And dull. However, I had no hopes of a solo part, my voice is nothing exceptional. Those who did have hopes were in a fever of excitement, waiting to hear whose names would be called.

'We will have just five soloists,' Don Antonio went on. 'First, the old seer, Mopsus. This would normally require a man's voice, but the part is in the tenor range, and I think Giovanna can reach the low notes. Stout Giovanna grinned, happy enough to play a man. 'Then, a Mother, an older woman. Giulietta, you will sing this role. With a shawl over your head. And a cane. And perhaps your spectacles? You sweep the floor with a broom.'

Giulietta is older than many of us, perhaps in her thirties. She has a lovely contralto voice, but is terribly short sighted, and partly because of this, extremely nervous.

'You will do this, Giulietta?' Don Antonio asked, quite gently for him.

'I will try,' Giulietta whispered, petrified.

'Then we must have a Wife. She washes clothes and takes care of the children. Perhaps we can borrow two of the little girls from the school, Ma'donna? They need not be singers. I think a mezzo soprano for this role. I would have chosen you, Chiaretta, but I need you to lead the orchestra as I understand Barbara is still indisposed. Albetta? You are rather young to be a wife and mother, but we will see how you do!'

Albetta gave a little jump, and a squeak of excitement.

'Now the Sweetheart. She is waiting to marry her handsome fisher boy. Meanwhile she sits making lace to adorn her wedding gown. I need a full bodied soprano for this part. Lucrezia? We will try you.'

Only one role left to be filled. Beside me, I could sense rather than see, Marta digging her nails into her palms.

'And lastly, the Daughter. She is a young girl whose mother has died, and she keeps house for her father. She gathers flowers every day in the meadows. Offerings for the shrine of the Virgin. For this role I need a high, sweet, girlish voice.'

There was a tense silence, while he looked round at us, thoughtfully. Perhaps he really hadn't made up his mind who should sing the daughter. Or perhaps he liked keeping everyone in suspense? Before he said anything however, the door opened, and Signora Amelia hobbled in. Behind her, came a short procession of laundresses, one carrying a small wash tub, one a folded sheet draped over her arm, one a pillow case, and one a handful of clothes pegs and a bundled washing line.

'Here they are, then, Don Antonio! Them things you asked for. Where d'you want 'em?' Signora Amelia demanded.

The Prioress and Sister Angelica (who clearly did not approve of the way parts were being allocated, but was resigned) looked questioningly at Don Antonio, who threw up his hands in exasperation.

'Over there, woman! Give them to the Signore!'

I had not even been aware of Harry, but now I saw that he was standing in the doorway to the copyists' room, a notebook and pencil in his hand. What *his* role in all this was to be, I was curious to know.

The laundry girls made quite a performance of carrying the things they had brought over to Harry, and setting them down at his feet; first the wash tub, then the sheet, folded once more and laid inside it, with the pillowcase, the clothes line, and the pegs on top. I think they hoped to stay and watch what was to happen next, but Signora Amelia, though she was enjoying provoking Don Antonio, must have decided it would be wiser not to exasperate Mother Prioress, and hurried them away.

'These things are for you, Albetta,' Don Antonio explained as the door closed behind them, 'in your role as the Wife. We shall have to find a hooded robe for Giovanna, as the sage. Sister Domenica has promised a broom for Giulietta, some lace bobbins for Lucrezia... and, *hmm*, possibly some silk flowers for you, Marta, as the young girl'.

Marta's hands flew to her cheeks, and she gave a most unmusical squeak. 'Me!'

'Marta? You think Marta, for the young girl?' queried Sister Angelica. I'm certain she would have greatly preferred someone else.

Yes, yes! Did I not say so? No, I was about to, when Signora Amelia's army besieged us. *Now*, the chorus.'

I wasn't even chosen for the chorus. Third violin in the accompanying small orchestra, alongside Chiaretta and Cecilia. I knew I shouldn't feel disappointed. I'd had my moment of glory, at the Foscas' party, and I was pleased for Marta, who would now have her chance to shine. Now only Maria-Regina stood on the side lines looking distinctly put out, apparently not chosen for anything. But she was not forgotten. Don Antonio, having placed the orchestra to the right of where, we were told, a small platform was to be erected, insisted that plenty of space must be left, behind the strings and woodwinds, for timpani.

'We shall need some ferocious drum rolls to signify the storm! Maria-Regina? I look to you to provide them.'

Our music salon is of a size to seat an audience of thirty or more. At one end is an arched 'loggia' of wood, with a triple gallery above, accessible from a stair in the copyists' room, where a choir, or in this case, the chorus, can stand, one tier above the other. Don Antonio sent them clattering up there, so that he could see how they would look.

'Black concert dresses, and stoles of green or blue fabric, to represent the sea, I think,' he announced. I watched Harry write something down. Perhaps he was charged with making a note of everything? Then I saw that others were watching me watch him, and looked hastily away.

Don Antonio sent the soloists to stand, one in each of the four central arches of the loggia. Giulietta at the left hand end, then Albetta, then Lucrezia, and lastly Marta, nearest to the orchestra. They stood in their spaces, looking like self-conscious saints on an old altar predella. Giovanna, as the seer, would wander on from either side to sing her part.

'We shall need nails to suspend the washing line across the loggia,' Don Antonio now addressed Harry directly. 'A stool for the betrothed girl and her lace pillow. And another for the wash tub to stand on. And a shrine. A shrine to the Virgin in this last arch on the right, where Marta will lay her flowers.' Harry was busy scribbling all these things down. 'And here, to the left of the platform, is where you will place the images of the boats.'

'*Boats?*' interrupted Sister Angelica, awfully. 'Why do we need boats? Surely the fishermen do not, in fact, appear? They are 'off stage', I believe the term would be?'

Don Antonio waved this away. 'Signor Harry here, has drawn some designs of fishing boats, which he will paint on canvas, mounted on light wooden frames. We may need a few of the commoners, Mother Prioress, to hold them from behind, and whisk them away, symbolising the fishermen setting sail. The music indicates this, soloists and chorus sing them 'Farewell and God speed'. Then, at the end, they reappear, sailing back to harbour, as it were, for the final thanksgiving. The effect will be simple, but charming.'

'I'm sure it will,' said the Prioress, smiling. Sister Angelica pressed her lips together, and raised her eyes to the ceiling.

'And now,' said our *maestro*, happily, 'If the copyists have finished, all that is needed is for you all to learn your parts!'

And that, over the next few days, is what we did, first of all in our separate groups in the practise rooms, orchestra, chorus, and soloists; then together in the music salon. Disastrously, to begin with, but then gradually our miniature opera began to take shape. Don Antonio was in his element, bobbing back and forth, breaking down now and then into fits of coughing and wheezing, but always recovering sufficiently to carry on. Helga and Juanita refused even to play in the orchestra, and to everyone's surprise, Don Antonio excused them without a murmur. I had hoped to speak to Juanita, but now I never saw her, except in chapel. She did not come, even to the practice rooms.

'You'd think Sister Helga would want to take part,' said Marta, 'She's from Bavaria. He's *her* Prince, this Ferdinand!'

'Oh, but her Mother Superior, an *opera* never would permit!' mimicked Ambrosina, and we all fell about laughing.

'La, how wonderful it must be to be so pure, so holy, as she!' snickered Carolina.

When we processed through the *cortile*, on our way to chapel, rehearsals, or meals, I saw Harry there on his knees, together with his monkey-faced friend, Luca, hammering nails into canvas and wood, until they had created what looked, at first sight, like several small squat doors, in fact rectangular panels, on which Harry then sketched out in charcoal the outlines of fishing boats with sails partly furled. Presently, when rain threatened, he disappeared indoors, and Lucrezia, who had been to confession, said he was in the vestry, painting them, and the oil paint smelt horrid.

'He's got the boats quite well,' she added, 'but the waves don't look very convincing. He *is* rather a charmer, isn't he? He gave me ever such a sweet smile, when I peeked in. I don't wonder that he's taken your fancy, Paola! When is the wedding to be?'

'Never! His family are *Barnabotti*!' Marta had told me this. I forced myself to make a joke of it. I tried to take this teasing in good part, but I know my face flamed to the colour of my hair. I had said nothing to Marta or anyone else, about the events at Ca'Fosca, but the *Coro* had decided that I was in love with Harry, and until they found some other poor soul to mock, I would just have to smile, and pretend I didn't mind.

'That Sister Juanita is a strange one, isn't she?' Lucrezia went on, typically, flitting like a butterfly on to the next subject. 'She was in the chapel, just now. Not praying or reading her missal, just wandering up and down, and poking about in one of the side chapels. They say the Prioress has had her up in her office and threatened to send her away. I don't know what she's supposed to have *done*. She never seems to do anything much, except live in Sister Helga's pocket — she had that *thing* for Barbara, of course. Perhaps she's love sick!'

'Which side chapel?' I asked.

'I don't... San Stefano, I think, why? Do you think she has a special devotion to him? Surely she should favour San Sebastiano! Isn't he the saint for people who prefer their own sex? Why do you want to know?'

'Just curious,' I replied. 'Perhaps Stefano was a Spaniard?' Although I was pretty sure, despite not having always paid as much attention as I should have in Sister Benedetta's classes, that he wasn't. *Sonia used to sit with the school staff, next to the side chapel dedicated to San Stefano.*

I had half forgotten, in all that had happened since she died, that she had mentioned a paper, a letter, that she wanted me to read. I think I had assumed it was from her brother, or her father, inviting her to come and keep house for them, perhaps containing some Slovenian words. But why should they write? Her brother had made contact with her in person, while she was out running errands. This must be something else, something that by her possession of it, threatened someone. It might have been amongst her belongings, but I thought I would have heard a rumour, if the lay sisters had found anything unusual — and that reminded me, also, that I had never heard mention of that gold coin. If Sonia had wanted to hide something from prying eyes (of which, in her dormitory, there would be many) might she have concealed this object in the care of San Stefano? No one would question a girl who went a few minutes early to chapel, to offer up a few private prayers.

'Marta,' I said, once Lucrezia had gone on her way, 'Will you come with me? I want to have a good look around San Stefano's altar. I think Sonia might have hidden something there.'

Chapter 21

In which the secret that the saint was keeping is uncovered

Rehearsals for the opera had quite disrupted the usual timetable of our days, so Marta and I were able to find a quiet moment to slip down to the chapel between Vespers and supper, without anyone asking where we were going.

'What will we say if someone catches us here?' Marta muttered, getting cold feet.

'We'll say we're praying for the success of Don Antonio's opera!'

'Nobody is going to believe us!'

'Nobody can prove we aren't.'

'I'd wager they'll think they can!' she responded gloomily.

The little side altar dedicated to San Stefano had a cluttered and untidy air. I found this surprising, because at all times of day, there always seem to be several commoners in the chapel, dusting and polishing. What had San Stefano done to be so neglected?

'Oh, the school must be expected to take care of this one,' said Marta, glancing around. 'The laundresses look after Santa Veronica, because she's the patron saint of laundry workers, and the kitchen staff take care of my namesake, Santa Marta, patroness of cooks, but we don't seem to have a saint here with particular responsibility for school teachers and their pupils, so I suppose they got this one by default.'

'And *I'll* wager Sonia offered to look after it,' I said, wondering where to start looking for a hidden letter amongst the clutter of vases, long dead flowers, spent votive candles and crumpled lace. 'It would be like her. That way she could come trotting down here whenever she fancied a break from her work, "to tidy the altar".'

'And to hide whatever she wanted to hide,' agreed Marta. 'But since she died, no one's taken it on. Let's start by straightening up this altar cloth, and then we can see what's here.' She gave it a tug, and nearly dislodged a flower vase and the statue of the saint. They rocked and clunked together, alarmingly.

'We'd better take all this stuff off first,' I said, hastily. We were in the midst of doing this when we heard footsteps.

'Oh, no! I knew we'd get caught,' Marta hissed, but it was only Spotty Cristina, who had appointed herself chief 'runner' and property mistress for the opera, hoping, I think, to be allowed to take part, if only to stand behind one of Harry's 'fishing boats' and hold it upright. I thought, rather meanly, that Sister Domenica probably found it only too easy to spare her.

'Marta Rovigo!' she panted, 'I've been looking for you *everywhere*. Don Antonio wants another quick run through with all the soloists!'

Marta dropped the candle stick back onto the altar with a clatter, and hurried away without a backward glance. Nothing mattered to her, at this moment in her life, except *Il Mopso*.

Fortunately Cristina, who hurried after her, hadn't seemed in the least interested in what we were doing in the chapel, but I couldn't be sure she wouldn't mention it to someone. If I was going to find the missing letter, and whatever else Sonia might have secreted here, I had better do it now, on my own, and quickly.

I took each item from the altar I had never done this, was it sacrilegious? Surely not, Sister Domenica's work teams must do it all the time, and laid it carefully aside. None of the vases or candle holders contained anything but the odd dead insect. I considered the image of San Stefano. The statue was tall, and looked heavy, but the lace cloth went underneath it, so it must be possible to lift it, to remove the cloth for laundering. Soon it would be removed altogether, when all the altars would be cleared and laid bare for Lent. How to lift the saint, on my own, when he was at least a third of my height? Yet I must do it, if I was to see what was behind him. I grasped him around the waist, and heaved him up. And nearly dropped him! He was much lighter in weight than I had expected, and now I had him in my arms I could see that, between his shoulders, he was hollowed out. Perhaps there had once been some means of fixing him to the wall, but this had been removed, leaving a hole in his back.

I set him down, with some difficulty, on the altar step, and wriggled a finger into the hole. Straight away I felt the edge of a folded paper, and then something moved in there. I hastily withdrew. An angry spider, very much alive, crawled out, dropped to the floor and ran off.

'Ugh! Horrid thing!' I could not stop myself exclaiming aloud.

'Ha, Signorina Paola!' said an amused male voice, and there was

Harry, watching me. 'How is it that *you've* been demoted to dusting saints?'

I was too flustered and embarrassed to say anything.

'I was looking for a couple of young women,' he went on, sounding, now, rather embarrassed himself. We hadn't spoken to each other, apart from a few brief words after Sonia's funeral, since the night of the party. 'There are usually at least two or three girls here in the chapel, at any given time,' he went on, 'and I was hoping to get them to come and hold my canvas for me. Whilst I look at it, to see if the waves look any better,' he went on. 'Sister Domenica doesn't seem to mind me borrowing her girls for a spell, as long as I take two or three to chaperone one another. Signorina Marta isn't here somewhere, is she?' he enquired, glancing around. 'You and she could come and hold it for me. The vestry's no good, the room is too small. I need to bring a panel through to the back of the chapel, so I look at them from a proper distance. The fishing boats have come out reasonably well, I think, but the water... is proving difficult.'

'Yes, Lucrezia said so,' I blurted.

'Lucrezia? The one with the ...?' he pointed to his eyes.

'Eyelashes?'

'That's the one. She looked in earlier, but again, there was only one of her.'

'Marta, Lucrezia... the soloists are rehearsing just now,' I said, not knowing what else to say.

'And you're searching for something?' He looked down at the statue. 'This saint has been hiding something?'

'San Stefano. Yes, he's hollow, here, between his shoulder blades. I think Sonia may have... put something in here for safe keeping. It's a letter, a document of some kind. Something she shouldn't have had, something dangerous... perhaps. She told me she had it, but she couldn't make out all the words. She wanted me to read it for her. We'd arranged to meet, but she never came. She died, and I never saw it. Perhaps she died because she wouldn't give it back to the person she took it from. I'd like to find it and... discover who it belonged to.'

'You think it's still in there?'

'Yes. I felt the edge of the paper just now, but then a spider jumped out.'

'That's easily dealt with.' Harry picked up the saint, turned him upside down, and shook him. Out fell a number of coins, a string of beads, several pieces of tightly folded lace, and a comb. I scurried after the rolling coins and gathered them up.

'The spoils of Sonia's blackmailing campaign I suppose?' said Harry, continuing to shake San Stefano in a disrespectful manner. 'She was doing well, amassing a tidy sum!' Finally, the edge of the paper appeared, and he pulled it out between finger and thumb.

We sat down on the step, San Stefano standing between us. 'Our duenna,' said Harry, patting his carved wooden robe. 'Now what do we have?'

I unfolded the letter. It was hand written, in an ornate style, such as I believe they use in convents, for copying sacred texts. Beautiful to look at, but not necessarily easy to read. A few of the words I could make out, but not many.

'I see why Sonia couldn't read it,' I said. 'I had wondered if it might be Latin, a legal document of some kind.... though why anyone here would...?' Latin words are familiar to me, from singing Masses, but I don't really understand it. Still, Sonia would have expected me to know more of it than she did. 'It seems to be a letter.' I handed it to Harry.

'Definitely not Latin. I *do* know Latin. My tutors at home in England drilled it into me. No, this is Spanish. Like you, and like Sonia, I can make out the words that are similar in Italian.'

'Oh!' I said, thinking furiously. This must be what Sonia took from Sister Juanita, and demanded money to keep quiet about. She must have known enough of the contents to realize that it was incriminating. Or perhaps she hadn't. Perhaps she simply guessed, from Juanita's reaction, that it contained something no one must see. Oh, greedy, foolish Sonia! I looked sadly at the pile of coins I had stacked on the floor beside me. Amongst them gleamed the golden one that she had accidentally allowed me to glimpse that day in the *cortile*, but most were small coins, dearly saved, and unwillingly parted with, by girls within the orphanage who had probably never seen a gold coin, never mind possessed one. Harry was perusing the letter.

'We can guess who wrote it,' he said.

'Sister Juanita. She's the only Spanish person here. She comes from a convent near Tarragona, where I expect she might have learned that kind of script. Is it... a love letter?'

'No. Quite the opposite. She's renouncing someone.' Harry

looked uncomfortable, and I assumed this must be because he was reading a private letter, but he said, 'I do know a *little* Spanish.... a kind Spanish lady in Naples undertook to teach me... things.'

'Oh,' was all I could think to say. I could imagine well enough what these *things* might have been. I'm not a complete ignoramus. Sister Berta, one of the lay sisters, used to be a midwife in the city, and she gets us all together from time to time, to instruct us. She says if we have proper knowledge of our bodies, and the physical relations between men and women, we *might* manage to avoid the mistakes our mothers made.

'She's telling this... Sister Manuela, that all must be at an end between them — the direction on the outside is to someone quite different,' Harry went on, 'because now she loves only... *Barbara?* This would be your Signorina Barbara? And she has hopes of persuading her to come with her to her convent, when she returns.'

'Oh,' I repeated, yet again. I couldn't think of anything else to say. No wonder then, that Barbara was in distress. She had seemed embarrassed by Juanita's too public attentions, but perhaps in private...? I couldn't imagine myself falling in love with another girl, but love is such a strange emotion, as I was finding out for myself. Everyone praises Barbara, admires her for her great musical gifts, but has anyone ever told her they love her, just for herself? I suppose it is something every one of we orphans wants, in her heart, to hear. And if you had waited all your life to hear it, might you be tempted to respond to it, whoever was saying it?

I peered round San Stefano's carved robes. 'So what would you advise me to do, Signor Harry, destroy it? Or give it back to Juanita?'

Before he had time to reply, purposeful footsteps approached. Sister Serafina, passing the open door to the chapel, must have heard our voices.

'*Well*, and what might you two be up to?' We both flushed scarlet to the roots of our hair.

'Nothing.... *wrong*, Sister,' I mumbled.

No? Perhaps not, since I see San Stefano has jumped down from his altar to prevent it! I suppose you are about to tell me that you both had headaches, and recalling that he can be invoked for this complaint, came to ask him for relief? *That's* the story I had from the person I found here earlier. I have lemon balm, and an excellent feverfew concoction in the dispensary, both efficacious for headaches, but no one seems to think of coming to ask me for them.'

'*I* was merely hoping, Sister' said Harry, scrambling to his feet, 'to find two young women to hold my canvas, whilst I look at it from a distance, to see how it will look to an audience, but *unfortunately* I found only Signorina Paola here.'

'What a smooth tongued fellow you are,' countered Sister Serafina. 'If Mother Prioress had not enough on her hands, trying to fend off those who think they should have been invited to meet His Royal Highness, and if we didn't need you to complete the scenery in time for the performance, I would be forced to report you.'

Harry looked abashed, but I noticed that although her eyes remained stern, a tiny muscle quivered at the corner of her mouth. Sister Serafina was laughing at our confusion!

'So, what *are* you doing?' She looked down at the pile of coins and other items at my feet. 'Ah, you've found where Sonia kept her ill-gotten gains?'

'Yes, Sister. She hid them in the back of this statue.'

She nodded, considering the items spread at her feet. 'That comb belongs to Giulietta. Yes, that surprises you! She's been receiving notes and little packets of bon bons from a fishmonger who has a stall on the *riva*. Her voice singing Mass has bewitched him! Silly chit, she thinks we don't know. His intentions are perfectly honourable. He's a widower, and if she wants him, she shall have him. There was no need for her to pay tribute to Sonia!' She bent, and picked up the necklace of glass beads.

'These, I think, belong to Annetta. A gift from the young scoundrel who fumbles her when he comes for the pig swill. He's a ruffian, but then so is she. Sister Domenica would raise no objection if they want to make a match of it. The lace — it's harder to guess who that belongs to, and the money — I think I should take charge of it, do you not? I shall let it be known, quietly, that I have these things, and if anyone wishes to reclaim them, they may come and ask me for them.'

Harry looked at me, and I looked at Harry, our eyes enquiring, 'should we give her the letter?' Harry was holding it behind his back.

'There's something else?' Sister Serafina had guessed there was. I glanced at Harry again, and nodded. He held out the letter, and she took it.

'It's in Spanish,' he said.

'Yes, it would be,' she replied, giving it the briefest of glances. '*Now* Paola, on your way to supper, take that altar cloth, and drop it in a laundry cart. I'll ask Sister Domenica to get someone to tidy up here.' We were dismissed.

As I dropped the cloth into the cart, I remembered the candle stick I had thrown there on a previous occasion. There had been several little glass containers for votive candles on San Stefano's altar, but only one brass candle stick. There should surely be two? And the cloth... as it fell from my fingers, I saw it had two small stains (brown now) in one corner. I knew, didn't I, who had murdered Sonia? I knew why, and where, and what the weapon had been. But *how* could she have done it? How could such a frail, sickly looking creature have carried Sonia's body out through the laundry and pitched it into the canal? Unless there had been someone else to help her.

Chapter 22

In which Harry receives advice about his life and career, some of which he has no intention of taking

The whole orphanage took a great interest in my scene painting. Too much, for my liking. Heads, which kept popping round the vestry door to see how I was progressing, were shaken sorrowfully over my struggles to depict the waves (as though any one of them could have done any better!). A calm sea, I might have managed creditably, even a tumultuous one, but what was needed was something in between. Choppy, we would say in English, I never discovered the Italian. My ocean must not look too rough when my fishing boats set out at the beginning of the piece, and neither should it be too calm, once the operatic storm had died down, and they limped home to harbour. Even Luca, my most loyal supporter, was unimpressed when I showed them to him, and Frediano, who called in one morning, ostensibly to make a small donation to Don Salvatore for conducting Sonia's funeral Mass, shook his great turnip head and rolled his eyes in alarm. He stood around in the vestry for some time, looking profoundly uncomfortable, and I supposed he was trying to think of a way to tell me how little he liked my painting, but then when the girl universally known as Spotty Cristina appeared with a mug of watered wine and a panini for my lunch, he flushed beetroot red, and began to breathe noisily with his mouth agape, and it dawned on me that he had been prolonging his visit in the hope of seeing some of the young women. The bevy of charmers he had seen at the funeral had evidently awakened in him a desire to see more of them.

After I began to scrape back the canvases for a third time, old Don Salvatore became alarmed. So much so, that one morning I arrived to find he had called in an expert (whom, he said, just happened to be passing). He was a slim individual of medium height, wearing a black floppy hat with a feather. I had met him before. He was Giovanni Canaletto.

'My young English friend! I am pleased that my instruction helped with the boats, at least!' he remarked, grinning. I felt myself flush, guiltily, because I had taken the drawings of fishing boats he had sketched so quickly, that day on the *riva,* as the templates for my little fleet. However, he seemed not to resent my borrowings. He stood a long while before the canvases, turning the brim of his hat in his hands, considering the waves.

'I tend to avoid seascapes, myself,' he remarked. 'I stick to the canals and flat calm. My esteemed colleagues, the brothers Guardi, now. They're your men for stormier waters! However, time, I gather, is short. You permit?' he gestured that he would like my sketch pad, and once again I handed it to him, and he made a few quick slashes with a pencil, and there were my waves, just as they should be, neither too steep nor too sluggish.

'Add a plume or two of spray, thrown back from the sides of the boats, like this. Use white sparingly for the wave crests, the merest feather stroke, don't overdo it,' he said, handing the pad back to me. 'I was a scene painter myself, and my father before me,' he explained. 'It's a good way to practise your craft, though it won't make you rich. Good fortune with it, my friend!' and, clapping me on the shoulder, he was gone. He was right, of course. I scraped back my canvases for the last time, and copied his sketches. The results were not masterpieces, but a great improvement on what had gone before.

Discipline within the Pietà, it seemed to me, became at this time somewhat relaxed. The girls, particularly the *Coro,* went about more freely, without close supervision. There was, of course, the disruption to the normal order of things caused by the rehearsals, and the approach, outside in the city, of the last, most hectic week of carnival, infecting the inmates, though they could not be part of it. Perhaps, too, the nuns were simply too busy, fending off those who wanted to be presented to His Royal Highness, and dealing with a sudden outbreak of chickenpox amongst the younger children. Groups of choristers chose to call in at the vestry at regular intervals to encourage me in my work, and then stood about in groups, twittering like flocks of starlings. (Frediano had been unlucky; he had called at a time when they would all have been in rehearsal) Don Salvatore, who ought, in my opinion, to be considered by the Holy Father in Rome for beatification when he passes away, did his best to chase them away, otherwise the scenery would never have been completed at all.

Paola and Marta came one afternoon. Paola smiled, wistfully, but said little. Marta, on the other hand, was so wound up about her role in the opera, that she whirred like a clock about to strike. She was full of it. Don Antonio this, Don Antonio that. A hooded robe had been found for Giovanna, but her false beard, waggling within it when she sang, looked so ridiculous, and made everyone laugh so hysterically, that it had to be abandoned. Don Antonio was insisting that his seer should be taken seriously, not greeted with shrieks of mirth. Giulietta was so nervous her top notes wavered. Albetta was far too skittish as the Wife, and Sister Angelica had threatened to have the role given to someone else. Four little girls from the school had been tried as the Wife's children, and all of them had broken out in chickenpox from head to toe, and so on, and so on, and so on.

'Has anything more happened,' I asked Paola, when Marta's busy tongue at last showed signs of running down, 'about our Spanish acquaintance?'

'I haven't seen her. People say she is confined to her room, as a punishment, no one knows for what, and must not venture out except to come to services in the chapel. The Prioress and Sister Serafina visit her, but for what purpose, I don't know.'

'Perhaps she denies she did it,' offered Marta, flippantly. She was not, I judged, really interested in the matter anymore, one way or the other, since the opera had taken over as the most important thing in her life, 'and they want to make her confess?'

'Perhaps. I'm sure she had *some* part in it, after all she wrote that letter, but I don't see how she could have done the whole...' replied Paola, seriously. Our eyes met, and I shook my head, acknowledging that though she and I might still be concerned, it was of no use to expect others to share our interest. We might have spoken further on the subject, but just then Cristina of the spots (they were not really so very bad, poor child) appeared once more, and called them back to rehearsal.

Later that day, I was surprised to receive a visit from the Prioress herself. I assumed she had received alarming reports of my struggles with the fishing fleet, and wished to see for herself that all was now well, but after glancing only briefly at the canvases and nodding, she took the seat Don Salva found for her.

It's a pleasure to take the weight off my feet,' she said, 'I've been so busy all day. So much to do, so many troubles, both great and small, which require my attention. All our poor little school children, suffering so with this wretched chickenpox. Sister Serafina has her assistants hard at work making salves for them, and sponging the blisters, but their distress is pitiable. And Barbara, our most senior chorister, has made herself quite sick with anxiety, worrying over her desire to take the veil, but convinced she is somehow unworthy, so much so that she is confined to bed. We're at our wits end to know how best to help her. Then today, on top of everything else, though this was a more cheerful thing, I have been out to inspect the fishmonger's house. Perhaps you heard? He is to marry Giulietta, once Lent and the Easter festivities are past.' Evidently the fishmonger's suit had been successful.

'How fortunate for us that you have been able to help us with this project, Signor Harry,' she went on. 'I'm certain tomorrow's presentation will be a great success! By the way, I have sent your drawings of the chapel to the bookbinder, they will be a part of the Pietà's history in the years to come. But alas, after this we cannot afford to give you any more employment once this scenery is finished, so I suppose you will be moving on. Will you leave Venice?'

'Possibly,' I said, carefully. 'I'm not sure of my plans.' In truth, like Don Antonio, I hoped something might come of this operatic venture. I had never previously considered a career in scene painting, but perhaps one of the many theatres here, with their constant round of plays, masquerades and musical entertainments, would be willing to take me on? Luca and I together might offer our services...?

The Prioress regarded me, thoughtfully. 'I have heard — these things come to my ears — that your family are of noble descent, but have been unfortunate financially?'

'That is the case,' I admitted. I suddenly realised that I was being interviewed — but could not fathom why.

'Money, or lack of it, is not the source of *every* evil,' she went on. 'Misfortune can come in many forms. I myself was born into a family in comfortable circumstances, but as a baby I developed a tumour behind my eye. The disease burnt itself out, but half my face was destroyed. My parents knew I could never live a normal life in our city, so they placed me here. I was quick-witted, and proved to have some musical ability, and it was the best decision they could have made for me, in the circumstances. Though it did not always feel so, as I was growing up.' She sighed, and then smiled.

There was something about this lady that encouraged one to confide in her. Long practice with countless young women, no doubt.

She had shared her story with me, now I could see she wanted to hear mine. So I told her, about my father's support for James Stuart and the Catholic cause. About my older brother and his devil may care tendency to lose money on horse races and at cards. About my three sisters, who were dowerless, and forced to live the restricted lives of unmarried females at home.

'Though I am not so unfortunate as those poor fellows I see wandering around the San Barnaba district, here,' I explained. 'Unlike them, I am not dependent on the charity of others. My birth does not prevent me from earning my living.'

'Are you permitted to marry? It is forbidden for the *Barnabotti*, here in Venice.'

'I *may* marry,' I said, ruefully, 'but I am expected to trade my family's name for a young woman who has her own fortune.'

'Ah, so you must look for a girl... perhaps less nobly born, but whose father has done well in business?'

I found myself telling her about Lydia. Mother Prioress was, as I have said, a very easy person to confide in, and I had gone so many months without speaking of it. Of being unable to speak of it, but now at last, I had mastered the language. I found myself telling her how my parents had hoped that I would marry my mother's cousin's child, on the understanding that I would assist Cousin George in his business. The offer was a generous one. Cousin George would require me only to deal with his correspondence. He was highly capable in all practical business affairs, and already employed clerks to calculate his money dealings, but knew himself to be a poor hand at the wording and drawing up of contracts. These would become my task, and in return Lydia and I would have a comfortable income, and the rest of my time would be my own, to dally with my pretty bride, or paint water colours of Lancaster's waterfront and the hills around, as I pleased.

'But I found I could not stomach his trade,' I told Mother Prioress, 'Oh, not through pride! If he had been a ships' chandler, or a sail maker or a... cheese monger!'

'You would have wed this Lydia? What was it about his trade that so disgusted you?'

I stretched my mouth in a grimace. 'He sends ships to Africa, Ma'donna, to capture slaves, and then transports them to Jamaica and sells them to the sugar planters. He keeps one or two to wait on him in his house. He does not regard them as human beings, but as animals, to be trained, as a dog might be, to do his bidding. He treats them abominably. He sees nothing wrong in this. Nor does Lydia.'

'Many do not; we have many slaves here in Venice,' said the Prioress, quietly. 'I understand your repugnance. Sister Teodora, too, would agree with you. She met delegates from the Ethiopian church, whilst serving with our order in Rome, and declares them to be fine upstanding Christians, though their skins are black as pitch. So, you lost your chance to marry an heiress?'

'I caused great distress to a girl who had expected to be my bride, and forfeited my family's good opinion. Now I must work for my living.'

'Dear me, that was unfortunate indeed. But perhaps in the future things will be different. You may make your name through your painting. Fortunes do change...' she got to her feet. The interview was drawing to a close. She began to walk towards the door, but turned and spoke.

'Yes, fortunes *do* change for the better on occasion. Our Giulietta, who never expected to marry... and today I've had an offer for Paola Rossa. Oh, not to *marry* in her case! But a woman came to see me. She was at the Fosca's party and saw Paola there... and thought... Well, I must not break her confidence, but I believe she imagined she recognised Paola, as ...a child *someone* in her family had given up to us in babyhood. Unfortunately, I had to tell her that this cannot be the same child. The date of *that* baby's birth did not match Paola's. She was disappointed, but not dissuaded, and would like to become her patroness.'

I must have raised my eyebrows questioningly, not having heard of these patronesses before.

'Oh, many of our most talented girls *do* acquire patronesses, wealthy women who ask them to their homes in return for recitals for their friends,' she told me. 'Sometimes they invite them to stay at their villas on the mainland during the August heat. Of course, Paola is only just beginning her career, she's still very inexperienced, but it will be good for her to have... a mother figure. I gather this woman, Felicia Lodi, has no children of her own. So, you see, fortunes *can* improve! Who knows, in a few years' time, you may come back and tell us you are a wealthy man!'

It was not until after she left the room that I realised what the interview had been all about. The Prioress had been considering me as a prospective husband for Paola! Unlike the fishmonger and Giulietta, no wedding, thanks be to God, was to be arranged for us immediately after Lent. But I was not being dismissed entirely. If I cared to go away and make some money, Mother Prioress would listen sympathetically. For a moment I was furious at her presumption, and then burst out laughing!

Don Salva, who had pottered about in the background whilst she was present, enquired what had so amused me. I told him.

'But Paola is a charming girl!' he protested, 'I thought, that first day, when the two of you talked together in the chapel... after you had been so mistreated... how well you two would deal together. *Now*, if this Signora Lodi the Prioress spoke of is wealthy,' he said, tapping the side of his nose, confidentially, 'very likely she will leave Paola something in her Will, or at least give her a substantial wedding gift. She's...' he thought a moment, how to put it, 'Paola is a *good* girl. You understand? Not just charming, but *loyal*. Look how she grieves for her friend, Sonia. She would be a *loyal* wife... if you happened to be looking for one.'

I shook my head in dazed amusement, imagining myself explaining to my parents that, yes, my bride is a foundling, daughter of who-knows-who, brought up in a Venetian orphanage, but see how talented she is, and with a dowry too, and consider this lavish money order from her patroness, showered on us as a wedding gift! Then I thought, the whole thing is ridiculous. I don't know Paola well enough. to... An image floated into my mind. Of Lydia. Of Lydia, when she thought no one was watching her, poking her maid with the sharp end of her embroidery needle, because the girl failed to fetch her fan. (The poor child, newly brought from Africa, had no idea what a fan might be.) That was the moment when my boyish affection for her had shrivelled and died. I hadn't known Lydia as she truly was, until that day, even though we had been in each other's company from babyhood. Would Paola treat another girl like that? Somehow I knew she never would.

I picked up my paint brush. 'Well, Father, before I can even consider taking a wife, *any wife*, I must improve my financial position. Mother Prioress was quite clear on that point. And to do that, I must finish this scenery. Tomorrow, the opera goes ahead!'

'God's plans for us are sometimes very mysterious,' Don Salvatore remarked. 'If that poor child Sonia had not been killed, we would never have met you, and made use of your gifts, and thus would have no scenery for Don Antonio's opera... Paola will not be the only one to miss you, when you go.'

Chapter 23

In which an opera by the esteemed Venetian composer Don Antonio Vivaldi is performed by the choristers of the orphanage of Santa Maria della Pietà, in the presence of His Royal Highness Prince Ferdinand of Bavaria. (and the sad mystery of a young woman's death is finally unravelled)

'Paola! I'm terrified!' Marta whispered, as we waited together in an ante room for the Royal party to be seated. 'This is my big chance. Oh, not the prince, he isn't going to invite me to Bavaria! Some of the Governors have connections with the opera houses. If I do well, tonight, they might...'

She did not elaborate on what they might do. I did not point out that Don Antonio had connections with the opera houses, and so far had shown no sign of inviting Marta to sing there.

The prince, I have to say, was a disappointment. Somehow, they always are. In a children's tale they are young and handsome, in reality, I have never found this to be the case. This one was a military man, not young, very upright, very severe in his manner. When he clicked his heels and bowed to Mother Prioress (we watched, from behind a curtain) the many medals on his dress uniform tunic clanked together.

Our little 'stage set' looked very well. Giorgio and Nardo Piccoli had been prevailed upon to create a sturdy dais for the soloists (not too high, lest the Prince or any of his party be offended by a glimpse of their ankles) but raising them up, so that their heads and shoulders, at least, could be seen from the seats at the back of the salon. The dais had been covered in green baize, to represent the island, scattered with the silk flowers Marta was to pick, and fringed with real sand brought over from the Lido. Harry, Luca, Spotty Cristina, and a girl with a hare lip called Lisbetta, stood concealed behind the panels representing the fishing fleet, holding them upright. Harry and Luca had created, out of vegetable crates, and a bolt of fabric begged from Sister Domenica's sewing cupboard, the shrine to the Virgin at the end of the loggia closest to Marta. There was another at the opposite end, containing, according to Don Salva, who had found him at the back of yet another cupboard, an image of

San Ferdinando in his Franciscan robe. A compliment to the Prince, though he showed no sign of recognising his name saint.

We of the orchestra filed in, took our seats, opened up our scores and began to tune our instruments. It seemed strange that Chiaretta, rather than Barbara, was to lead us. True, she had done so at the Fosca's party, but this was a far more important occasion. At one of our rehearsals, Ambrosina had daringly asked Sister Angelica if Barbara would be returning, but received only a tight lipped shake of the head. I had not seen her for days. I even wondered if she had already left, for a convent on the mainland, without wishing us goodbye.

Then, once the audience was seated, and quietened down, Signor Fosca made a speech, as he always does, as Chairman of the Governing body, welcoming the Prince and his party, and assuring them that they were about to witness a splendid entertainment. Now Don Antonio made his bow, the chorus filed in above, and the soloists took their places under the arches of the loggia. Marta might be inwardly terrified, but no one would have known it by looking at her. Albetta, I was glad to see, did look a little nervous. She had shown off tiresomely at rehearsals, but the sight of the music salon filled to capacity with fashionable people, had sobered her. Two small girls, newly released from the sick bay, their faces still marred by fading scabs, clung meekly at her side. Giulietta, who had looked impressively elderly at rehearsals, in shawl and nose pinchers, tonight looked less convincing, glowing with happiness now that her betrothal had been announced. Lucrezia, as always, fluttered her eyelashes, and looked sweetly pretty.

Don Antonio tapped the floor with his stick, and we were off! The music wasn't a great challenge. Much of it we had encountered before, as part of other compositions, particularly *La Tempesta di mare*, which I believe he wrote several years before I was born. However, I suppose it was entirely possible that the Prince had never heard it. Harry's boats sailed away on cue.

Our soloists did us proud. Giovanna's deep voice almost convinced as a man. Giulietta's top notes were perfect, even if she appeared rather too blithe today, about the fate of her supposed son. Albetta wrung their hearts over the probable lot of her children, if her husband should be lost, and between them they managed the hanging out of the bedclothes most creditably. Lucrezia made good use of her voice as well as her eyelashes — and Marta! Marta sang as I had never heard her sing before. She was easily the best actress (true daughter of the theatrical troupe), lithe and graceful as she picked her flowers, demure and devout as she prayed at the shrine. The chorus sang up the storm, waving their blue and green stoles most effectively, to represent the churning waves. All in all, a triumph, once again, for Don Antonio Vivaldi, and the Pietà.

It was difficult to tell if the prince enjoyed it. Perhaps he did, but he looked tired, ill even. Maybe he was. I heard he died, not so long afterwards. However, he clapped heartily, once the final 'Gloria' had been sung, with Harry's fishing boats safely back in harbour.

Don Antonio was then formally presented, and we heard the word 'Vienna' spoken. I imagine the Prince was suggesting he might visit his uncle there. We all know that our *maestro* has hopes of a big commission from the Emperor. I hoped he wouldn't go, but I think it's a vain hope. If the invitation comes, he'll go.

Now we could all relax. Perhaps we might even be offered a titbit or two from the splendid cold collation that the kitchen workers had slaved for hours to produce. That is, once the Prince, his followers, and the cream of Venetian Society (for they certainly so considered themselves) had eaten their fill.

I offered to pack up the scores, and fold the music stands. I always dread this part of a concert, when we're expected to make polite conversation with people who aren't in the least interested in us, until Sister Angelica hustles us away. I hoped to be able to tell Harry, as I passed by with a bundle of scores, how well his boats looked, but in this I was frustrated. The Prince, looking more animated than he had all evening, abandoned Don Antonio, and now buttonholed Harry, and was talking to him, in German, with one of his entourage translating. Harry was listening intently, but he did notice me, as I passed, and closed one eye, and tweaked the corner of his mouth into a tiny grin. That made me smile, that he should favour me with a wink, and I was still smiling when I found Marta, in the ante room, looking as pale as death.

'Paola! Oh, I feel dreadful.'

'Why ever? You sang superbly!'

'But now I feel like I'm going to die!'

I looked at her. She was flushed and shaking, as though she had a fever. On one of her cheeks, I noticed, a small red blister was forming.

'Marta, did you ever have chickenpox?'

'No. I don't... didn't we all have it when we were in the school?'

'Sonia and I did, but I'm fairly certain it was the year before you came. I think you've caught it, probably from one of those little girls who were tried out as Albetta's children.'

'As long as it isn't smallpox. *Please* tell me it isn't smallpox, to ruin my face for ever!' She slumped against the wall, seeming hardly to have the strength now, to stand.

'Let's go and find Sister Serafina,' I soothed. 'You're shivering. She'll put you to bed with a warming posset.'

'No! My career. I wanted... the Governors... to have them take note of me!'

'They've taken note,' I said firmly. 'You were the best of all. They'll remember! Come on.'

She clung to my arm, as we made for the door. Sister Angelica raised her eyebrows, but she must have seen that Marta looked deathly pale, and didn't stop us.

Outside the brightly lit music salon, the corridors and stairways were dim and shadowy, lit frugally by occasional wall sconces. Our footsteps echoed on the stone stairway, as we made our way upstairs, Marta shivering violently now that we had left light and heat behind. As we made our way to the infirmary I was half aware of a distant sound. Someone, somewhere, must be ill or in pain, I thought, but I could not pay much attention to it, being too anxious to deliver Marta to Sister Serafina, or one of her assistants.

Sister Serafina herself answered my knock at the infirmary door. Marta took a step towards her, and fainted to the floor.

'Over excitement? Or couldn't reach a note?' Sister S enquired, as she and I lifted her onto a bed.

'No, Sister. She sang brilliantly, but I think she's caught chickenpox.'

'Ah, of course.' She glanced at the red patch on Marta's cheek. 'Yes, the last epidemic we had would have been just before she came. I well remember it! You and Sonia, covered in blisters from head to foot! Don't worry, we'll take care of her. You hurry back to the celebrations, child. I hear it's all gone off splendidly.'

I wandered back along the corridor. I didn't particularly want to go back to the celebrations. The only person there I wanted to talk to was Harry, but that wouldn't be allowed. In the distance, I heard the sound of sobbing, louder now, and interspersed with the muffled groans of someone in real pain or distress. This seemed to come from the corridor on the floor below me and to the right. As I descended the stairs, I saw two little figures in nightgowns, hovering on the landing. I recognised them; Bella, the little blackamoor, and Maddelena, her friend with the fearsome squint. Maddelena was crying, though the sobs and groans did not come from her.

'Paola!' hissed Bella. 'Tell Maddi it *isn't* a ghost. Making that noise. She says it's a ghost, but my Papa says there ain't no such things as ghosts!' The groaning stopped.

'Your *Papa?*' I asked, astonished by the idea. She giggled at my shock.

'I have got a Papa, I *have!* His name is Angelo, and my Mama-was-an-African-Princess, and-he-won-her-in-a-card-game,' the child recited. 'She died, cos' it was too cold for her here in Venice, in winter. My Papa's a sailor, and he's going to come and get me, when I'm bigger, and we'll run a lodging house together!' She beamed, her teeth gleaming in the dark, proud of this imagined parent. Or I supposed it might even be true? If her father *was* a sailor, and had no one to leave her with. I had felt desperately sorry for this child, fearing she had only a future of drudgery ahead of her, but not every Pietà child is unloved and unwanted. There are a few girls here whose families would care for them if only they could. For years, while I was growing up, I hoped that one day someone might reclaim *me*, but now I know they never will, and I must, as the nuns tell us, make the best of what I have. Perhaps I should be saving my pity for scrawny little Maddelena, with her crossed eyes and runny nose? Sister Angelica was unlikely to choose *her* for the *Coro*. Just then, we heard the groaning sound once more.

'It *is* a ghost!' wailed Maddelena.

'No, Bella's Papa is right,' I assured her. 'It's probably just someone with toothache.'

To be honest, I'm not sure whether I do or don't believe in ghosts. When I was Bella and Maddelena's age it was a great game to scare ourselves with the notion that there might be a ghost in the gloomy East wing privies. I never saw one, then or since. Somehow, however, I knew *this* was a living person in torment.

'Why don't you two go back to bed, where I'm sure you should be. Who's on duty in your dormitory?'

'Elena, but she's gone down to sneak a look at the Prince,' replied Bella.

'Go quick then, before she gets back! I'll go and see if I can help this person with the toothache,' I suggested, trying to sound braver than I felt.

'I *said* we should be in bed, Maddi! We've had the chicken spots!' confided Bella. 'Maddi's had lots and lots.' Once again, we heard the low moaning sound.

'Back you go, both of you! You'll go down with putrid fever, standing about on this draughty landing in your nightgowns!' I listened to their little bare feet drumming on the floor as they scampered away. Then I set off along the corridor in the opposite direction. To find the ghost.

And I found one. Or at least I found a shadow. The shadow of a proud Spanish girl who had once been Sister Juanita. She was standing in the corridor, still but alert, her eyes burning in her sallow, unhealthy face. As I approached she tensed, as though she intended to block my passage, but when I continued walking towards her she stepped to one side, holding up her hand before her face to block out the sight of me.

'Sister Juanita? I've come to see what...' I asked, puzzled, because she didn't seem to be weeping, and somehow, although I could not have explained why, I knew the voice I had heard sobbing and groaning was not hers. Suddenly she lurched forward, arms raised, her hands claws, ready to rake my face with her finger nails. I flinched, ducking my head, to avoid the coming attack, but then, just as suddenly, her strength seemed to leave her and she spun away, croaking, 'She won't see you! She won't even *speak* to me! You are wasting your time, stupid bitch!' and then she turned and ran down the corridor, and I turned to a half open door, beyond which a single candle flame lighted the dark room.

Even hoarse from sobbing, her voice was recognisable. Otherwise, I might not have known her, standing in the doorway, her hair a tangled curtain, half concealing her face, so swollen with weeping. I had known, everyone knew, that there were two young women within the Pietà, who were in a state of distress. Juanita was one of them. Until tonight I hadn't thought about the other one, and what her distress might mean.

'Barbara?'

'Paola,' she said, her voice barely audible. She stepped back into the tiny bedroom. A Senior Chorister is entitled to a room of her own. She did not invite me to follow her, but seemed to expect it. I went in. She slumped down on the bed. I took the stool, and sat down.

'How was tonight's concert?' she asked, her voice was a frog's croak; she had cried so much.

'It was... excellent. But never mind that, what's wrong, Barbara?' She stared at me through her curtain of hair, her eyes angry, as though I was being deliberately stupid. Suddenly she slumped forward, burying her head in her hands.

'Oh, I killed her. You've guessed. I knew you would.'

'Sonia?' I noticed that my own voice didn't sound surprised, just puzzled.

'It was an accident, Paola, I swear it was! Before God and all His saints! You knew that Juanita, the novice... had a thing about me? When she first came I tried to befriend her. I talked to her about her convent and her novitiate. I wanted to know what it was like, how she had discovered her Vocation, and what had decided her to take vows, because these last few years I've felt drawn to the idea of a life in religion. But I soon realised I had made a mistake in encouraging her. She began to act strangely. She was too familiar, always touching me... I never encouraged her, never! But she wrote a letter, to someone at her convent, saying... that I would go back with her to Spain... and she gave it to Sonia..'

'She *gave* it to Sonia! But why?' This was astonishing news, but the reason turned out to be quite commonplace.

'She was afraid to ask for a frank. She told me Mother Prioress reads any correspondence the novices send, to their families or their convents. I suppose she would read any letters *we* might send, but since we have nobody to write to.... But Juanita learned that Sonia went out on errands, and she asked her to take it to the office of the Spanish Envoy, to be forwarded, to a friend who would give it to... the person she was writing to. She gave her a gold coin, and told her to sew it up — she didn't have any sealing wax. She thought of Sonia as a servant — in her convent she was used to having a maid, there to do her bidding, and not ask questions.'

And Sonia, being incurably nosy, and not liking the assumption that she was Juanita's servant, read the letter. Or tried to. Very wrong of her, but the part of me that had loved Sonia was glad to know that it had been given to her. She hadn't stolen the letter.

'And Sonia, well *you* know what she was like. She must have realised that whatever was in the letter was... something that could get Juanita... and me... into serious trouble. She told Juanita she couldn't find the place where the envoy has his office... but she wouldn't give the letter back!'

'She asked for more money to keep quiet about it?'

'Yes, and Juanita gave her some, but she still wouldn't return the letter. Juanita was desperate, and so was I, when I realised how it would look, if Mother Prioress, or *anyone* here got to know of it. I *hadn't* promised anything, but it would be my word against hers. Then Juanita told me she'd asked Sonia to meet her in the chapel, and would I go with her, and make Sonia understand that she *must* give it back? I wanted someone else there. I didn't like being on my own with Juanita anymore, so I asked Helga. She and Juanita were always together. Helga seemed to have taken charge of Juanita — I think she bullied her a bit — and I thought she'd found out about the letter anyway, from something Juanita had said.'

'So, what happened?'

'Sonia had arranged to meet her by the altar to San Stefano. She came, all out of breath, saying she couldn't stop, she'd arranged to meet *you*, Paola. I remember she said that. And she said she was going to show you this mysterious letter, and ask what *you* thought she ought to do with it! Helga started telling her what a wicked girl she was, and how in *her* convent she would be thrown into a punishment cell, and kept on bread and water — you know how Helga goes on? That made it worse! Sonia yelled at her to be quiet about her stupid convent, and stop pretending she was so holy and superior. She was shouting! I was so afraid that someone, one of the nuns, would hear, and come to find out what was going on. Then everything would have come out, and people would think...' Barbara's head sank on her breast, and I thought she was almost too weary to finish her tale. There was silence for a moment or two, but then she spoke again.

'In a panic, I grabbed the first thing... a candlestick, and hit out at Sonia. Just to stop her noise! She fell, and caught her head on the corner of the altar. She just lay there. I couldn't believe I'd killed her! Helga bent down, and said she thought she was dead, now what should we do?' Juanita and I were too shocked to reply. Helga said, 'It was just an accident, Barbara. It wasn't your blow that killed her, it was the fall. She was a wicked girl, and Our Lord must want her dead, or He wouldn't have allowed her head to strike San Stefano's altar.' She was so *calm* about it, as though she knew exactly what Our Lord would want. I suppose that's why we let her do what she did. I wanted to believe her. I didn't want to think I had caused the death of another human being!'

She fell silent again, weeping softly.

'So what did Helga do?' I asked, although I was beginning to guess.

'She sent Juanita to get one of the laundry carts, and they lifted Sonia's body into it, and put the bundles of sheets that were in it, down on top of her, and Helga said later, when all was quiet, they would take her... I just stood there, frozen to the spot. I couldn't think, I couldn't move. Sonia didn't stir when they lifted her. I've thought since, she must have been dead. *Mustn't* she?'

I said nothing. I was back in the vestry, that dreadful morning, hearing the Watch Captain say, 'She was hit over the head here, see? Then they dropped her into the canal, where she drowned.' I stretched out my hands, and took Barbara's in mine.

'Barbara. *You* didn't kill Sonia. Helga did.'

'You can't know that for sure.'

'But I believe it.'

Sonia must have been deeply unconscious, even if she wasn't dead at this point, her skull damaged by the fall. It was impossible to know if she might have recovered. Perhaps I *wanted* to believe it was all Helga's fault, for Barbara's sake?

'What will you do?' she asked.

'Go to Mother Prioress, first thing tomorrow morning, and tell her the whole story, Barbara. I think I must.'

Barbara pushed her matted hair back from her eyes. She looked infinitely weary, but calm now, ready for sleep.

'Yes,' she sighed, 'that would be best. If *you* tell it, as Sonia's friend, and say to Mother Prioress that it was an accident... then... it will be better than it would have been. I think she already suspects that Juanita and I...'

'Had something to do with it,' I finished, nodding. I did not say anything about Helga. Helga, who evidently felt no guilt at all. Juanita and Barbara had both fallen into great anguish at what they had done, but Helga had carried on as though nothing untoward had happened. God may forgive Helga, I thought — I'm sure *she* thinks He will — but I *never* will, not until I'm an old woman on my death bed. And only then if the priest says I must.

Just as I rose from my stool, and turned to go, Barbara said, 'I'm sorry, Paola, about the chandelier. I never explained properly, did I? Sister Angelica kept on at me, telling me I *must* play, but I just couldn't. I left her in the courtyard, saying I was sick to my stomach and needed the privy, and I went and hid in the corridor, and then that youth... the younger Fosca son... came, and grabbed hold of me, and tried to kiss and fondle me. Men think all we Pietà girls are easy meat, *figlie di puttane*.' She shuddered at the memory.

'We struggled, and I seized hold of the rope, it was the only thing I could think of. I thought, if the chandelier shook and all the candles flickered, the servants would come running from the salon, to see what was happening. I didn't mean it to fall, but he snatched at the rope and I lost my grip, and...'

'Don't worry,' I said. 'No one was hurt, and I've got a new concert gown! Go to sleep now.'

Chapter 24

In which Paola acquires a patroness, intercedes for those who caused Sonia's death, and realises she must bid Harry farewell

I had spoken boldly to Barbara of going to the Prioress first thing next morning, but many difficulties were set in my way. First I must sing during Prime, or Sister Angelica would demand the reason for my absence. (She gave an exasperated snort when I told her Marta had succumbed to chickenpox). I was willing to forgo breaking my fast with the usual roll and coffee, but when I went to the Prioress's office, I was told she had gone upstairs to her quarters to break her own. Hanging about outside her door is not encouraged, so there was nothing for it, but to go and practice violin with Chiaretta and the rest of our section. I played badly, with so much occupying my mind, but Albetta played worse, tired out and petulant after her triumph of the previous evening. Even Chiaretta seemed listless, and hurt by our inability to improve under her instruction. She is a better teacher, in truth, than Barbara, though not such an accomplished performer.

'You'd better rouse yourselves, girls,' she told us. 'Sister Angelica wants a general choir practice after the break, and I warn you, she is not in the best of tempers.'

This was bad news indeed. We had all worked so hard on the opera, and, I believed, given one of our best performances ever, but there was to be no respite. A general choir practice, with many halts for criticism and sharp set downs, would be exactly what she thought we needed. Dall'Olgio still being sick, and Don Antonio resting after his exertions, she would enjoy taking this herself. What should I do? I had promised Barbara I would talk to the Prioress, she was depending on me, but Sister A would certainly notice if I played truant.

There are occasions, (Dear Santa Paola, hear my prayer) when only a lie will serve. I went to Sister Angelica and told her, with downcast eyes, that the Prioress had sent for me. Since she always suspects me of unsteady conduct, she believed it. I made my way back to the Prioress's office. There to encounter a further obstacle. A small ante chamber containing a writing desk stands immediately in front of the Prioress's door. The lay staff sit there when they have lists to make, or copying work. They also regard it as their business to prevent people from troubling the Prioress, and today, Sister Agnes, who has very little patience with any of us, was seated there.

'See Ma'donna? Certainly not, she has someone with her!'

'But I must see her; I have very important information to give her!'

'Concerning?' I pressed my lips together, and shook my head.

'Come, girl, you may as well tell me! Ma'donna is busy. *I* may be able to help you.'

'No, Sister. The matter is... confidential, and concerns... another person. I am only at liberty to speak to Ma'donna. I will wait.'

'You had much better not! It may be an hour before she is free....'

And so we might have gone on arguing, but the Prioress's door opened, and she stepped out. Seeing me there, her visible eye brightened, and she smiled.

'Paola! I was just about to send for you!' (Santa Paola, you might have hinted to me that my lie was unnecessary) 'Do come in. I have someone here I want you to meet!'

I followed her in a state of bewilderment. I had come to tell Barbara's story, the words, explanations, including my own part in it — all ready on my tongue. In the small hours before dawn, I had realised I must confess the lie I had uttered to the Prioress herself, whilst I had waited in vain for Sonia on the *terrazzo*.

'This is Signora Felicia Lodi, Paola. Signora Lodi, this is Paola, whom we call Paola Rossa, for reasons which will be obvious to you! Oh, and Signora Lodi has brought her dog. His name is Manfredi.'

Dazed by this turn of events, I attempted a curtsey. There wasn't much room for it, as most of the floor space was taken up by the largest dog I had ever seen. He was white, with black and brown spots and patches across his body and face. He opened one huge eye, looked at me, and then shut it again. Evidently eating me would be too much trouble. Beyond him, I now saw, sat a neat little person in an unbecoming lilac gown. Her own once red hair was faded and heavily flecked with grey. It was slowly coming to me that I had seen her before. On that occasion she had worn an equally unflattering gown of green crepe. She was the woman who had wept during my solo at Signora Fosca's birthday party.

She rose, smiling, and stretched over the recumbent Manfredi to take my hand.

'Don't mind Manfi,' she said. 'He's a darling. My protector, whenever I want to go about without my maid! I hope you like dogs, because I do so want you and I to be great friends!'

'Perhaps we should all sit down,' suggested the Prioress, who must surely have been able to see how bewildered I was. I took the stool, perching uncomfortably to one side, because Manfredi's hind legs took up the space where I would have put my feet.

Mother Prioress than began to explain the patronage system, as much for Signora Lodi's benefit as for mine. I knew about it, of course. A coveted recognition of a chorister's talent is the acquisition of a patron. Wealthy ladies who support the Pietà will offer to be patron to a particular girl. This means invitations to visit her home, and the occasional boat trip, perhaps a picnic on one of the islands in the *Laguna*. Even, if one was very fortunate, a stay at the patroness's country villa in the foothills of the mountains, during the August heat. The whole system is carefully supervised. The Governors and the nuns are very strict about it, and discourage too much favouritism, and the giving of lavish gifts. I had never had a patron, and had not expected to have one for many years yet, if ever. I was astonished to find myself chosen. Signora Lodi began talking about her husband, who she described as 'getting on in years, but so very kind', and her house in the San Polo district. My head began to swim, unable to take all this in.

'Unfortunately, I am about to accompany my husband to Vicenza, to visit his aged sister,' Signora Lodi was saying, 'which means I cannot invite you to my home immediately. However, Mother Prioress was just telling me that your best friend — Marta is her name? — has chickenpox, so perhaps you will not mind waiting for a week or two? Then the two of you can come together, and you won't feel shy on your first visit? I will send our gondola to fetch you! You may already have met our gondoliers, we had them row you home after the party at the Ca' Fosca.'

'Why thank you, Signora! I would like that, very much,' was all I could think of to say. I stood up to curtsey, being careful not to step on any part of Manfredi. 'He *is* a magnificent animal, isn't he?' I said, seeing she was smiling at my efforts not to tread on his huge paws.

'Oh, I knew the moment I saw you, and heard you play your violin so delightfully, that we should deal well together!' she responded.

'And, now dear Mother Prioress, I must be on my way. I have taken up too much of your time already.'

'And too much space in my office!' grumbled the Prioress, once Signora Lodi and the dog were gone, but she was chuckling. 'She strikes me as a silly creature, Paola, but very good natured. I believe her husband is a great deal older than she, and there are no children of the marriage. I think there may be some story of a lost daughter there. She may tell you herself. Be assured, however that she is *not your mother* — so if you find you do not suit one another, we can cancel the arrangement. The dog does not worry you?'

'No, Ma'donna. I am quite happy to try... the arrangement. And now, can I? I *must* tell you... what I was waiting to see you about? *Please?* I promised Barbara!'

'Ah, Barbara?' She quietly resumed her seat, and folded her hands into the sleeves of her robe. 'Sit down child, and tell me.'

Before I repeated the story, as Barbara had told it to me, I explained about the meeting I should have had with Sonia on the *terrazzo*.

'I did not entirely credit your tale at the time!' was her only comment. 'And this letter, which you passed to Sister Serafina,' she touched a paper on her desk, and I saw that she had it there already, 'was the cause of all. Let me see if I understand the sequence of events in the chapel. Barbara hit Sonia a blow with a candlestick. Sonia fell back and hit her head on the altar's corner. Helga pronounced her dead. Barbara was too horrified by what she had done to protest. Helga and Juanita hid her in a laundry cart, placing bundles of used sheets over her, and later, once everyone had retired to bed, took her to the laundry, and from there, tipped her body into the canal. That is quite possible, I suppose. There is rarely anyone working in the laundry after dark, and the doors can be opened from inside, if two people are available to lift the bar. But how would those two novices have known that, unless...?' She paused, gazing into space, thinking, and then answered her own question. 'Helga might easily have known. She is always complaining that *something* is not up to the standard of her own religious house! She came to tell me that the laundry don't starch her veils correctly. She said she had already spoken about it to Signora Amelia, who was rude to her. Helga is a prompt riser, so she probably went there early one morning, when the girls were taking down the bar. So... she knew.'

We sat in silence. I discovered I was crying, my throat was choked with tears, and I could hardly breathe. I fumbled in my sleeve for a handkerchief, and blew my nose.

'Do you think, Ma'donna ... *was* Sonia dead when they put her into the canal? The Watch Captain said she might have drowned... which would mean... ?' My voice choked again, I was unable to go on.

Mother Prioress brought her hands together in an attitude of prayer, her elbows on the table, and laid her forehead on her clasped hands. 'I pray, for the sake of Helga's immortal soul, that she *was* already dead. Otherwise it does not bear thinking of! She may even have been smothered by the bundles of sheets, if the injury to her head hadn't already killed her. If *only* they had called Sister Serafina! Now I'm afraid we shall never know, for sure, whether she could have been saved.'

'What will happen?' I whispered, 'to Barbara.... and Juanita?'

Mother Prioress raised her head, and stared at the opposite wall, the visible half of her mouth a rigid line.

'They will have to go. All three. Barbara has been saying for some months that she thinks of entering a convent. I've been corresponding with the Poor Clares in Padova, who need someone to train their choir. I shall have to tell them all this — or she will. In her case, it does seem to have been an accident, she never meant to kill the girl, and she had been very much harried and provoked. I *think* they will still take her, if she does sufficient penance. Juanita, I have already arranged to send to a Spanish foundation in Naples, and from there they may send her on to Tarragona, or not, as the nuns there think best. With an accompanying missive about her unacceptable behaviour, which I had already written, but must now amend.'

A moment of pity for Juanita stirred in my breast. All she had done was fall in love with the wrong person, and write a silly letter. Barbara would get what she wanted, in time, and perhaps even find some measure of peace and contentment in serving her convent. Juanita, I feared, never would. It did seem to me that God and his saints had laid a very heavy burden on Juanita.

'And Helga?'

'Helga goes back to Bamberg, if I have to drag her over the mountains myself! This Mother Superior she talks about is her aunt. What they will do with her, I cannot imagine. She seems to believe she knows Our Lord's Will better than Our Lord Himself! She told me she knows Juanita is a sinful person, but she has been wrestling with her soul! She! I doubt my ability even to make Helga see she has done anything wrong, although I suppose, with Don Salvatore's help, I must try.'

We sat silent again for a few moments. I fished for my handkerchief in my sleeve once more, and wiped my eyes.

'I will go now, Ma'donna, but... Sister Angelica is holding choir practice... and I don't think I could sing just now. May I have your permission to go to the chapel?'

'Certainly! You are a good girl, Paola. A little giddy at times, but a loyal and faithful friend. Say a prayer for me too, whilst you are there. *I* must send for these wretched girls, and... deal with them.'

As I rose to go, she pulled a small cloth bag from a drawer in her desk. 'Oh, as you are going to the chapel, take this to Don Salvatore. It's the money we owe to Signor Harry. He is packing up his things I'm told, as he leaves tomorrow, early, to travel with the Prince to Munich. I had hoped to see him, and give it to him myself, but,' she heaved a deep sigh, 'instead I must deal with *this* situation. Don Salva will thank him, and wish him well in my stead. Perhaps you would also like to say farewell to him... on behalf of the *Coro*? Without his help with the scenery our little opera would not have looked half so well.' She smiled her sweet half smile, granting me permission to speak to Harry one last time.

Chapter 25

In which Harry bids farewell to Paola and to Venice, and finds himself making a promise to return

Having bundled up my art materials, and sent them with a servant to the *palazzo* where the Prince was lodged, I was roaming about the vestry, so much my home of late, wondering whether I should return some of these last few half used pots of paint and broken sticks of charcoal to those who had lent them to me. I had paid my landlord in full, much to his surprise, retrieved my shirts from the washerwoman, and spoken my adieus to Luca. I had offered to enquire if he could come with me to Munich as my assistant, but he declined, ungrateful youth, saying he did not care for clambering over mountain passes, and he was very hopeful of at least a walk-on in Signor Goldoni's latest play. I was musing on what else I must do, when Don Salvatore came to tell me there was someone waiting on the *riva* who wished to see me. I followed him out through the chapel, into the soft morning sunlight.

'I hear you're leaving for Germany?' said Frediano Størje, clasping my hand in a massive paw. 'The old besom in the laundry's spreading it about the district,' he added.

'And saying how glad she is to see the back of me, no doubt!' I laughed. 'Yes, I am sorry to leave Venice, but the Prince has offered.... a princely sum, if I will come and paint Venetian scenes for a *ridotto* he plans to give immediately after the Easter festivities.'

'I'm amazed he is to attempt to cross the Alps so early in the year,' worried Don Salva. 'I understand he has been some months on an embassy to his Spanish relatives in Naples over the winter, but now wants to return home to Munich in time for Easter. I trust we shall not hear that your whole party is lost in an avalanche.'

'Hannibal crossed the Alps in winter,' I said, lightly, although I was somewhat uneasy about this myself.

'Indeed, but he had elephants.'

'So he did, but Prince Ferdinand holds the rank of Field Marshal in the Emperor's army, and no doubt supposes he can do it without them. They say the thaw will hold. Spring has come early in the mountain passes. If the worst were to happen, he has any number of men in his entourage to dig us out.'

'I am sorry you are to leave, and my father will be sorry too, when he hears of it,' said Frediano.

I doubted the old scoundrel had even registered my existence. Seeing my raised eyebrows, he went on, 'He is gone over to Koper, to see whether one of his *other* daughters will come and keep house for us. But I think none of them will, they know him too well. We shall have to hire someone, and Papa hates to pay out money. I had hoped,' he continued, wistfully, glancing from Don Salvatore to me, and back, 'that you might have news of what happened to my sister?'

I looked at Don Salva, who pursed his lips, and looked vague for a moment, but then said, 'I believe... I think significant progress has been made, Signore. Mother Prioress is looking into the matter, rest assured. Once she has all the facts in her hands, she will undoubtedly send for you.'

'I suppose that is all I can hope for,' he replied.

We stood, not speaking, for a few moments, a group of three men, taking the air on the *riva*, appreciating the spring sunshine, the light dancing on the tiny wavelets in the *bacino*, gondolas sliding by, the warm red and gold brickwork of the *campanile*, the squat grey domes of *San Marco*, the shining white marble of the *Salute*. We could have been figures in one of Signor Canaletto's *veduti*.

'Tell me, Frediano,' I said, idly curious, 'What were you and Sonia arguing about, that first time I saw you, out here?'

'*I* wasn't arguing,' he protested. 'I was wanting her answer, would she come and keep house? Since Mama died, I've tried to keep things straight, but I'm a poor hand at it. And Papa resented paying to have cooked food brought in. No, it was Sonia who was arguing. She said I was (here he used a Venetian word I did not know, but I think our Lancashire equivalent would be, *mithering)* mithering her, that everyone mithered her. She had been out on errands. One of the sisters — she said 'sister' but I don't know which one, had wanted her to go to some foreign envoy with a letter, but she hadn't been able to find this person, and now this 'sister' would very likely kill her. She seemed... agitated. I thought she enjoyed working herself up into a frenzy, and would come round in the end. Our mother was the same. I didn't want Papa to know I'd asked her to come to us, until I had her promise that she would.'

He shook his great turnip head sadly, thanked me yet again for rescuing his disreputable parent from drowning, shook my hand once more, bowed, and began to walk away, back, I suppose, to take care of business at the wood yard. Just then a young woman in a heavy cloak, carrying a marketing basket beneath the curve of her arm, came hurrying along the *riva*, threading her way through the fish stalls, past the wash tubs and the carnival masks. Just for a moment, she might have been Sonia, as I had seen her that first day. Frediano must have thought so too, for he halted, startled, and then he smiled, and blushed, and removed his hat with a flourish and bowed. The girl's free hand came up and she pushed back the hood of her cloak, smiling and blushing too. Then I recognised her. It was spotty Cristina, who seemed to have taken on the running of errands for the Pietà, which had once been Sonia's task. So, here was a little romance blossoming before my eyes. I wondered how old man Størje would react? Perhaps, if Sister Domenica were to give her a few extra cookery lessons, all would be well.

She hesitated a moment, but then turned and went to ring the bell to be let in. Frediano watched her, as he had once watched his sister do the same, and then walked away.

I remained where I was, marvelling at the beauty of Venice laid out before me. How I would miss this! A trader, bound for the East, with sails still partially furled, was moving gently out towards the lagoon on the tide, whilst men in a tug boat strained at the oars. Shrouded gondolas, tied in a bunch to a post on the quayside, swayed and bobbed back and forth on her swell. Don Salva constantly looked around him, raising a hand, or calling a greeting to passers-by he recognised. Between this old priest and Signora Amelia at the laundry door, there could be few in the *Castello* district, whose comings and goings went unnoticed.

'Ha, here is someone else who would like to see you!' he remarked, looking towards the orphanage building. I turned, and saw a slender figure, her red skirts billowing in the breeze, standing in the doorway to the chapel. Paola. I walked towards her, assuming Don Salva would accompany me, but he was hailed by an elderly woman with a little dog, and stopped to exchange greetings with her.

'Good morning, Signorina! And how are you?' Drawing closer, I saw that her face was tear stained, and wished I had not asked. What a clumsy oaf I am around females. I could have bitten off my tongue.

'Oh. Good morning, Signor Harry,' she seemed both embarrassed and confused. 'I.. that is, the Prioress asked me to give this to Don Salvatore, to give to you... but since he is conversing already, and you are here... I suppose I may give it directly into your hands?'

She held out a small cloth bag, in which coins chinked, encouragingly. 'Your payment, for the scenery, with Ma'donna's thanks, and from all of us in the *Coro*,' she said, as I took it from her. 'She would have wished to thank you herself, but... after I told her what I discovered from Barbara.... she has to see those girls.... and tell them what their fates will be.' She gulped, and I thought she was going to start crying again, but she fought against it and won.

'Tell me. Don Salva can see us — and if he, a man in holy orders, can gossip with an old lady, surely I may speak with a young one?'

She managed a watery smile, 'And *we* are almost in church!'

We stood side by side in the doorway, and she told me the whole. A warm breeze ruffled our hair, and tugged at our clothing. Before our eyes was nothing but beauty, graceful gondolas floated by, another huge sailing barque, newly arrived, perhaps from the far Indies, manoeuvred to berth in front of the customs house, holds already thrown open for inspection — but inwardly we saw only darkness, and the horror of a young woman thrown into the canal like a parcel of refuse, who might not even have been dead.

'It's Helga I cannot forgive,' Paola said. 'What the other two did was wrong, but they were paralysed by fright. She took charge, and convinced them it was God's doing!'

'What *will* happen to them?'

'To me it's very dreadful, but perhaps it's the best they can hope for. At least they are not to be handed over to the city authorities and taken before the Doge's court! Barbara is to go to a convent in Padova, if they will still have her. It was already being negotiated, since she had expressed a wish to become a nun, but she may have to do months of solitary penance before they accept her noviciate. Juanita is to go to a Spanish Foundation in Naples. Mother Prioress said 'perhaps' they will send her back to Tarragona, but I think very probably they will not. She may remain there, a prisoner in effect, walled up in a convent that is not her own, hundreds of miles from her own family, perhaps for years! And Helga will be sent back to Bamberg in disgrace. It grieves me that *she* may get off lightly, since it seems it is her aunt who is Mother Superior there.'

'Do not be so sure,' I said, to comfort her. 'As I understand it, she has constantly complained, throughout her stay here at the Pietà, and even if the Prioress has somewhat censored her letters, Helga cannot have given the impression she thought everything perfect here. But no letter seems to have come back, supporting her complaints, or asking to recall her. May it not be that her Reverend Aunt knows full well what she is like, and sent her here to give her nuns some peace?'

'I had not thought of that!' She managed a real smile at this, and as I wanted to introduce her to more cheerful topics, I changed the subject.

'When I spoke with the Prioress, a day or two ago, she mentioned to me that you are to have a patroness? This is something new for you, is it not?' This time she laughed. A little.

'Yes it's true, a Signora Felicia Lodi — she has the most enormous dog I have ever seen! When I first saw him in Mother Prioress's office, I thought it was a bear!'

'Ah, I have seen her walking with it through the Piazza. An eccentric! Was she not at the Fosca party, too, now I think of it? She didn't have the dog with her on that occasion.'

'No, or we might all have been too terrified to play! I didn't tell you, did I, that it was partly Barbara's fault that the chandelier fell? She didn't intend any harm to me, or to Don Antonio. She was desperate to distract Sister Angelica, who was following her everywhere, trying to persuade her to play. She was hiding from her in the corridor near the privies, but then Bruno Fosca tried to… well, I expect you can imagine what he tried! She thought, by grabbing the rope she would cause the chandelier to shake and all the candles to flicker, and then people would come running to see the cause… but then, struggling with him, she lost hold, and the whole thing came crashing down.'

'Poor girl. And all because she was afraid to stand up to Sister Angelica.'

'Well, we all find that difficult. To Sister Angelica, you see, the *Coro* is the most important thing in the whole world.'

'Indeed. She has given her whole life to it, Paola. Even I, on a very short and sour acquaintance, can see that! If she had remained with her order, within a convent, she might be a Mother Superior by now.'

'No. I don't know anything of her background, but I think the important posts in a convent go to those women whose families, outside, are wealthy and have influence with the Church. I suspect she didn't have that. In a convent she would be choir mistress, and the nuns would sing beautifully, but she wouldn't be known, outside those walls. Barbara would be happy with that, but not she. She *pretends* that our public concerts distract us from our real work in the chapel, but really...'

'She glories in your fame, knowing it couldn't happen without her? That your teachers need supervision — they go sick, they leave for more lucrative positions. Don Antonio trots off to direct the opera, and forgets the lessons of girls he dislikes...'

'Yes. Even Don Antonio will leave — if the call comes from Vienna. They say the Emperor's Kapellmeister is growing infirm... and you too, will go.' She turned away, but not before I saw her eyes fill with tears.

I found I wanted to put my arms around her, but one cannot do that on the steps of a chapel, in full view of everyone who is out and about on the *Riva deghli Schiavonni*. Which constitutes a great many people, in the middle of a bright spring morning. Don Salva had found another old crone to gossip with, but I knew he was watching us, being discreet.

'Yes, even I must go, with the Prince,' I said, quietly. 'I have given my word. Like those fellows in the folk tales, I must journey away. For a year and a day — most probably. But then I hope to come again, and see how... you all go on!'

Her face brightened, though a tear still trickled down her cheek. 'You will come again to Venice?'

I took the letter I had received that morning from my pocket, and glanced at it. The British Consul in Rome had held it some weeks, trying to establish my direction.

'This was brought round to my lodgings, just now. If I had received it a day earlier, I would not have given word to the Prince. However, I should still have needed to return to England, and his money will pay for me to travel in comfort. My Godfather, a cousin to my father, has died, leaving me... not a fortune, Paola, but a competence. So, once I have undertaken this hazardous journey over the Alps, and painted sufficient gondolas to please His Royal Highness, I must go to England, see the lawyers, and claim my inheritance. Then, I must settle one or two of my father's more pressing debts, and — if I can — do something for my sisters...'

'And then you will return!'

'Paola, I will.' It was a promise I had not intended to make. It held in it, the suggestion of a commitment, to a girl I had only known for a very short time. But I made it.

She laughed, and it was a pleasant sound, not that irritating tinkle so many drawing room misses cultivate, and I noticed for the first time, a dimple in the corner of her mouth. She had changed, even in that very short time. No longer a green, awkward girl, but one who had known sorrow and success, anger, and a measure of forgiveness, and now she looked out, not just on the bustling *Riva della Schiavonni*, on a radiant morning, but on a future which might hold many things, perhaps more than she had ever dreamed. She seemed to realise that.

'A year is a long time, Harry. If Signora Lodi and her husband grow to like me, you may find me married to a rich merchant, and smelling of cinnamon and cloves!'

'That would be a *much* better match for you, than an artist with only a competence!'

I lifted her hand, and placed a kiss on her fingers. Don Salvatore saw me do it, and shook his head, pretending to be scandalised. Romantic old fool. Had he not told me, that from that first day — when, both of us shocked and distraught — Paola and I had talked together, that he had thought how well we would deal together?

Historical Note

The Orphanage of Santa Maria della La Pietà in Venice was founded in 1346, and existed until the 19th Century. In the early days, boys as well as girls were accepted, but by the time Antonio Vivaldi worked there, only girls were admitted. The orphanage, although staffed by nuns, was in fact financed by the city of Venice, and the orphans were considered to be 'daughters of Venice' since they had no families of their own. The Coro, or choristers, those girls who showed an aptitude for music, were trained to sing, and also to play a variety of instruments. In the eighteenth century, when Vivaldi was at the height of his powers, attending one of their concerts was a highlight for many visitors to Venice. The Coro enjoyed considerable status within the orphanage and the city, almost as pop musicians might today. This must have left the other girls, those whose talents were not sufficient to be chosen, and who were trained instead to do laundry work, lace making, or to care for the younger children, feeling less than valued. In fact some of the work they did, notably that of the skilled laundresses, actually brought in more money to pay for the day to day running of the orphanage than did concerts by the Coro.

It is known that Vivaldi did compose an 'opera,' Ill Mopso, for the girl musicians of la Pietà, to perform, perhaps for the visit, during Carnival, of Prince Ferdinand of Bavaria, although even that is doubtful, because the dates don't quite fit. The plot of Ill Mopso seems to have been roughly as I have described it, but it has been lost. This is fiction; I couldn't resist including the performance in the story.

Printed in Poland
by Amazon Fulfillment
Poland Sp. z o.o., Wrocław